Rock My Bed

A Black Falcon Novel

By

Michelle A. Valentine

This is a work of fiction. Names, characters, places, and incidents are either the product of the author's imagination or are used fictitiously.

For questions or comments about this book, please contact the author at michellevalentineauthor@gmail.com

Dedications:

To the readers: You all are my cheerleaders and I love each and every one of you. If it weren't for your support I would never have the courage to keep on writing. Thank you for being so awesome!

Rock My Bed

(The Black Falcon Series, #2)

By *Michelle A. Valentine*

Michelle A. Valentine

Black Falcon Series Reading Order

Rock the Heart (Black Falcon, #1)

Rock the Band (Black Falcon, #1.5)

Rock My Bed (Black Falcon, #2)

Chapter 1

AUBREY

I tip my head back, listening to the beat of the music echoing down the hallway and readjust my backstage pass. This isn't the piece of cake first assignment for my best friend, Lanie, although I thought it would be. I just hope she isn't beating the crap out of Noel Falcon on the other side of that red door.

The brick wall is cold against the bare skin on my shoulders as I lean against it. This is such a fucked up mess. If I'd known things would get this heated between Lanie and Noel I might've agreed with her that she shouldn't take Diana Swagger, our boss, up on her offer to head up his children's literacy campaign. Seeing an ex is never easy. I can't even imagine what I would do if my ex became a rock-god and I was forced to work with him in order to advance my career.

She's definitely got her work cut out for her.

Rock My Bed

A few screams at the end of the hall draw my attention. I stiffen against the wall as my gaze lands on Riff, the lead guitarist of Black Falcon. Women rip open their shirts for him to sign their chests as he moves gracefully among them down the hall. My eyes rake over his body. I can see why women line up to throw themselves at him. He's really, really sexy.

The hair on his head is perfectly styled into a tall Mohawk that alternates between blond and black chunk stripes, while his wife-beater tank top shows off a vast array of tattoos covering his broad shoulders and impressive forearms. Riff grins as he signs a couple of bare breasts with a silver Sharpie while another fan kisses his cheek. Everything about him emits raw sex appeal, and it's impossible to tear my gaze away.

I bite my bottom lip just as Riff glances up and notices me. Every instinct in my body advises me to look away because this guy is trouble—the kind I've sworn off since the last bad boy I messed around with broke my heart. Guys like him aren't good news.

He holds my eyes with his for a few seconds and when I don't break our stare, a slow, cocky smile spreads across his lips.

Oh shit. Why do I have the feeling that look means I'm in for it?

Riff leans over and says something to one of the security guards then claps him on the back before he stalks towards me alone.

Security holds the crazed fans back. The girls behind him continue to scream out Riff's name as he leaves them standing there still starving for his attention, but he never looks back. His gaze pins me as he heads right for me.

I swallow hard and my heart hammers inside my chest. The moment is surreal. Since getting to know Lanie in college and learning about her connection to Black Falcon, I admit Riff is the one band member that's always caught my eye. Everything about him that screams naughty sex on a stick, and I can't believe he's heading my way.

My knees grow a little weak beneath me as he stops a couple feet in front of me. Riff smirks as his eyes trail over my body unabashedly, lingering a good while on my breasts beneath my form fitting halter-top. "You're tits are amazing."

I flinch and my mouth drops open. It's not like I'm dressed like a skank, but this form-fitting halter doesn't do anything to disguise that I have a large chest. It doesn't give him the right to be so crude about it. "*Excuse* me?"

His grin widens as he leans into me and braces himself against the wall with a hand beside my head. "I knew it. Redheads are always feisty, and they *never* disappoint in the sack."

Where does he get off? I'm not a prude. I'm down for having all kinds of fun with a random hottie, but just because he's a fucking rock-star doesn't give him the right to treat women like random pieces of rump-roast, especially ones like me. I'm not a usable doormat.

Any other pick-up line would've given him better shot at getting in my panties. Now, he's just pissed me off.

"Um, ever heard of personal space?" I place my hand on his chest and give him a gentle shove.

Riff's hand shoots up and he wraps his fingers around my wrist. "Feisty *and* brave. I can only imagine what a night with you would be like. I bet you're a regular wildcat. Here. Take this." He reaches in his back pocket of his jeans and pulls out a golden piece of paper and slips it into my palm. "Meet me out by our bus. Let me have just one night to fuck you senseless. I guarantee I'll have you speaking in tongues before the nights through."

I stare down at the paper, which looks like a pass to an amusement park ride. My fingers crumple the golden ticket in my fist. "What the hell is this?"

He moves his other arm and places his left hand on the other side of my head, effectively pinning me against the wall. Both of his knees bump into mine as he leans into me. I feel my own lips betray me as they part when Riff dips his head low, like he's about to kiss me. I close my eyes and my chest heaves with anticipation. Damn my stupid body for getting turned on by this beautiful asshole. This is wrong on so many levels, but a rational reason to not allow this to happen doesn't enter my brain.

The door across the hall startles me as it slams shut, and a very pissed Noel Falcon flees from the room. Riff watches the back of the lead singer of his band storm down the hall, obviously distraught as he grips handfuls of his own hair in his fists.

Riff shifts his gaze back to me. "Use this ticket and come find me. Security will let you through as long as you have it. We aren't done with this conversation."

I open my mouth to protest, but he leans in and kisses me so passionately my knees below me nearly give out. The warmth of his tongue gliding over mine causes a tingle in my belly that spreads down between my legs. Riff cups my face in the palms of his hands and gives me a final peck on the lips. "Find me."

Without another word he pulls away and heads toward the direction of his band-mate. I watch his retreating backside with my mouth gaping open.

What the hell just happened? Did he really just offer to fuck me for sport and then kiss me breathless?

My heart still hammers in my chest as I unclench my fingers and stare down at the golden piece of paper in my hand. That's one man I need to stay far, far away from. I just know my sanity and my heart depends on it. Good thing this is the last time I'll ever see him.

I shake my head to wake myself out of the daze Riff just put me in and stare at the door across the hall. The way Noel came tearing out of it tells me Lanie's little chat with him didn't go well. Time to do a little damage control.

The door creaks open, and I spot my friend with her

head hung low. More than anything I want to comfort her. I know it can't be easy facing a messy past head-on like she just did. She's got some big lady balls, I'll give her that.

I rest my hands on her shoulders. "Did you get your answers?"

Lanie nods, but she doesn't turn to face me. She sniffs a little, trying to fight back her emotional pain. "Everything I needed to know."

My heart instantly breaks for her because I can tell she's not referring to our job. This weekend jaunt hasn't gone anything like what I imagined.

RIFF

What the fuck is wrong with me? Why am I chasing down the one person I hate, instead of working on seducing that fine piece of ass back there? Two more seconds and I would've had her heading back to the bus where she would've been happy to cash in that golden ticket.

What a waste.

I follow Noel out the exit doors into the Texas summer heat and watch as he paces in the parking lot. The cool demeanor he usually sports is gone, replaced by a wild look in his eye as he huffs and growls with his hands on top of his head.

"What the fuck is your problem?" Not that I really care anymore. Anything that's bothering him, he probably brought on himself.

Noel glances up to the sky and bites his bottom lip like he's searching for answers from up above. After a couple long moments he shakes his head but still allows his chin to be tilted up. "You ever wished for something so much that when it actually came true you ruined it without even meaning to?"

I scrunched my brow. "I have no clue what the fuck you're talking about. You're not using again are you? Babbling like this was always a sign before. You know you shouldn't be doing that with a baby coming and all. You need to keep your shit together."

Noel's eyes meet mine. "You know I don't touch that shit anymore."

I cross my arms over my chest. If it weren't for needing to keep Black Falcon together, I would've told him to go fuck himself two months ago when I found out he fucked my girlfriend and got her pregnant.

I actually do hate him for going behind my back. Sophie I expected that kind of shit from. I knew from the jump she and I were never going to be serious. She was merely the chick I kept around for a good fuck when I needed it. Finding a random groupie night after night gets pretty taxing.

But Noel on the other hand, his ass was supposed to be my brother, and I never expected that shit from him. If he stabbed me in the back for a quick piece of ass, what else is he screwing me over with? The moment Sophie told me she was pregnant by him, the trust between us was gone. And so was our friendship.

I stand here now, trying to talk to him out of obligation to the band, nothing more.

Noel rubs his hand over his face and sighs. "Lanie Vance was at our show tonight."

My eyes widen. "The cold-hearted slut you dedicate *Ball Busting Bitch* to at every one of our shows?"

He nods. "That's the one. I never thought I'd see her again, and how the fuck did she end up backstage?"

Things start to click. "Is that who was in there with you when you came flying out? No wonder you were pissed. The one chick that carries your balls around in her purse finally confronts you for calling her ass out in front of thousands of people. Nice."

I laugh and his face twists. Karma is a bitch named Lanie Vance apparently. Life couldn't get any fucking sweeter.

Noel glares at me. "That's not why she came after me."

"What other reason would she have? You haven't seen her since high school, right? Keep your wallet in check, dude. Sounds like a gold digger to me," I say.

He shakes his head. "No. She isn't like that. Believe it or not she needs me for a job."

Like that doesn't sound like a load of shit. "What kind of job?"

"She's working for Center Stage Marketing. Apparently, I'm her first client."

"Fuck. That blows. Can't you just hire someone else to handle your children's literacy thing so you won't have to deal with her crazy ass?" This band doesn't need any more fucking chick drama to come between us.

"That would be the easy thing to do, but the thing of it is, man, she knows me. She knows all about my struggle with dyslexia, and as much as I hate to admit it, she's actually the best person for the job."

I stare at this pussy-whipped douchebag in front of me and know exactly what he's trying to get at. He's told me all about how this woman was the great love of his life. I know Noel Falcon well enough to know he has a side agenda for keeping her around. God knows he'll screw anything that walks at the drop of a hat, why not fuck an old flame that crushed you once just to prove you still can. If I was him, that's what I would do.

I shake my head, trying to rid myself of the thoughts. Who he sleeps around with is none of my concern. It just makes him look like a jackass even more if he starts stringing along this Lanie chick while he knows he's got another woman knocked up. "Well, good luck with all that."

"Whatever you're thinking, don't. I'm keeping my word to Sophie. I will be there for the baby. Lane coming back into my life won't change the fact that I'm responsible. I'll take care of her and stick by her side throughout the pregnancy just like I promised."

I hold up my hand. "I don't give a flying fuck what kind of arrangement you and Sophie have worked out. All I know is that neither of you can really stand the other. How you two are delusional enough to think you'll be able to come together as some sort of cohesive family unit is beyond me. Thoughts like that prove to me how screwed up your concept of family is."

"You don't have to understand it—"

"And I don't have to listen to you talk about it either. Like I told you before, the days of our personal friendship is over. You ruined that when you couldn't keep your dick out of my girlfriend."

"I told you I don't remember sleeping with her. I didn't do it on purpose, I was drunk. It happened. I'm sorry—"

"Save it. I've heard this song and dance from you before, and frankly I'm sick of it. You did it. Man up and admit it. Don't play the victim card here."

"God, Riff, are you ever going to accept my apology? I didn't mean to hurt you, man."

Hurt me? He has no fucking clue how much it actually takes to hurt me. My life has never been sunshine and rainbows, and I learned a long time ago in order to keep heavy shit away. If you don't let people in, they can't hurt you. Things are so much easier when you can keep the caring part of you locked away from the rest of the world. The idea of Noel hurting me is laughable, and it pisses me off that he thinks he has that much influence over me.

"Whatever. I hope she rips your heart out again for fun and I'm there to laugh when she does." A little harsh I know, but it gets my point across.

Noel flinches as I turn around, not giving him a chance to reply. I trudge toward the security of our bus, Big Bertha, and I whip out my phone to check the time. The night's still young. I hope that fiery, wild cat doesn't make me wait too long. I need a good fuck to take my mind off shit.

Chapter 2

AUBREY

A couple days after the concert in Texas, I'm back in my comfortable little cubicle at Center Stage Marketing working away. Sometimes the work as an assistant is a little tedious, but typically, I don't mind. My new boss, Isaac Walters, and I seem to be hitting it off.

Isaac is an up and coming hotshot at the firm. Even though he's fairly green to the marketing world, he's proven that he knows his stuff. Already, he's landed major accounts that the old bloodhounds around the firm would kill to represent. I can learn a lot from him, and hopefully one day this place will give me a shot to run a few jobs on my own.

I stare at my computer screen. Ever since that crazy-random kiss from Riff, he's been constantly hoarding every spare minute in my brain. I've tried to convince myself that he's a total jackass and to forget about him, but I can't.

Stupid body for getting turned on by him.

After a few simple clicks, I pull up a social media site. It feels a little creepy and a slight bit stalkerish, but my curiosity is intense. I type in Zackary Benjamin Oliver, the name behind Riff's stage persona, and hit search. Two seconds later a few names pop up, but none of them are the man I'm looking for, which disappoints me.

I lean back in my chair and tap my bottom lip. He must only use his nickname on these types of things so his fans can follow him. I try again, only this time typing in Official Riff. The person with the most followers lands at the top of the list. It's him. I could spot that signature, crazy hair anywhere. His page fills my screen after a few clicks and I study his profile picture. The green in his eyes is striking, and I lean in to study the rest of him. His strong jaw line, prominent nose paired with his kind eyes give him that I'm very approachable vibe, but all the tattoos scream rocker badass, quickly reminding me of his true nature. His plump top lip curls into a slight snarl, almost like he's growling, while his hands grip his guitar in a suggestive pose.

I bite my bottom lip. Damn it! Why does he have to be so sexy?

If only things had gone better between Lanie and Noel, I wouldn't have missed out on what I can imagine would have been an amazing one-night stand. All the what-ifs flow through my mind. If he fucked half as good as he kissed, I know it would've been mind blowing.

I sigh. Maybe it was for the best I didn't hook up with him. A night like that would've probably ruined me for all other men and it would've meant nothing to a man of his stature. I'm sure he sleeps with models, actresses and any other beautiful women he wants. Compared to them I would only be a blip on his radar.

Rock My Bed

The mouse in my hand hovers over the 'Friends' button. I debate on opening a can of worms by connecting with him, but decide to click it anyway because what are the odds that he'll actually remember me?

The phone on my desk rings. "Yes, Mr. Walters, what can I do for you?"

"Aubrey, can you please come to my office for a quick meeting."

I start grabbing my tablet and pen as soon as he mentions needing to see me. "Sure, I'll be right there."

I shake my head. It's best if I forget about Riff. As much as I would love to experience a night with a sexy rock star, that's one pipe dream that will never happen.

My mother is probably right, I need to find a nice respectable man with a good job—a man that's good for my future. She's been on me for years to leave the bad boy types alone. They always break my heart, and she's always been there to pick up the pieces.

I hook my pen into my legal pad and stand up just before an audible ding from my computer attracts my attention.

RIFF

My eyes widen as I spot my redheaded wild cat on my laptop screen. I didn't think I'd ever see her again after she stood me up the other night, so I'm totally caught off guard when I see her picture pop up as one of my new friends on one of my fan sites.

I click on her photo and it instantly fills my entire screen. She's just as beautiful as I remember, long auburn hair trailing over her shoulders, complimenting her green eyes and fair skin. She's the absolute model of fucking perfection—one I'm desperate to bed. Everything I like in a woman *she* has: sex appeal, and fire. Those things combined are a rare find and my libido drives me to possess it.

This request excites me. It's another shot—a do over—for me to try to get her. She doesn't hate me, that's clear, or she would've never sent me a friend request. I minimize her profile picture and click on her personal information section. The name Aubrey Jenson rolls off my tongue as I read her name aloud. I finally have a name to go with the beauty I've been dreaming about the past couple of nights.

It says she lives in New York, which throws me off a bit because I met her in Texas. I shrug it off and continue reading about her and then my heart pauses for a beat.

Fuck!

She works for Center Stage Marketing? That's the same company that Noel's heartbreaker came down to talk to him about. Holy Hell.

Things start clicking as I think about the few stolen

moments with Aubrey in the hallway. Noel flying through the door in a rage after arguing with Lanie flashes before my eyes. My dream girl was there on business, and I treated her like one of my random groupies that was just looking to get laid because of that shirt showing off her tits.

No wonder she stood me up. She's probably not the type of girl who sleeps with rock stars who ram their tongues down her throat on a whim. This chick is different from the rest. She's classy, not some hooker that will suck my dick on command.

But then again, she did just search me out. Maybe she's down for a night of hot, sweaty sex after all.

I chew on my thumb as I debate over what to do. The fact that I want to bang her doesn't change, but my approach will definitely need to be different. This will take more finesse than I'm used to shelling out in order to get laid.

Knowing that we've got a common connection almost ensures that I'll see her again at some point. And when I do, I want her to be so desperate for me to fuck her, she'll practically tear off my clothes the minute she lays eyes on me.

Yes. This chick will take some wooing. This will be fun. Girls playing hard-to-get is one of my biggest fucking turn-ons. I love a good challenge and I rarely have that when trying to get laid anymore.

I sigh and start putting a plan of attack in my mind. First things first, I need to gain her trust.

AUBREY

The fact that Isaac's waiting on me to come into his office to take notes presses into my brain as I plop back down in my seat. A private message from Official Riff just dinged into my inbox within a couple minutes of requesting his online friendship.

My fingers shake a little as I click to open it.

Hello Wild Cat,

I haven't been able to stop thinking about you since the other night…that ticket never expires, just so you know. See you soon.

Riff

I swallow hard at the realization that he remembers me. I don't know whether to be flattered or scared. He's sexy as hell, I'll give him that, and my god, I bet he knows what he's doing in the bedroom. I love a man that's forward and goes for what he wants. It's one of the biggest reasons why I always fall for bad boys. Nice guys just don't have that edge I need to keep me interested.

Rock My Bed

My phone rings again, and I glance down at the number.

Shit. Isaac again. He's probably wondering where the hell I am.

I gather my things and head for his office across the hallway. Luckily for me, my boss typically works with his door shut, so I don't have to explain why I was sitting in my cubicle with my mouth hanging open staring at a computer screen instead of immediately jumping at the call to come into his office.

I knock once before I hear Isaac call "come in" on the other side of the door.

His office is in perfect order, as always. I never knew a man could be so neat until I met Isaac Walters. He's hard at work on his computer, typing furiously with his blue eyes narrowed through his glasses. The blond hair on his head lays perfectly in place. His gray suit jacket fits snugly across his broad shoulders. He's only older than me by a couple years, but he has a refined presence about him that makes him seem so much wiser.

I catch myself staring at him, ogling his chiseled cheekbones and sculpted nose before I shake my head and remind myself that this man is my boss, and a little bit too uptight for my taste. Yes, my boss is model perfect with a little touch of O.C.D. and makes for good eye-candy while I'm at work. This is the type of guy my mother would love for me to bring home, but he's totally not my style.

"Have a seat, Aubrey. I'll be right with you," Isaac says, never tearing his eyes away from his work.

I take my seat across from him and tug down my black skirt as I cross my legs. His ultra-modern black and glass desk gleams from the afternoon sun shining in from the wall of glass windows behind him. There's nothing better than New York in the summer time. Anything you could possibly want is in this city.

I adjust the yellow legal pad on my lap and click my pen, ready to jot down the list of notes I'm sure he's about to fire at me.

Once Isaac is satisfied with whatever he's working on, he turns his chair to face me directly. That's one thing I've learned from him. Direct eye contact lets people know you mean business. It's hard not to give him one hundred percent of your attention when he turns his gaze in your direction.

He folds his large hands together on his desk and clears his throat. "I was curious how it went this weekend with Black Falcon."

Oh shit!

This is surprising. We never really make small talk, and it kind of shocks me he's interested in an account that doesn't belong to him. Maybe Noel has called Diana and demanded that Lanie be fired, and I'm automatically going down too because of association.

I take a deep breath and internally cringe. "It went okay,

I think."

Isaac nods. "That's good. So, you think you're up for working with them a little more then?"

What? "I guess so."

"Excellent. I've been assigned to create the design for the Noel's children's literacy campaign, and I'm going to need a lot of help from you on this one since you had a chance to meet with the band and hear Noel's vision directly."

My shoulders relax, even though I'm still in shock a little bit. From what Lanie told me, Noel Falcon couldn't get away from her fast enough. I figured we'd be in some deep shit for losing such a large account for the firm, but from the way Isaac is talking, Black Falcon is still our client.

"Of course, anything you need."

Isaac leans back in his chair. "It's funny you say that, because what I actually need from you requires a bit of… discretion."

"Okay. No problem."

"I know you're close to our intern, Lanie Vance, and I'll need you to obtain some information from her."

I scrunch my brow, confused on where he's going with this. "What kind of information?"

"It seems that Noel Falcon is quite smitten with her, and has requested that she alone handle this account for him. Diana smoothed things over with him and led him to believe that was exactly what was going to happen. She even agreed to send Ms. Vance on the road with Black Falcon, at his request, for two weeks to appease him, but naturally we can't allow an intern who's still wet behind the ears run a million dollar project."

Things start to click. "So, you're going to work on it here, while Noel is left to believe that Lanie's in charge?"

He smiles. "Precisely."

"How am I involved in all of this?" I don't like the way this sounds. It feels an awful lot like he's asking me to lie to my best friend.

Isaac leans in and rests his elbows on the desk. "You're going to keep me on the inside track. Get her to tell you things about the band, and then report back to me."

I swallow hard. "I'm sorry, Isaac, but that feels like a huge betrayal of my best friend's trust."

He nods and scoots his chair back and walks around to the front of the desk. His tall frame towers over me as he leans back against his desk while both hands rest on either side of him. "I know this sounds bad, but it's not exactly what you're thinking. Diana was going to give this account to someone else until I threw my hat in the ring. I didn't think it was right to pull the rug out from someone like that, so I figured if I took the account, that since you know her, you could get her ideas. That way, we can still implement some of them…if they're good. She'll still get some credit."

"That seems awfully nice of you, but I can't help but wonder why you would get involved."

He shrugs. "Because you work for me, and I would like to keep it that way. If your friend quits because she gets angry over the Black Falcon account, I don't want her to convince you to quit with her. I like having you around."

That's kind of sweet, in a weird twisted way, but I'm not sure why he would go through all the trouble. It's not like we talk much, other than when we have to for business-related things. This sudden act of chivalry causes me to raise my eyebrows.

"Isaac, even though I love Lanie, I wouldn't quit my job on a whim. Center Stage has been my dream place to work since my third year of college. I'm glad you put your faith in a new grad and hired me even though I had no experience. No one else would've given me a shot like that, so I'm grateful to you for the chance."

Isaac's face lights up and his smile brightens. "Good, because I really don't want you to go anywhere. Matter of fact, I would like to keep you around so I can get to know you better."

I meet his gaze with my mouth slightly agape. Why am I getting the distinct feeling he's trying to make a play for me? This is so not good. I can't get into a relationship with my boss —it could end my career.

Feeling a bit uneasy about the situation, I stand and fight the instant urge to run as fast as I can out of this office.

"Okay, well, will there be anything else?"

He pulls his lips into a straight line. "No. That will be all, Aubrey. Please keep me informed of Ms. Vance's progress on the campaign."

I nod curtly and flee from his presence.

Shit.

I flop down in my desk chair inside my little cubicle and run my fingers through my hair. How can I tell a man to take his O.C.D. ass and beat it because I'm totally not interested in dating my boss? They certainly never prepare you for this in college. They should teach a *When Your Boss Wants to Fuck You: 101.*

I punch the spacebar on my keyboard, ready to fire a message of warning out to my best friend, but the message from Riff still sits on my screen.

If I tell Lanie about this, she'll probably quit and ruin the one shot she has at getting her foot in the door here. Pissing off people as powerful as Diana Swagger is highly inadvisable. She practically runs New York's advertising world. If she wants to destroy you and make sure you never work in this town again, she will.

Besides all that, going on the road with the man she still loves, even though she denies it, might be the start of a beautiful new relationship for her. One that I can tell even as an outsider isn't completely over for either one of them.

I stare at Riff's message, and the thought occurs to me

that I cannot only get insider information from Lanie to help her out secretly with the ad, but I may have just won myself a new connection in the form of a sexy, tattooed rocker.

I hit reply and begin to type.

Riff,

I'm amazed and flattered you remember me. It's nice to know the golden ticket still stands. I am kind of curious as to what it grants me admission to?

Aubrey

I hit send before I have a chance to chicken out. Since my last break up, I swore off the bad boy type, but I can't help but to still be attracted to them. When I saw my mother over the weekend back in Texas, she went on and on about how at twenty-four *she* was done with college, settled down with my father, and was ready to start her family. She just can't understand that I'm not ready to settle down, or feel that I have to.

I'm still young, with my entire life ahead of me. Twenty-four isn't old by any stretch of the means. What's wrong with messing around with a guy for fun every now and then? It's not like this thing between Riff and I will ever turn into a relationship anyway. My mom would have a heart attack if I brought someone like him home to meet her. She would like nothing more than for me to find a nice, boring man like Isaac and pop out a few heathens.

I shudder at the thought. Not that there's anything wrong with Isaac, but I know me. He would bore me to tears, and the organization issues he has would drive me insane.

I shake my head. The last thing I need to be thinking about right now is men, especially my boss. I've got bigger problems than that—namely, how and if I can break the news to Lanie about what's going on in the dirty underworld of Center Stage Marketing.

Chapter 3

RIFF

It's been a couple days since I received my Wild Cat's reply. So many times I've stopped myself from answering and telling her to name the time and place so I can fuck her out of my system. I don't want to seem desperate.

It's been a long time since I allowed a chick to get under my skin this way. The last time was clear back in high school when I set my sights on the Prom Queen. I didn't relent in that situation either, not until I had her legs thrown over my shoulders and she screamed about how big my cock was while we were in the back of my Charger.

Sexy women that play hard to get are my downfall.

I lean my head back against the headrest of the captain's chair while Big Bertha rolls down the road and I fish my phone from my pocket. To hell with trying to resist her allure. It'll drive me bat shit crazy if I don't have her soon.

"Who you calling?" Trip, our crazy-ass drummer, flops down in the seat beside mine with a huge bowl of cereal.

I ignore him and open up the social media site on my phone "Not that it's any of your fucking business, but I'm not calling anyone."

Trip readjusts his baseball cap. "Damn, dude, just trying to make some conversation. This place is boring as shit with you and Noel not really talking."

I raise my pierced eyebrow and shoot him a sideways glance. "That's not exactly my fault, now is it?"

He takes a huge bite of his cereal and swallows it down before he answers. "Don't start this shit again. Are you ever going to let this go? You weren't in love with Sophie. You said that yourself."

I shake my head and search out Aubrey's message. "That's not the fucking point, and you know it. Regardless if I loved her or not, you don't go behind your friend's back and fuck his girl. Period. Drunk or not. That's no excuse."

Trip nods in agreement. "Yeah, yeah. I get that. And you're totally right, but you're going to have to find a way to get past this shit. We're still a band, and we're trapped on this tiny fucking bus for far too long to allow this tension to go on. What's it going to take to fix this?"

I flip my lip ring in and out of my mouth a few times while I reflect on his words. He's right. Things around here have been tense for the past couple of months. It sucks for everyone because Noel and I have completely zapped away all the fun of being out on the road together. Yeah, it's partially my fault for bringing a chick on the road with us, but both of them fucking knew better, and I completely blame him.

Her—I couldn't really give two shits about.

But what Noel did broke our brotherly bond. It'll be hard to forgive him for that, but Trip's right. We can't keep going like this.

"I think I need to learn to let it go, for the sake of the band, and quit being a total fucking dick to him all the time. He's apologized to me several times—still claims he was too wasted to remember sleeping with her though. It's hard to let it go. Every time I see him, I think about it."

"I've been friends with you a long time, man. You've been through a ton of shit with your family, and I know it's hard for you to trust people. Hell, if this had been anyone other than Noel, I would've helped you beat his ass myself. It was a dick move on his part—he knows that—and now he has to deal with the fucking mess he's gotten himself into by knocking Sophie up. Be the bigger man, and let it go. It's what's best for this band. We've worked too damn hard to get here to flush our careers down the toilet over some skanky hoe." Trip gives me a pointed look and then drinks down the remaining milk in his cereal bowl.

For the guy that's the goofiest motherfucker in the band, he's sure making sense out of this fucked up situation.

When he gets up to go to the sink, I open Aubrey's last message. The thought of exactly what I'll be willing to give her when she cashes in that ticket makes me smile. It's nice to think about her and get my mind off all the other shit I'm going through.

Wild Cat,

Why don't you come use it and find out for yourself? ;)

Riff

I press send and then stuff my phone back into my pocket. She'll either be intrigued or tell me to go to hell. More than likely it'll be the latter, but that won't stop me. It'll only push me harder to get what I want—a night with her tangled up in some sheets.

AUBREY

My phone chirps with a new message as I help Lanie pack her bags to get ready to go on the road with Black Falcon.

"Do you need to get that?" Lanie asks.

I shake my head. "Nah. It's probably just Mom. I'll call her back when we're done." I fold one of her shirts and stuff it into her suitcase. "Are you excited?"

She sighs and her green eyes drift across the room. "Yes and no. I'm scared more than anything, but at the same time I am grateful for the opportunity to work on such a large account."

My heart sinks a little. What Diana is doing to her is completely wrong, and as I open my mouth to explain everything to her, she gets another text on her cell. The excitement in her eyes is evident as she reads the message. It's obviously another one from Noel. That guy has been texting her non-stop since she went on a 'business dinner' with him, but she refuses to tell me any details about it, which leads me to believe it was more pleasure than business.

No matter if I think telling her about Diana's plan is the right thing to do, I can't rob my friend of the happiness I know she'll have once she admits to herself that she's still madly in love with Noel.

After we have her pretty well packed, we get comfy and decide to veg out and watch a movie together. I load up a bowl of my favorite double brownie ice cream and head into the living room just in time to hear Lanie's cell ring with yet another text message.

She definitely has the most attentive Black Falcon band member chasing her. It's been days since I've heard from Riff, not that I honestly believe that we'll ever be anything other than pen pals, but I do feel a twinge of jealously at all the attention she's getting from Noel.

I roll my eyes as she grabs her phone off the coffee table. "Mr. Wonderful, again? You still owe me some juicy details about your dinner date, you know."

She shakes her head. "A lady never kisses and tells.

Besides you already know nothing happened. It was strictly business."

That's rich. I wish she would quit kidding herself. I plop down on the couch beside her. "You, missy, are no lady. So, dish."

She shrugs. "Nothing happened the other night. I swear."

I fold my legs under my butt, take a bite of my ice cream, deciding I need to force her to try to see the bigger picture here. "Bull. You expect me to believe Noel Falcon makes a romantic date with you and after a couple of hours together nothing happens? He's texted you at least fifty times over the past few days, and there was no sex involved? I say bull. No man gets that sprung unless he gets a little somethin'-somethin' if you know what I mean."

She gives me a pointed look. "Getting romantic with Noel is the last thing on my mind."

Just as I thought: she's in complete denial. I lick my spoon and push for a little more details. "So he's PG-13, huh? That's kind of disappointing. Not much of a 'Sex-god' is he? I figured as much as you talked about him he'd have you out of your panties within the hour."

"Aubrey!" She smacks my bare leg. "I can't believe you just called him that."

"What? A 'Sex-god'?" I say around my spoon. "I got the name from you. That's how you always referred to him, but I'm thinkin' of revoking his title after the boring business date story you just told me."

She's quiet for a few minutes, and I fidget in my seat. I know that look on her face. It's the same look she used to get back in college when she was about ready to drop one of her brilliant ideas on me.

She sighs. "Well, there are other single guys in the band...Why don't you meet us at a show or something?"

"Are you serious?" My thoughts instantly flick to a second chance with Riff. Sleeping with a bad boy of rock and roll has always been one of my bucket list items, and now that I know he's interested there's no way he won't be down for a night of hot sweaty sex. After all, he's famous for one-night stands.

"Totally serious. I know how much you wanted to get backstage and meet the guys before, so I figure I kind of owe you."

I fight the urge to toss my ice cream on the floor and throw my arms around her and go into a total girl hugging and screaming fit of excitement. She really is my best friend.

That last thought causes my heart to twist a little and makes me feel like a complete jerk. Would a best friend keep a huge secret? Isaac is asking a lot from me, but I know deep down, he's right. Telling her now would only cause her to do something crazy, like walk out on Center Stage Marketing. Lanie's hot-headed, and when she's pissed she speaks her mind with no filter.

Before I can struggle anymore with the internal debate, her cell phone rings. Noel's calling her *again*. She answers with a sickly sweet tone to her voice and I shake my head with a grin on my face. Fight him my ass, that boy will have her in his bed before the week is up. For a while I sit and listen to how happy she is by merely talking to him and my thoughts are confirmed. I can't screw this up for her. If she knows the truth, she'll never go to him and possibly find happiness.

I whisper and tell her we can skip the movie and that I'm heading to bed. She waves me off and continues to talk to Noel. Yep, I give it a week tops before she's humping him.

I set my bowl on my nightstand as my cell buzzes with a new message. I had nearly given up hope of hearing back from Riff, so I'm caught off guard when I see there's a new message from him on our private message thread.

I gnaw on my lip as I read his words. Just as I thought, he's totally down for a one-nighter. Bad boys make the best lovers, and Riff is one that I can't wait to sample. I pull the ticket he gave me from my nightstand drawer and read the crude words.

One Night with a Rock Star

Admit One

I shake my head and laugh. It's clever, really. Handing out tickets like sex with him is a coveted prize. Suddenly, the silly 'golden ticket' song from *Willy Wonka and the Chocolate Factory* rings through my mind. Bad boy Riff has a sense of humor. This could be fun.

Riff,

Tempting…

Aubrey

P.S. What's up with the Wild Cat name? Do you call all the women you try to bed that?

Aubrey

I hit send and I hope this time it doesn't take him two days to respond. Five minutes later, another message dings in.

Kitten (since you seem opposed to Wild Cat),

You're my only Wild Cat. I knew from the minute you tried to resist me, that deep down there's a naughty girl inside you dying to bust out and cash in that ticket. You contacting me only proves my theory. So why don't you save us both a lot of trouble and name your time and place so we can fuck each other out of our systems.

Name the date.

Riff

I nearly choke on my ice cream as I read his words. Just like when he kissed me backstage, he's not afraid to go all out and say exactly what he has on his mind. I respect him for that.

I reread his message, and while I agree one hundred percent that we need to get this over with, I don't want to seem like one of his random sluts that can be used. I do want a little respect from him. If I can keep this little messaging game up for a bit, and make him wait, I'll stick in his mind. I'm fully prepared to give into his wicked ways when I visit Lanie on the road with the band, but I want to be the girl that blows his mind. The woman, when he looks back, who was most amazing in bed.

Dearest Cocky Riff,

You want me? You have to earn it. It'll be worth it.

Aubrey

Either he'll take the challenge or I'll never hear from him again. Before I have a time to toss my phone on my bed, another message comes in.

Name your terms, Kitten…

I nearly squeal with delight. Game on.

RIFF

Damn it. Only a few messages in and I've already let her gain the upper hand. This is so not good. I stare at the message I just sent her and bounce my leg while I wait for the floodgate to be unleashed.

Noel comes out of the back room or as I like to call it his throne room. It kind of pisses me off that because he's the front man everyone willingly handed him the only bedroom on the bus. See where his fucking privacy got him.

Trip turns around from the kitchen sink and acknowledges our band mate.

"What's up, man?" Noel says to Trip as he plops down on the bench seat attached to the kitchen table.

Noel slides the opened pack of Oreos that I left on the table away from him. At least he knows not to touch those. Too bad he didn't realize the same rule applied to the chicks I'm banging. Everyone knows not to touch my fucking cookies or I go ape shit. That's one thing I don't share with these assholes. They'd eat every single one if I weren't such a dick about it.

Noel clears his throat. "I need to have a band meeting."

I roll my eyes. Leave it to Noel to always be the one to call for a band meeting like there's a problem with the rest of us. Usually the problem is him, or caused by him. Ever since we dubbed him the band's leader—none of us wanted the responsibility of making tough decisions for the group—he's taken it to extremes. Calling band meetings is typically a way he gets to bitch at us for some stupid reason or another.

"Tyke! Get your fruity ass in here!" Trip yelled at his twin who's still back in his bunk.

"What?" Tyke calls back grumpy.

Tyke writes the majority of the band's songs, and likes to be left alone most of the time with his 'thoughts' so he can concentrate. I know he really just fucking sleeps when he's in there, using song writing as an excuse for us not to bother him. He probably busts out the songs right before we get in the studio. I'm down with all his tricks.

"Noel wants to have a band meeting. Hurry the fuck up!"

I shake my head. I've known Trip and Tyke since junior high school. I know everything about them, and they know everything about me. Sometimes that's a real pain in the ass when all you want to do is forget your fucking past.

Tyke fumbles out of his foxhole and shoves his blonde hair out of his face. "What the fuck did we do now?"

I laugh.

Noel raises his pierced eyebrow and cuts me a look that tells me he's not amused by our distaste of his leadership. "Look, guys, there's going to be a guest staying on the bus with us for the next couple of weeks."

"Who?" Trip asks.

"An old friend of mine that I've hired to run my children's charity campaign."

I shake my head. "Hell no! You aren't bringing another chick on this bus."

Noel's gaze flicks to me. "It's already done. She'll be meeting up with us in Columbus tomorrow."

"This is fucking horse shit." The idea of Noel bringing his ex-girlfriend on this bus so he can have at her for two weeks behind Sophie's back is sickening. He's a bigger fucking douchebag than I thought. "Don't you have any morals at all?"

"I haven't forgotten my responsibilities, if that's what you're referring to."

"That's exactly what I'm talking about. All you do is use people!" I seethe.

Noel jumps up from the table and his nostrils flare. "You obviously don't know a goddamn thing about me. I don't fucking use people."

The muscles in my jaw work under my skin. "What the fuck do you call Sophie then, huh? You're telling me you didn't use her?"

He runs his fingers through his hair. "How many fucking times can I say I don't remember sleeping with her? If it happened, it was a one-time thing that meant nothing to me. It's not like I set out to deliberately hurt you! You think I like fucking fighting with you?"

I shrug. "You seem too. That's all we ever do is fight over this."

"That's because you won't let it go!" Noel shouts.

"All I know is you knocked Sophie up, and you promised to stick by her through this pregnancy. How's it going to look when you're banging your ex on the bus for two weeks?"

He shakes his head. "Lane can't stand me anymore. She's only doing this because I backed her into a corner at her job. If she doesn't come on this bus with me now, she'll get fired."

"What do you mean she'll get fired?" Tyke chimes in.

Noel scratches the back of his neck. He only does that shit when he's nervous. Whatever he's about to drop on us isn't good.

"I kind of promised the owner of Center Stage Marketing rights to all Black Falcon ad campaigns for the band in exchange for giving Lane this opportunity."

"What!?" Tyke exclaimed in the tone of voice he usually reserves when his brother does something idiotic. "Without consulting us, you made that big of a business decision?"

"There was no time. The owner of the company forced my fucking hand. She threatened to fire Lane because she didn't disclose that we knew each other. Long story short, if

Lane doesn't come on this bus, she'll hate me forever. I can't have that. I hope you guys can understand." He drops his head.

"I understand plenty," I say while I stand up. "This further proves you only think with your dick."

"Riff—"

"Shut the fuck up, Noel. Do whatever you want, 'cause you know you will anyway." I don't give him a chance to say anymore before I storm off and climb into my bunk, slamming the curtain closed.

It's really nothing against Lanie. I'm sure she's harmless, and can even be a good insight on Kitten, but I hate that Noel gets his way all the fucking time. Why should that guy get it so good?

The last thought causes my fists to clench. I know I told Trip I would work on forgiving Noel, but the more he does shit like this, the more I want to see fate turn around and kick him square in the balls.

"Riff?" Noel says on the other side of the curtain.

Doesn't he fucking get it? I huff and roll over to face the wall.

"I'm sorry, man. I know I should've talked to you guys first, but I was desperate…" he trails off like he's waiting on a response from me. When I don't say anything, he knocks on the wall at the top of my bunk. "Night."

I let out a sigh after I'm sure he's gone. Thank god. I hate fighting. That's all my family ever did and now that I'm an adult I want to stay as far away from bullshit as I can.

I close my eyes and will myself to sleep, but before I drift off, my phone vibrates in my pocket. I flip over onto my back and grin when I see Aubrey's name.

I only have three simple rules:

1. I determine the time and place

2. You have to make me want you

3. No falling in love

Those are my terms. Take 'em or leave 'em.

Aubrey

I chuckle to myself. I give her an open door and that's the best rules she can come up with? Number one is fine by me as long as she doesn't make me wait too damn long. The second one's laughable. She already wants me or she wouldn't be playing this little game in the first place, and third not falling in love? Is she kidding me? That's the easiest one on the list. I don't do love. Period. Not even with my own family. I don't love them and they don't love me. This chick has another thing coming if she thinks I'm some sad, sappy asshole. I'm not a guy that can be tamed. Ever.

Chapter 4

AUBREY

I double-check my phone again before tossing it back into my purse under my desk. Riff hasn't responded yet. He probably thinks I'm completely lame now. I mean, I've never claimed to be witty, or someone who's good with coming up with ideas on a whim, so I panicked a little last night. If I put more thought into what the rules were, maybe they would've been better—made this game between us more fun.

It's not like I can call Lanie up either and tell her all about this. I don't want her trying to play matchmaker while she's on that damn bus because I don't want a relationship with Riff. It's a good thing I didn't mention the kiss between Riff and me to her either. I would've never heard the end of it about how I let men walk all over me and how I always pick the wrong guy.

Sometimes she sounds like my mother.

I get so tired of hearing what people think is the right thing for me to do with my life and my relationships. People don't get that I'm not looking for a guy to settle down with. Not really, anyway. I like freedom and being crazy if I feel like it. I like sex. I like slightly kinky sex even more, which is why I think Riff will be down to play a few naughty games if given the opportunity.

I open a new file on my computer and get busy typing up a memo about the Black Falcon charity that Isaac assigned me earlier in the day.

Speak of the devil…

Isaac gives me an easy smile as he strides up to my desk. "Hey, Aubrey. You got a minute?"

I nod as I take in his polished features. The skin on his cheeks appears smooth and soft, with no hint of stubble. He probably takes better care of his skin then I do. I bet he smells pretty great too.

I lean in a little as I stand before him and take a whiff, hoping it's not obvious. I grab the things off my desk. Yep, there's definitely some type of woodsy cologne sprayed on him, which is off because nothing about him screams lumberjack.

I follow Isaac into his office, and he shuts us inside once I'm seated. "How have you been?"

One of my eyebrows shoots up on its own accord. This

is unusual. "I'm fine, and you?"

He shakes his head as he sits behind his desk. "Not so good. Diana's breathing down my neck wanting preliminary details for the marketing plan. Did you get any information from Ms. Vance about the vision from the project?"

My lips pull into a tight line. "She just left this morning to meet up with them."

Isaac sighs. "I was afraid you were going to say that. This project has to get rolling, and since we don't have any information from Lanie, I have to move on without her input."

I bite my bottom lower lip. "Do I still have to keep this secret from her?"

He nods. "Think of the damage walking out on a company like Center Stage will do to her career. I know she's your friend, but the best thing you can do is keep this from her. If she gets upset, she won't think rationally. Plus, Diana would probably fire me if this got back to Lanie and we lost the Black Falcon account."

I slump a little in my seat. I hate that he's right so damn much. Lanie Vance is one of the most hotheaded people I know. I've never met someone so willing to fight at the drop of a hat if she knows she's right or feels she's being wronged in some way.

I want to tell her, but I think maybe I need to keep this from her while she's on the road because I don't want her to go crazy. If she quits, Isaac and I will probably be fired for telling her. This is Diana Swagger's company and she's not known for being understanding.

I stare into Isaac's big blue eyes. There's concern in them marked by crinkles on the outer edge of them. In the two months that I've been here, not once has he shown me any real concern, merely been a friendly coworker.

I sigh. "That's true. I just hate keeping things from her, especially since she's my roommate, but I don't want her to ruin her dream because Diana refuses to have faith in her work abilities."

Isaac stands, his black suit hugging him in all the right places, and then walks around his desk. I stiffen a little as he gracefully takes the seat beside me. "I'm glad you're being so reasonable about this. You're a strong person who cares a great deal for her friend. That's very attractive in a woman."

I swallow down the lump in my throat and my pulse quickens. This closeness between us feels very intimate—like we're entering into new territory. One that will end up with us spending late nights with me bent over his desk if I'm not careful.

I nervously tuck a strand of my hair behind my ear and curse myself for having these thoughts about my boss. I'm sure he's just being nice and is in no way trying to flirt with me. I'm reading into him sitting next to me all wrong.

My eyes flick to his. "I understand. I promise I won't mention this to her."

He smiles, and still holds my gaze. "Thank you."

I feel his eyes on me as I stand and walk out of the door, hating that I promised to keep this from Lanie.

Back at my desk, I fire up my computer and get to work on a couple projects Isaac gave me for the afternoon. An hour later I'm so totally absorbed in my work, the chirp from my phone causes me to jump a little.

I dig my phone up from my purse and can't fight back the grin on my face.

Kitten,

I'm down with any rules you want to throw at me as long as the outcome ends up with me and you getting hot, sweaty and naked.

R

A thrill shoots through me. We both have exactly the same thing in mind. I'm so glad he's not looking for more than sex with me. He'll make the perfect one last hurrah before I start down my path to becoming a Soccer Mom—one last fling with a bad boy before I start looking out for a man like Isaac who won't crush my heart.

RIFF

Crowds of women shove against one another in attempts to gain my attention. Cameras flash in my eyes as different arms are thrown around my neck, invading my personal space. I keep moving forward and push my way between them so I can make it up the steps backstage, where their access to me will be cut off.

A brunette yanks down her red t-shirt, effectively stretching out the neckline. "Will you sign me?"

She lowers the shirt enough for me to see a hint of her left nipple. This is her way of saying I can have her if I want. "Sure."

I hand her Sharpie back and a frown creases into her face when I don't say another word. I turn away and my eyes land on a fine piece of ass staring in my direction. My mind flashes back to that night in Houston when Kitten was looking at me with the same amount of curiosity. The brunette in cut-off jean shorts has killer legs, and I would love to get them wrapped around me. With any luck, she'll have that same fire that drew me in with Kitten and I can get over this stupid obsession I have over a girl I don't even know.

Security holds the mass of female fans behind me back and I lock eyes with Legs McGee. When she catches me staring, I give her my most cocky grin.

"Damn, you're sexy," I say as my eyes rake slowly over

her body. She has amazing tits. Tits are totally my weak spot on a woman.

Her eyes narrow as I stare at her chest openly. I try to make it very clear to women what I want from them, that way there's no misunderstanding between us. I don't do relationships.

She's glaring at me like she wants to kill me, which only makes me smirk. I love it when they play hard-to-get. I reach into my back pocket and pull out a ticket. She's earned it, and she'll make a great distraction. "This golden ticket grants you access into my pants when our set is over. Hold on to it tight and give it to security that guards the buses. They'll let you through. I only give away one or two of those a night. Consider yourself a lucky lady."

I stuff the paper into her hand, and she flinches at my touch.

Odd, that's not the typical reaction I get from a girl.

Leggy Hottie shakes her head and attempts to hand me back the paper. "No thanks."

"Not interested?" I laugh. She's hot *and* funny. "Sweetie, that's cute, but you don't have to play hard to get. I know why you're back here, and I can guarantee there's no better time to be had than the one you're going to get with me."

Time to up the charm factor.

I lick my lips and allow my fingertips to trace the skin on her bare arm.

Suddenly, she slams the ticket into my chest with enough force I actually flinch. "I'm waiting for someone, you asshole. I'm not some random fucking groupie."

Whoa. I raise my eyebrows. That wasn't exactly the reaction I had in mind. This girl may not be playing. She actually seems kind of pissed, which makes the challenge of bedding her even more appealing. I allow my typical panty-dropping grin to return to my face as I relax and brush off her harsh words. "You're feisty. I like that." I tilt my head and study her. She's stunning and would've made an awesome notch on my belt. "What a shame. We could've been pretty awesome together tonight. You know where to find me if you change your mind."

I step back and allow the piece of paper fall to the ground in case she decides she wants to use it after all. It lands between us by our feet and I wink at her before I turn and walk away.

What are the odds of running into a woman who reminds me a lot of Kitten? I hope I'm not turning into one of those saps that try to make every girl in the world seem like the one girl they really want. That would be pathetic.

I shake my head and roll my eyes at my own thoughts as I continue backstage to get ready for my show. I need to get laid, bad. I'm starting to feel emotions, and I don't like that shit. Emotions are bad, very bad. I have to get Kitten out of my mind.

After Black Falcon's set we all hang out with the

roadies and the opening act, Embrace the Darkness, backstage. That's one thing about being a rocker. You're never alone. There's always people who adore you and hang on your every word around. Take this chick on my lap for example. All it took for her to come to me was a crook of the finger.

The blonde giggles as I slip my hand into the waist band of her jeans. This one, like most of the others, offered no challenge when I pulled out a golden ticket. She eagerly accepted and offered to drop to her knees and blow me on the spot, which was a little awkward considering we were in a crowd of people.

Some women will do anything. Even though most of the time their willingness is welcomed, lately I haven't been feeling the whole groupie scene. I'm twenty-six fucking years-old. I should be having the time of my life, but I can't shake the feeling that there's something missing.

I blame the redheaded vixen that's gotten her hooks into my head.

Ever since her ass messaged me, all I've been thinking about is that kiss and what it'll be like to fuck the hell out of her. That girl earlier tonight reminded me a lot of Kitten. She would've made a good distraction if she hadn't told me to basically go to hell.

"Can I cash in that ticket now? You're so fucking hot," the tipsy blonde says into my ear, taking me away from my thoughts.

I pull back and gaze into her face. She's attractive with

her platinum hair and dark eyes, but she doesn't have that spark I'm looking for—that thing that's sometimes in another person that can light you up and remind you that you're alive. This chick is here for the ride, which is fine, and I'll happily give her what she craves, but it'll only be instant gratification for me. That few seconds of bliss that makes me forget about everything else, but the here and now. I'm addicted to forgetting. My life is something I would love to sometimes forget.

She leans in and runs her tongue across my lips. "I want you."

She's persistent. I'll give her that. The quick flicks of her tongue against mine causes my dick to grow hard and strain against my jeans. "Come with me."

I nearly toss her off my lap before I take her hand and pull her into the next room. It's a cleaning supply storage closet, but there's enough room in here to get the job done.

Blondie is eager. She goes right to work on freeing my cock from my jeans. It springs up once she shoves my jeans and boxers down a little. She wraps her fingers around me and gives me a couple quick tugs.

I suck in a quick breath. "Jesus."

She's done this before. You don't get great hand job skills without some practice.

She drops to her knees, but I pull back. "Not without a condom."

Rock My Bed

I never let random hookers lick my dick without one. It's probably not the most pleasant experience for them to basically suck rubber, but I don't have any sexually transmitted diseases and I would like to fucking keep it that way. I don't know where the fuck her mouth's been. I don't even know her name for fuck's sake.

I tear the foil package with my teeth, pull the rubber out and then roll it onto my cock.

She runs her tongue up and down my length. "You have a huge cock. I want you to fuck me with it really hard."

I know this is a further ploy to turn me on, but I hear the same lame ass lines from different chicks every night. I stare down at her as she swirls my dick around her lips, before taking me into her mouth.

She's slow at first with a nice, steady rhythm, but I know I don't want to be trapped with her very long, so I grab a handful of her hair and coax her into sucking faster.

I close my eyes and try to forget where I am, and even who I am, focusing only on how good I feel. That's when I'll be damned if Kitten doesn't pop back into my mind. I can see her leaning against the wall where I first spotted her. The feel of her smoking hot body shoved against mine, and the little moan she let slip into my mouth when I kissed her plays in my thoughts. Suddenly, I imagine us naked against that wall, with me driving my cock balls-deep into her.

"Fuck!" A tingle takes over my entire body and I clench every muscle in my body as I come hard.

A couple shudders ripple through me as I untangle my hand from the blonde's hair.

"Can you go again? I didn't get anything out of this," she whines.

I shrug. "Better luck next time, sweetie. I'm done with you, so you can go ahead and go." I nod towards the door.

She stands with a scowl on her face. "Fuck you!"

I shake my head, but refuse to make eye contact because I'm actually kind of embarrassed. I didn't mean to lose my shit so fast, but I have to play it off. No one wants to be thought of as a one-minute man. "No thanks. It was hard enough coming for you the first time. Now leave."

"Asshole!" she shouts before she slams the door, leaving me alone finally.

Fuck. I rub my forehead. What the fuck is wrong with me? I feel like I'm losing my fucking mind.

Exhausted from the mind-fuck I just went through, I drag my ass inside of Big Bertha, ready to pass out. When I reach the top step, the sight in my kitchen stops me dead in my tracks. Bending over going through our cabinets is the hot brunette with nice tits and legs. Her presence is surprising considering her reaction to the ticket when I gave it to her. She must've decided to use it after all. There's no other way she could've gotten on this bus.

"I knew you'd be here," I say and she stands instantly and stiffens. "The ladies never turn down the golden ticket."

Rock My Bed

I grin as I balance my weight against the top cabinet and peer down at her. Her eyes rake over my shirtless chest, lingering a couple seconds too long on my tattoos and nipple piercings to hide her interest. I flick my lip ring between my teeth a couple times and she attempts hide some of the bare skin on those sexy legs by tugging at her shorts. A slow grin pulls across my face as I inspect every curve on her voluptuous body. She shakes her head vigorously as I pull my arm down and take a step towards her.

She holds out a shaky palm up. "Stop right there."

I reach for her hand, craving contact with someone real, but she snatches it away from my grasp. "Baby, I told you. No need to play hard to get. I won't tell anyone that you fucked me."

Her eyes widen like she can't believe I would say such a thing to her. This only excites me more. "You're really full of yourself, you know that?"

I smirk. She's one hell of an actress. "Only when it comes to women."

She rolls her eyes. "I hate to be the one to break it to you, but not every woman on the planet is willing to sleep with you, Riff."

"Maybe." I shrug. "But I can tell that *you* want me." I take another step towards her and she backs away, trying to put distance between us. She bumps against the cabinets behind her and I close in.

She shoves her tiny hand into my chest and shakes her head again. "No, I don't want you. I'm here with—"

"Shhhhhhhhhhhhh." I try and sooth her while I stroke the soft skin on her shoulder. I want her to show me she wants me. No more games. Time to be real. "No more talking."

"What the fuck do you think you're doing, Riff?" Noel growls from the hallway, wearing a low-slung towel around his hips, while water beads speckle his chest. Oh shit. Is this his piece of imported ass? How the hell did he get so fucking lucky?

I pull my hands off the woman and gaze into her eyes. Now I know why he's so crazy over her. She's hot, but what makes her even better is she's Noel's one big heartbreak. "You're Lanie?"

She nods and glances at Noel. "I've tried to tell you. I told you I was with someone when you first tried to shove that ticket thing in my hand."

Noel's eyes narrow at me. "You gave her one of your fucking golden tickets? I'm going to fucking kill you."

Noel's face twists with rage and he lunges for me, but I'm quick enough to avoid him and shove his hands away. I don't know why he thinks he owns this chick. She left him, and obviously we have no guy code between us, so as far as I'm concerned she's fair game. Matter of fact, I love the idea of paying him back by sleeping with his girl.

Lanie throws her hands against Noel's chest. "It's okay.

Let it go. He made a mistake." She looks over at me like she wants me to apologize to defuse the situation. She has no idea that isn't going to fucking happen. "Right?"

I stare Noel down. If he thinks he's scaring me off right now, he's got another fucking thing coming. To drive it home, with as much sarcasm as I can muster, I say, "Yeah, we wouldn't want to accidentally steal each other's woman, would we?"

Lanie flinches at my tone. I'm sure she has no clue what's gone down between us. As much as I would like to spill the beans, and tell her all about the secret I'm sure Noel's hiding from her, I keep my mouth shut. He'll eventually hang himself.

The muscle in Noel's jaw clenches. "You stay away from her. Or so help me God, Riff, I will end you."

It takes everything in me not to laugh in his face. He may be sporting a look of pure malice, but that shit doesn't intimidate me. He and I both know we're pretty evenly matched. If he comes at me he better be ready for a fight.

Noel and I continue to stare each other down, neither of us ready to be the first one to back down. Lanie being here ups the stakes between us, and he knows that. He knows I can pull chicks and this girl already hates him, so snagging her away will make a fun game. He just added fuel to our never-ending feuding fire.

Lanie pulls on Noel's arm and he tilts his head down and gazes at her. "Come on, Noel. I want to show you something." She grabs his hand when he doesn't immediately respond. She obviously doesn't want us to come to blows and she's doing her best to diffuse the situation.

Noel stares at me, like he's daring me to let everything out—to tell Lanie his secret and ruin his chance getting her back.

Finally, after he sees I'm not going to say another word, Noel nods and follows Lanie down the hallway, leaving me alone in the front of the bus.

I lean back against the cabinet and sigh. Jesus can my life get anymore fucked up?

My cell buzzes in my pocket and fish it out to read the message.

Riff,

Hot, sweaty and naked? Really? That's the best line you got? I expected more from one of the world's biggest players? I guess I can cross 'has suave game' off the list of your qualities. I can't believe women respond to that lameness.

You want to bed me? Impress me.

Aubrey

I laugh and shake my head. Kitten is really headstrong. What I wouldn't give for her to be here right now so I can show her how well lines like that can work when whispered into a horny woman's ear. I bet I would even forget my own name when I'm with her. She's exactly the distraction I need.

Chapter 5

AUBREY

I close myself inside the car and direct the driver to take me to LaGuardia airport. The tiny shoebox apartment I share with Lanie seems so much bigger now that she's away. Not in the good way either—more like the lonely-you're-all-by-yourself way. It's sort of depressing, so I'm glad to be out of it for a few days.

It's only been a few days since Lanie left to tour with Noel, and sadly the only company I've really had was my co-workers and sporadic messages from Riff.

I pull out my phone and reread the last message he sent me.

Kitten,

On the road again. This bus ride would be a lot more fun with you here. Please name the date when we can hook up. I'll fly you out to wherever I am. Say the word. The wait is driving me crazy.

R

I smile. I like the idea that it's me that's driving him crazy and he's so desperate to have me he'll come to me wherever I am. It's odd how connected I feel to him through this little message exchange we've been having even though I really don't know him at all. Even though I know he's a bad boy heart breaker type, he makes me feel special—wanted. What girl wouldn't love that?

My fingers itch to tap out my reply and let him know that my best friend has arranged for me to meet up with her and the rest of the band today. It's only for a long weekend, and once I told Isaac where I was going he practically shoved me out the office door to leave as quickly as possible. Hopefully, Riff would be excited to know our agreed upon one-night-stand was going to take place sooner rather than later.

The flight passes by fairly quickly. I couldn't sleep. My excitement level won't let me, but I know I should. Something tells me tonight will be a rather long one with Riff.

I hail a cab and quickly shut myself inside and give him my destination. My pulse races under my skin as we make our way down the freeway. I can't believe I'll be meeting up with one of the world's hottest rock bands soon and possibly sleeping with one of its members.

Crazy.

The parking lot behind American Airlines Center concert hall is filled with a group of crazed fans hoping to catch a glimpse of the men of Black Falcon.

The cabbie stops the car near the gate that's clearly marked 'authorized personnel only' and turns to me. "That'll be forty-seven fifty." I pass my money up through the slot and let the wave of excitement pass through me as I instruct him to keep the change. I can't believe I'm actually here and am about to follow through on a commitment of a one-night stand with Riff. I've never done something as bold as agreeing beforehand to purely have a sexual relationship with a man. This will definitely be something new for me, but I'm sure this won't be a big deal at all for him.

I guess I'm nervous enough for both of us.

I set my suitcase down and stand at the edge of the crowd waiting for the tour bus to roll in. Several of the women walking about are practically wearing nothing but beach attire and stiletto heels. Like me, they're basically here to have a romp with a rocker, but at least I have enough decency not to announce it to the rest of the world. I think I still look pretty cute in my low rise cut off shorts and a black tank top. It's fairly close to what I was wearing the last time I caught Riff's attention.

The gate opens and the brakes squeak as the bus pulls to a halt alongside the crowd. Cameras instantly flash while the onlookers hold up their 'we love you' signs and scream out the names of the guys in the band.

A scantily dressed blonde beside me turns to her friend and says, "I'll take Riff tonight and you get Noel. I'm ready to sample some of that Mohawk hotness."

I don't know why, but her words instantly make my blood boil and the words 'not if I get to him first' flash in my brain.

Patience is not my strong point after I don't see a sign of Lanie coming out to meet me. I pull my cell from my pocket and dial her number.

"I was just getting ready to call you," she answers.

"Good thing because I'm already here," I tell her as I strain my eyes to try to catch a glimpse of her through the tinted bus windows. "I think this is the bus you're on."

"I see you! I'm coming out," she practically squeals in my ear.

The bus door flies open and Lanie bounds out of the door. I push past security and grab her up in a tight hug. "I've been waiting for freaking ever." I release her and shove my hair over my shoulder. "It's good to see you too. I've missed you."

She grabs my hand. "Come on. I want you to meet the guys before they all take off on their two day reprieve."

A giggle escapes me as I find it impossible to contain my excitement. I grab my luggage and she pulls me up the bus steps. Three of the band members, Trip, Tyke and Riff stare openly at me once we step inside. Curiosity burns in their eyes as they soak every inch of me in. I swallow hard and look away.

Shit. They all know I'm here to sleep with Riff. He must've spotted me and told them I was his designated sex for the night. I inhale deeply and allow my gaze to land on Riff. He's just as unbelievably sexy as I remember. His tall, muscular frame leans casually against the counter beside him while he bites his plump bottom lip. There's a sparkle of mischief in his green eyes as he grins at me.

My insides jitter as I get the distinct feeling he's going to cause me to walk funny before the night's through.

Lanie pulls me beside her. "Guys, this is my closest friend, Aubrey. Aubrey this is Black Falcon. This is Trip"—she points to him—"he's the drummer. And this is his twin brother, Tyke—also the bass player. And last but not least—"

"Riff." He steps forward and takes my hand into his like we've never met before.

His eyes glue to mine and I grin like an idiot and even let another nervous giggle slip. I need to get my shit together and play it cool. He's going to think I'm a giggling bimbo if I don't stop this. Riff's gaze falls to my lips and heat rushes to my cheeks, surely flushing them red and exposing my embarrassment.

I bite my lip as he continues to shake my hand. I'm sure Lanie and the other guys have noticed our rather lengthy hello. I hope she doesn't drill me about this later.

Trip slaps Riff on the back. "Later, man."

Trip and Tyke head off the bus, but Riff doesn't even flinch or tell them goodbye. It's like he can't tear himself away from me.

Lanie clears her throat, and I finally let go of Riff's hand. "So, um, Aubrey, what do you want to do today?"

Reluctantly I pull my eyes away from Riff and say, "Doesn't matter."

"How about we all hang out," Riff says, not giving Lanie any chance to suggest something for the two of us alone to do.

Heavy boots clomp onto the kitchen floor. Noel's showered and looking downright sexy in tight jeans and black t-shirt. The material clings to his chest and shows off his body perfectly. Lanie's the one biting her lip now. I give her a second to ogle him before I grin and elbow her for an introduction.

"What's going on?" Noel asks as he grabs a bottle of water from the refrigerator.

"Noel this is my friend, Aubrey. The one I was telling you about."

He gives me a nod and then points his attention to Riff, who hasn't taken his eyes off me since I set foot on this bus. "You're going out with these two?"

Riff blinks hard a couple times, like he's breaking out of trance. "Yeah, I mean, if they're cool with that."

Before Lanie can object, I answer, "Absolutely."

Riff grins at me again and then puts on his sunglasses while he heads for the bus door. "Awesome. Let's get this show on the road."

My heart does a double thump as I turn to immediately follow him, only to be halted when Lanie grabs my arm. "What the hell are you doing?"

I shrug and try to play it off like I just met Riff and we don't already have plans to hump like rabbits. "He's hot and seems into me. What's the problem?"

She frowns at me. "Nothing, I guess. Just be cautious. I don't want to see you get hurt."

I lean in and kiss her cheek to assure her I'm not going down the same road with Riff as I have in the past. She knows most men have a track record of tearing my heart into pieces. "I'm a big girl, Lanie. I'm just here to have a good time, not get married. I know what I'm doing."

She throws her arms around my neck and says into my ear, "Of course, have a good time."

I grin at her—glad she understands and doesn't judge me before I follow Riff out the door. As soon as he spots me, he pulls away from signing autographs. His Mohawk standing at full attention as a slow smile spreads across his face and he holds out his hand to me.

"Why didn't you tell me you were coming?" he asks as he pulls me toward a black Escalade.

I shrug. "I wanted it to be a surprise."

He opens the door for me and then yanks me flush against his chest. "Oh it's a surprise all right, but it's nothing compared to the one you're going to get later."

His lips hover above mine for a few seconds and all I can think about is the feel of his lips on mine again. As he leans in, I hear a female call his name, totally ruining the almost moment we shared.

I pull away and huff, causing Riff to chuckle at my annoyance of his adoring female fans. He helps me into the middle row of the SUV with a hand on my ass and follows behind me.

Once the door is closed and we're alone inside, I open my mouth to ask him about the ticket, but I never get the chance. He practically attacks me before I even have a chance to settle into my seat. His lips and hands are everywhere. It's like he's a starving man and I'm a juicy steak he can't wait to tear into. Both of his hands settle on my hips before he turns me to face him. My back rests awkwardly against the door, the armrest digging into my neck as he shoves his body against mine. The weight of him is forceful and I don't have to guess what's on his mind.

"I've never had to wait this long to have a woman," he says against my lips. "You've already got me so fucking hard."

I pull away and pant. "Just a little longer. I promise."

I know letting him basically have his way with me in the backseat of a random car isn't the best way to stand out amongst the bimbos he's typically with, but it's hard to resist him.

He cups my cheeks and stares into my eyes for a split second, like he's drinking me in, before his lips crash into mine. His tongue enters my mouth and slides effortlessly over mine. Riff presses himself into my thigh, allowing me to feel how much he wants me. To know I have so much power over such a sexy beast of a man sends a thrill though me.

A heavy knock on the window causes us both to jump apart. I sigh heavily as I readjust my tank top to cover my stomach back up.

When the hell did he practically expose me?

Riff smirks at me before he winks. "To be continued."

I sit up as he slides over next to me on the bench seat after he opens the door for Noel and Lanie to crawl into the back seat. He reaches over and scoops my hand into his, threading his fingers through mine before kissing the back of my hand.

Such a sweet gesture from him shocks me a bit. I guess I didn't expect him to be sort-of caring. I figured our entire time together would be a lot like what we were doing in the SUV. No talking, just getting down to the hot and sexy nakedness he messaged me about.

I study his features. The smile on his face is one of pure contentment and it draws me into him even more. For a split second I wonder what he's really like behind his bad boy persona. Is it possible that the entire world, including me have him pegged all wrong?

Just as the last thought floats through my brain he moves my hand to rest over his still erect penis.

I totally take back my last thought. Looks like he's exactly the person he shows the entire world.

RIFF

Her delicate hand fits perfectly in mine. I can't believe she's actually here. She's been the one thing that's been occupying my mind the last couple weeks, and now the reason we've been talking has come to a head. I'll miss the little friendship we've built up over the past few days. She's been a great distraction and I hate to give her up. Once I give her what she came here for, there will be no reason for her to continue talking to me. She'll figure out soon enough I'm an unlovable asshole who will only disappoint her and ruin her life somehow. Better to show her that right off the bat.

I readjust our hands and bring her hand to rest squarely on my crotch.

She whips her head in my direction and raises her eyebrows but doesn't make a move to jerk her hand away. There's a challenge in her green eyes, almost like she's saying 'is that the best you got'. I knew she would be an excellent distraction.

A few minutes later Noel's bodyguard, Mike, pulls in to a local Mexican restaurant. Kitten pulls her hand away the moment Lanie leans up from the backseat to chat with her about going shopping later in the evening together.

I hop out of the vehicle and turn to help Kitten out. I grab her by the waist and hoist her against my body.

She giggles. "Put me down."

I shake my head and lean in to whisper in her ear, "Get used to it, babe. You're about to spend a whole lot more time in close proximity with me."

"Shhhhhhh," she says, "Let's not announce that to everyone."

I tilt my head and quirk my pierced eyebrow at her. "Why? You ashamed everyone will find out you want me to fuck you senseless?"

Her eyes widen. "Why do you say things like that?"

I give her my most wicked grin. "Because it makes all you ladies soak your panties."

Kitten opens her mouth like she wants to say something else, but quickly shuts it when Noel starts complaining about us moving out of the way so he and Lanie can get out.

"Sorry, bro. You know women can never get enough of me." The easygoing tone in my voice catches me off guard. It's been a long time since I've been that friendly to Noel.

Kitten smacks my chest and shakes her head as I set her down.

She folds her slender arms across her chest and I can't help but to notice how unbelievably cute she looks when she's pissed. If she keeps this shit up, I'll be taking her into the bathroom of this restaurant and locking the door so I can have my way with her.

Rock My Bed

For the next hour Kitten and I listen to Noel and Lanie reminisce about stories of their childhood. It's funny how different Noel is around her. He's like this whole other guy—a nice one. One I would be proud to call my friend if he hadn't fucked me over in the past.

While Noel distracts Lanie with another margarita, I allow my fingers to roam over to Kitten's lap and trace the bare skin on her inner thigh. Instead of pulling away like I figure she'll do, she scoots closer. Her knees drift apart, like she's welcoming my touch and encouraging me to do more.

I readjust in my seat as my cock twitches in my pants. Damn. This girl is like the perfect fucking chick for me. She's unbelievably sexy, has a rack I would give my left nut to get in my mouth, and then there's that whole naughty-good girl vibe.

I slide my hand up and allow my fingers to rub the center stitch of the crotch of her cut-off jean shorts.

I rest my elbow on the table and prop my chin up with my free hand. Kitten scoots even closer to me and leans in to pick up her drink before taking a long sip. Her cool demeanor surprises me. Most onlookers would probably never guess there's anything out of the ordinary going on by the look on her face.

I steal a glance at our tablemates. Lanie looks like she's feeling no pain while working on her eighth margarita and Noel is too googlie-eyed by her to notice much else.

The next thing I know, Kitten's hand rests squarely on the crotch of my jeans. She doesn't waste any time. She's going straight for my junk.

She seems totally into a little naughtiness and doesn't flinch when she seizes the moment to unzip my pants. My entire body stiffens and I quickly throw a couple napkins in my lap to hide things from view. Suddenly I'm thankful for the extra wide table. It's bad enough Noel and Lanie are sitting at the same table as us, but thank God I'm not too close to them.

My heart races inside my chest. It's been a while since I felt such a thrill with a woman. While I know getting off right now isn't probably going to happen, I don't mind the little bit of cock teasing she's doing. It's going to make me fuck her that much harder when I get the chance.

Kitten turns toward me and licks her lips before giving me a little wink. God, she's the sexiest thing I've ever seen. It's taking every bit of my self-control not to throw her down on this bench seat and fuck her on the spot right here in front of everyone.

She bites her bottom lip as she pretends to listen to Lanie and Noel talk about themselves, but I know that little grin she's hiding is for me.

She's just as fucking excited by this as I am.

I take a deep breath to calm down as she snakes two fingers inside my pants and then finds the opening in my boxers. I suck in a quick breath the moment she touches the sensitive skin on my shaft. My cock jerks hard and she smiles as she takes another sip of her drink. I melt back into the booth and try to think about anything other than the fact she's touching me right now. My fingers ache to touch her—to feel her warm, wet flesh.

My dick throbs and more than anything I want to take her someplace private so we can get down to business.

Her mouth drifts open as she manages to get her entire hand in and wrap it around my cock. It's the hottest fucking thing I've ever seen.

Kitten moves her hand up and down my length. This is too much. I can't keep quiet while she jerks me off. Everyone in this restaurant would know the moment I came because sex with me is never quiet. I don't have that much self-control.

I grab her wrist and hold her still and Kitten makes a very subtle noise of surprise.

Lanie's gaze snaps in her friend's direction and Kitten's face flames nearly matching the color of her hair.

"These drinks are so good," Kitten tries to play it off and I can't hold back from laughing.

Lanie raises an eyebrow and then turns her attention back to Noel. Kitten instantly relaxes her tense shoulders and sighs.

I chuckle as I pull her hand from my pants. Her eyes land on me and I wink to let her know how much fun I thought that was. She twists her pink lips in response and then I feel her fingers on my thigh.

Fuck me. She's relentless.

When I come for her for the first time, I want it to be when I'm buried deep inside her and I can grunt all the obscenities I want to because it feels so fucking good.

I grab her hand as her fingers trace the bulge in my jeans. She scrunches her brow and tilts her head.

"Later," I say.

That explanation seems to pacify her as she shrugs and takes another sip of her drink.

A few minutes later, we make our way out of the restaurant. Noel practically drags a very intoxicated Lanie along and then helps her into the backseat of the SUV. Kitten and I pile into the middle seat, sitting so close together she's practically on my lap.

She stares up at me with her sexy, green eyes under long lashes and I'm reminded of how sweet she is. How she's not another groupie, but a career-minded lady. Someone that's actually too good for me, but I'm damn thankful she gives me the time of day anyway. Her hands rest on my chest and her warmth sets my skin on fire as I think about her touch earlier.

I tangle my hand into her thick, red curls and try to forget our friends are getting a free peep show behind us. "You're so fucking beautiful. I can't wait to get you back to the hotel."

She bites her lip and her gaze moves to my lips like she wants me to kiss her. I lean into her and bury my face in her hair.

"Tonight you're mine. I'm going to fuck you in so many positions the Kama Sutra will be asking us for tips," I growl into her ear.

I pull back in time to watch her wide eyes return to normal and those luscious lips of hers pull into a sexy smile. "That's what I'm counting on."

Dammit, can't Mike drive this thing any fucking faster? This is one girl I can't wait to test out.

Chapter 6

AUBREY

The bodyguard pulls the SUV into the back lot next to the Black Falcon bus. Lanie crawls out of the vehicle and then staggers away from the group. I watch as my friend zigs and zags her way inside the bus.

"She's going to be sick. I've never seen her tipsy," Noel says.

I laugh. "That's because you missed her college years. Trust me, this is very mild."

Noel frowns and instantly I feel bad. This man is crazy over her. Any sane human can see that by looking at him.

He rubs the back of his neck. "You think she's all right?"

Noel's concern is adorable.

I turn to Riff, taking Noel's hint. "I better go check on her."

He nods and then smacks my behind and I jump at the unexpected contact. "Hurry back."

The two men behind me laugh as I walk through the

parking lot.

I follow Lanie into the back bedroom of the bus as she fumbles through her clothes. Why is she changing? "Aren't you going over to the hotel with the rest of the band?"

She shakes her head. "I can't afford a room over there, and I'm tired. All I can think about is sleeping."

Odd. I tilt my head and stare at her, trying to figure out why she's fighting against Noel so hard. "Sleeping? After the way you were flirting with Noel tonight, you want to go to sleep?"

She shrugs like the little bit of P.D.A. tonight was no big deal. "Yes? What's so wrong with that?"

I bite my lip to keep from telling her to wake up and see that Noel is still crazy in love with her. "You two have this whole connection thing vibing between you. Aren't you the least big curious as to what it can turn into?"

"No. This is business, Aubrey. It can't be anything more than that between us. You know that."

I sigh. She likes to hold her grudges and stick to her guns. I've told her in the past that sometimes fighting against something so hard only delays the inevitable for a little while. This relationship between her and Noel is going to happen, even if she's not ready to admit that to herself yet.

I wrap my arms around her to show she has my support no matter what because I know denying her feelings for Noel is killing her—I can see it in her face. But she won't listen to anyone. She'll only come around when she's ready. This is a simple fact I know about my best friend. "I love you, Lanie, but sometimes you need to loosen up and say fuck the rules. A job isn't everything. Live a little, you know."

She laughs and tries to change the subject. "Like you are with Riff?"

My face heats up and I can tell it's probably matching the red shade of my hair. "I can't help it. I've always thought he was the cutest in the band. Gah! He's a really good kisser, too."

Lanie grins and then childishly plugs her ears. "I so don't need to hear these details."

I pull her hands down and laugh at her crazy drunk antics. "Trust me, by this time tomorrow I'll have more details about Riff than how he kisses."

She smacks my arm. "Go then, and slut around, if you must."

I smile and then wink at her. "Oh, that's a definite must."

When I return to the parking lot, I find Noel and Riff talking in a hushed, seemingly heated discussion that quickly dissipates when I'm within earshot.

Noel looks down at me with his clear blue eyes. "She okay?"

I nod. "She's fine. Just drunk and a little grumpy."

Noel laughs. "Great. Catch you guys later."

Once Noel heads in the direction of the bus, Riff grabs me around the waist and yanks me against his hard body. "What was that little stunt in the restaurant, huh?"

I give him my most wicked grin and try to portray confidence. "Just trying to get you excited."

He bites his bottom lip and sucks in his lip ring. "All you have to do is look at me and I'm turned on like a fucking light switch."

I run my hands up his sculpted chest and then allow my fingertips to linger on the exposed skin above the neckline of his t-shirt. I peer up at him and find his green eyes set on me. I lick my lips as nerves hit me a little. Back at the restaurant I'm not sure what possessed me to feel him up in public like that. The only thing that kept going through my mind is the need to stand out. I want this night together to be as memorable for him as it will be for me. I'm sure he's done far worse with a woman and that wasn't a big deal to him, but for me that was major. Being around him makes me do things I normally wouldn't do.

I swallow and realize I've got him exactly where I want him—desperate to have me. It's now or never. I've come this far. I can't be nervous now. "How far away is the hotel?"

Riff growls as squeezes me against him. "Keep looking at me like that and we won't be making it there before I have my way with you."

My heart does a double skip in my chest and my knees grow weak. I've been with the bad boy type before, but Riff is like their king. He's so straightforward and it's unbelievably sexy.

"You guys need me to drive you over to the hotel?" Mike asks from behind me.

Riff tears his eyes away from my face long enough to shake his head and say, "No, man. We're good. I've got my bike."

"All right. Later," Mike says before I hear his boots hitting the blacktop walking away from us.

I quirk an eyebrow. "A bike? You're really the ultimate bad boy, aren't you?"

He throws his head back and a deep laugh rumbles out of him. "Kitten, I'm the baddest, bad boy you'll ever need. Come on."

The roadies roll Riff's motorcylce out of the back of one of the trailers that haul some of the band's equipment around. He jumps on, allowing his strong thighs to hold it up while he hands me a helmet.

I take it and my eyes instantly search for another one. "Aren't you going to wear one? Isn't that a law or something?"

He shrugs. "I never do. I believe it's called living dangerously. Besides, we're in too many different states for me to keep track of each one's laws."

Rock My Bed

The engine roars to life after a couple seconds and I flinch. I've never been on a bike before, but I can't let a little nerve stop me from fulfilling my last hurrah weekend.

I hop on behind him and grab his sides, allowing my legs to rest against his hips.

Riff shakes his head. "You have to hang on tighter, babe."

He grabs both of my hands and wraps them around him. I open my mouth to ask why, but instantly snap it shut as he guns the motor and heads out onto the street. He roars through the city streets and the cars pass by at such a frightening speed I'm pretty sure my claws are raking his skin through his t-shirt. The only thing going through my brain is hoping we don't wreck and die considering there's absolutely nothing protecting us.

I try not to think about it as I attempt to bury my face into his back.

A couple minutes later we pull into the hotel parking lot. Riff parks the bike in the lot and cuts the engine. My entire body tingles and feels numb as I jump off as fast as humanly possible. I have to say that's one thing on my bucket list I can do without ever doing again.

I yank the helmet off and my hand shakes as I hold it out to him.

He laughs as he takes it from me and tucks it under his arm. "Did you like that?"

I tip my chin up and fake my best smile so he doesn't know that scared the shit out of me. I don't want him to think I'm a total wuss. "It was awesome."

Riff grins as he props his bike up on the kickstand before hoping off. "Good to know you're a bad liar."

I throw my hands on my hips. "I am not lying."

He touches the tip of my nose with his index finger. "You're sexy when you're feisty. I hope you keep this attitude up in the room." He holds out his hand. "Let's go get checked in."

The moment we step inside, I follow Riff's gaze towards the hotel bar. Loud bouts of laughter echo through the blaring rock music around the lobby. A party is in full swing. A couple of women dressed in tight, short shirts and halter tops loiter near the entrance while they hang on the arms of a couple road-beaten roadies who look like they haven't shaved in a month. Some women will apparently sleep with anyone associated a band to get to the talent. I bet the rest of the guests in this place love the idea that a bunch of rock stars are partying it up in here while they're on a family vacation.

Riff wraps his arm around my shoulders and leans into my ear. "Head on over to the bar while I take care of stuff at the desk. Order me a beer, would you?"

I nod and he lets go of my hand and we part ways.

The crowd in the small room is amazing. It's hard to believe that many people are working behind the scenes of this tour. Nearly every seat in the place is taken, sometimes even double occupied. The dim lights and sheer amount of bodies make it difficult to make my way to the bar. I shoulder past a few, mumbling my apologies as I finally step up to the bar.

I run my fingers through my wind-blown hair as I wait for the stocky, male bartender to make his way down to me.

"Can I buy you a drink?" a man's voice asks to my right.

My head snaps in his direction and my eyes land on an incredibly handsome man. Blonde shaggy hair drifts over his brow and he shoves it back as he grins at me. His blue eyes drink me in slowly as he waits for my answer.

I return his smile with a polite one of my own. "Thank you, but I'm with someone."

He leans in closer and completely blows off my refusal. "I'm Donovan. You might've heard of me?" He pauses for a brief second, but when I give him a blank stare he continues, "I'm the guitarist for Embrace the Darkness."

I nod. "I've heard of you. You're the opening act for Black Falcon, right?"

Donovan smirks. "Not for long. They'll be opening for us soon enough."

He turns, practically pushing his chest against my arm and I take a step away. "Pretty sure of yourself, aren't you?"

He shrugs. "Why not? I'm great at what I do and my band kicks ass. What's so wrong in taking pride in something you know you're good at?" Suddenly, I feel his hand on my ass. "Why don't you do yourself a favor and come upstairs with me?"

I yank his hand off my ass and shoot him the death stare. "Like I said, I'm with someone."

He makes a big show of looking around me. "Oh, yeah? Where? I don't see anyone. Chicks don't come around places like this alone unless they're looking for a good time. So tell me, where's this mystery guy you're here with?"

I open my mouth to tell him off, but before I get the chance Riff's voice cuts through the loud bar music. "Right fucking here."

I don't know who tenses more, me or Donovan.

RIFF

I stand back as long as I can. I want to see the way Kitten reacts when other men approach her. I want to know if her hard to get act is genuine or if she's just another groupie ready to slut it up with any rock star that moves.

Donovan creeps up on her and uses the same fucking lines I see him do night after night on the fans during the after-parties.

Sheer delight envelopes me when Kitten yanks his

hand off her ass and tells him to beat it. That doesn't sit well with Donovan. His chest instantly puffs up and his face twists. He's not used to rejection, and girls like Aubrey throw us resident man-whores off our game.

The moment he raises his voice at her, testing to see if she's really alone like she claims, I step in. I can't help it. I don't want him to get the idea he can put the moves on her or force her into something she doesn't want to do.

This urge to protect what's mine surges through me and before I know it my hands ball into fists and I say, "Right fucking here."

Donovan's eyes widen. "Sorry, dude. I didn't know she was one of your hoes."

Aubrey flinches beside him the moment the insult leaves his mouth. For some reason him referring to her as a piece of sexual garbage pisses me off. "Don't ever fucking call her that."

He raises his hands in surrender. "Easy, man. No need to get all swollen up in the chest. There's plenty of tail to go around."

My eyes narrow. "Then you better go find some elsewhere."

We stare each other down for a long moment. My shoulders tense more each second we stand here. I haven't had much problem with Donovan in the past, but the front man of his band, Striker has tried to get at Noel every chance he gets. It's always some sort of pissing contest to see who has the bigger balls and the most fame. I think those two would fight over a penny if it came down to it.

Embrace the Darkness is a label built band, and all those douchebags care about is climbing their way to the top. They have no sense of camaraderie or brotherhood like we feel. Well, like we used to feel. Noel did a good job fucking that up for us.

Donovan smirks after he sees I'm not backing down. "This one's too uptight anyhow. Enjoy your blue balls."

I grit my teeth and fight back the urge to crush his face with my fist. The label's already warned us about fighting, so I inhale deeply through my nose as Donovan shoulders past me. Noel and Striker threw down after our first couple shows together and the label threatened to disband the tour. We all knew those were idle threats because let's face it, our shows make too much money for that shit.

Aubrey hands me a beer. "You didn't have to do that, you know. I'm perfectly capable of handling myself when it comes to assholes."

A small grin plays across my lips. "I don't remember you fighting against me too hard when we first met."

She shrugs and takes a sip of her drink. "You really didn't give me much time to react, let alone launch a full-on war against you."

I eye her over my bottle as I down half the beer. A

blush creeps up her cheeks. The wall in her confident façade cracks a hair. I figured a girl like her wasn't used to being a booty call, but she's doing her best to fool me into thinking she's been down this road before. I can see right through it. "It's okay to admit the idea of fucking me turned you on. We both know you wouldn't be here right now if it didn't."

I set my empty bottle on the bar and lean into her. I push her auburn strands away from her neck and allow my fingers to trace the delicate skin right before her ear. She stiffens at first and I can see her struggle internally before I feel the tension leave her.

Her shoulder pushes into my chest as I dip my head and trace her jaw with my nose. It's such an intimate move to make inside this tight bar where there's probably fifty eyes trained on us, but I don't care. If I wait any longer to get close to her, I might explode.

When I reach her ear, my tongue darts out and I taste the flesh of her earlobe. She squeezes her eyes shut and her mouth drops open a bit. The smell of her fruity shampoo and perfume fills my nose and my cock jerks.

I lick my lips and reach around to play with the hem of her shirt. "I don't think I can wait any more."

She turns to face me, our noses nearly touching. "Then don't. Tonight I'm yours, remember?"

"Mine?" I swallow at the sound of that word in my head. I've never tried to claim a woman before and I have no fucking clue why I told her she was mine earlier tonight. But it feels right, which is completely fucked up, because I know I don't deserve anything good in my life. I ruin everything I touch. Every person that's ever mattered in my life has told me that at one point or another, so I know a future with anyone is out of the question. God strike me down for wanting to get to know this girl. I'm no fucking good for her.

I take her beer from her and toss it into a nearby trashcan before taking her hand into mine. "Let's go."

I need to fuck her—the sooner the better. It's the only way I know that'll get her out of my system.

Chapter 7

AUBREY

Riff swipes his room key in the door and it flashes green. That looks like a green light if I've ever seen one. I take a deep breath. It looks like it's go time—now's the time for me to make my mark.

He holds the door open for me and I step through the threshold backwards while grabbing a handful of his t-shirt in my fists. Riff's eyebrows shoot up for a brief second and then he grins devilishly. He likes me taking control. I can see it in his eyes.

The door closes with a bang and I throw my arms around his neck, crushing my lips to his. He doesn't hesitate, not even for a brief second, before he tangles his hands in my hair and deepens our kiss. We melt together and start peeling off layers of clothes.

Neither of us speak, which is fine by me. We both know what we're here for. There's no need for empty words or promises neither of us intend to keep. Instead, we both focus on the here and now, allowing our mouths, lips and tongues every opportunity to explore each other.

Once we are both down to our underwear, he steps back, allowing himself a moment to take in the sight of my nearly naked body. Unsure of what to do with my hands, I arch my back, throwing my plan to seduce him into action. My bare shoulders rest against the door and I run both of my hands into my hair, attempting to be as sexy as I possibly can. Confidence is key in any situation when trying to maintain power. I've learned that much from my new boss already. So, I keep eye contact with him and lift my chin.

It must be working because Riff bites his lip as his hungry eyes drink me in. "You are too fucking sexy for your own good."

Any games I remotely thought about teasing him with at the moment fly out the window. Riff grips my hips in his hands and pushes me against the door. The hard length underneath his boxers presses against my stomach and I lick my lips in anticipation. His lips fly over every inch of my neck before he dips his head and kisses the tops of my breasts. I throw my head back and a moan escapes me.

Why does his mouth have to feel so amazing?

My hands trail up the taut muscles in his back as he rises up and kisses my mouth. His expert hands undo the hooks on my bra quickly, before he peels it off, letting it fall to the floor by our feet. He runs his hands down my sides and pauses at my hips. I suck in a quick breath as he shoves my underwear down around my ass before gripping my bare bottom. This only excites him further. His mouth flies into a fury, tasting every inch of my skin that he can.

Instead of taking the time to slide my panties down, he

grabs one side and rips them at the seams. The loose, lacy material falls limply down my leg after a quick shove from Riff.

Riff growls against my skin as he grabs my ass and hoists me into the air. Instinctively, I wrap my legs around his waist as he balances my weight against the door and allow my fingers to run across the stubble of his recently shaved head.

He grinds his pelvis into mine and it's almost more than I can take to know only a thin piece of fabric separates me from the relief that only he can give me. "Oh, god, Riff."

It comes out almost like a plea and I can hear the desperation in my voice for him to take me.

"Don't call me that. Not in here," he whispers roughly in my ear. "Call me Zach."

I'll call him whatever he wants as long as he doesn't stop touching me. Every move he makes is right, turning me on to the point of nearly losing my mind—so much for taking control of this situation.

I kiss his mouth feverishly while the head of his penis rubs against my sweet spot. "Take me, Zach."

In any other moment, I would've laughed at myself for sounding like a cheesy twit, but they're the only words I can find that express exactly what I need.

I want him. Now.

Zach growls as soon as his name leaves my lips and he turns us around and tosses me down on the bed. I prop my weight up on my elbows to get a better look. He grins as he shoves down his boxers, putting himself on full display for me. I stare at him, taking in his god-like physique. Full sleeves of tattoos proudly cover every inch of his impressive forearms. Muscle lines every inch of him and his chest displays a vast array of artwork as well. My eyes pass over his nipple piercings and land on a line of script directly over his heart. The name Hailey stands out boldly against a series of hearts.

It makes me stop for a brief second and wonder about the woman the name belongs to and if she broke his heart. I kiss his chest near the tattoo and he freezes. I peer up as he squeezes his eyes shut.

I reach out to wrap my hand around his erect shaft, but he grabs my wrist and bends down to kiss my lips. "You first."

He gently pushes my shoulders back and kisses a trail down my naked torso. My breath hitches when he hooks the underside of my knee and rests it on his shoulder. His tongue darts out of his mouth, licking his way to my core.

His masterful mouth works its way around my folds, teasing me with every flick of his tongue. My arousal is out of control and when I reach the point of begging him to cure the ache that's building in me, he sucks on my clit.

The back of my head digs into the mattress as I arch my back and push my pelvis against his mouth. "Yes! Ohhhh."

My words are breathy and I probably sound like a lame porn star attempting to put on a good show, but I don't care. It feels too damn good to keep quiet.

Rock My Bed

An intense tingle spreads from where his mouth works diligently to the tips of my toes. Zach continues to work his magic until my legs shake and I scream out his name.

My entire body relaxes as I attempt to slow my breathing down. "That was amazing."

He grins devilishly as he crawls onto the bed beside me. His lips meet mine and I can taste myself on his lips. Even though I'm still feeling the euphoria of orgasm, I can't wait to see what else this night will bring. I know it's only just begun.

His hard length presses against my thigh as he leans in and kisses me deeply. I run my hand up his chiseled abs until I reach his nipple. I pinch it between my fingers and give the ring in it a little tug. A low groan emits from his throat and waves of giddy excitement flows through me.

Zachary "Riff" Oliver likes things a little rough, does he? Well, that's exactly what he's going to get—some downright kinky sexcapades.

I shove his shoulder, rolling him onto his back and he chuckles. "I knew you were a wild cat. This is going to be good."

I bend down and suck one of his nipples into my mouth. I swirl my tongue around his piercing and he bites his lip, trying to hold back a growl. I kiss his chest and then his stomach before he grabs a handful of my hair.

He's used to dominating in the bedroom. I have to flip the script on him.

Before I make it down to his cock, I look up at him and rest my chin on his stomach while my breasts touch his thighs. He gives his pelvis a gentle thrust, sliding his shaft against my chest.

He tries again, but I keep staring into his hooded eyes. "Why'd you stop?"

I smile. "I want to try something."

Zach raises a pierced eyebrow. "What do you have in mind?"

"Stay right here." I push myself up from the bed and grab my discarded black tank top. It's not exactly a blindfold and it probably won't fit around his head. I throw it back down when another possible item to use pops in my head.

I open the closet door and hanging inside are two fluffy white robes. I yank one of the belts free and shut the door.

When I turn around Zach grins. "Naked maid service? I like where you're going with this surprise."

I laugh and know I should be self-conscious about running around this hotel room naked in front of a mega celebrity like him, but the way he's staring at me makes me feel exactly the opposite. I feel desired and sexy. His green eyes tell me he likes what he sees and can't wait to get the chance to devour me fully.

I hold up the belt and he slowly starts to nod like he's playing in his mind what I'm about to do to him. "Kitten, I like your style."

I walk around the bed, gripping the thick material in my hands. I've never been one to take charge in the bedroom, but since I'm not in this for a relationship, I can let my freak flag completely fly. Women have probably attempted to dominate him before, so this shouldn't be anything new, but hopefully it's memorable.

"Sit up," I command. After he positions himself on the side of the bed with his legs over the edge, I order, "Close your eyes."

Zach fights back a grin and does as I ask. My hands shake while I cover his eyes and knot the belt at the back of his head. This makes a decent blindfold in a pinch.

"Now what?" he asks.

I press my index finger to his lips. "No more talking until I say."

A huge smile erupts on his face and he opens his mouth to speak again, but I pinch his lips shut. I bend at the waist and barely touch his top lip with my tongue. When I pull away Zach nods in approval and relaxes his weight against the palms positioned on either side of him.

I can feel the anticipation radiating off him. This is exactly what I want—to make him feel unsettled.

I rake my nails down his chest, not hard enough to leave any permanent marks, but enough to let him know I mean business. His mouth drifts open when I halt at his belly button. I'm really not sure what the hell I'm doing, but he doesn't need to know that.

I get on my knees in front of him and place my hands on his thighs. Zach's head lulls back and he licks his lips in anticipation.

RIFF

I think about stopping her. I've not broken my penis to skin contact rule since the band went big and I started banging random chicks after shows. But, the thought of finally having her please me outweighs my rational brain. Letting her blow me for a while isn't going to hurt anything. I think I can trust that she's got a disease free mouth.

Fuck it.

I let my head fall back and prepare to enjoy the ride for a bit. I have to hand it to her, blindfolding me was a nice touch. This isn't the first time a girl has tried to seduce me, but it is the first time it actually seems to be working a little. The mere thought of her hard at work in her office during the day in dress clothes, and being this naughty sex-kitten in the bedroom at night is nearly enough to make me nut on the spot.

Damn it. If I were into relationships this girl would be fucking perfect for me.

The moment her hand wraps around my shaft I want to moan, but I fight it back. I can't let her know she's won me over with a simple touch. I like this little teasing game she's playing.

The tip of her tongue swirls around the rim of my head—my most sensitive spot. I suck in a quick breath as she pops the tip in her mouth. "Fuck."

I know she told me not to talk, but I've never been very good at following rules.

A rush of air flows through my clenched teeth as I suck in a quick breath when she takes me in further. Good god. This woman is really trying to kill me. If she keeps this up I'm going to blow my load early again like I did the last time I got head. Then she'll be fucking disappointed and done with me.

I clamp my eyes shut and try to focus on anything other any how good she's making me feel. The baseball game I watched the night before with Trip pops into my head. It helps a little to distract me, but it doesn't really take away the warm sensation enveloping every inch of me.

I bite my lip ring and knot my fingers in her hair. "That feels so fucking good."

The minute the words leave my mouth, Aubrey's mouth pulls away. My entire body slumps at the loss of her warmth. Why would she pull away after I told her she was doing a good job?

I reach out for her, but can't find her with this damn blindfold. "Come back. Don't stop."

She pinches my lips shut again. "I told you no talking. You're ruining this."

I grin. "It's cute you want to play dominatrix with me, but babe, it really isn't necessary. I've fucking wanted you from the moment I laid eyes on you."

The mattress beside me gives under her weight as she sits down beside me. She slides the belt from over my eyes and tosses it onto the bed. Kitten's face twists like she's trying to hold back some disappointment and the urge to comfort her consumes me. "You aren't having fun? I wanted this to be memorable for you."

Not many people let their guard down around me to let me see that I've actually hurt their feelings. It's a nice change of pace to be around someone real.

I lift her chin so I can stare into her green eyes. "Just being with you is memorable enough." She smiles and her eyes completely light up. I lean in and press my lips to hers. "I do like the idea of less talk and more action, though."

Kitten giggles as I pull her down on the bed with me. Beneath me she looks so pure, and innocent. I can't even explain it, but there's something about her that's pulling me in. I run my hand down the length of her arm. Her skin's so fucking soft it causes my cock to twitch against her thigh.

Her almond shaped eyes stare up at me, waiting on my next move. The tip of my finger traces her chin. Too bad this night with her has to be a one-time thing. She's a girl I would like to keep around for a while. One time with her, won't be enough. I can already fucking tell. But she would never sign up to stay on Big Bertha as my fuck-buddy. She's not that type of girl. She has a life.

I kiss her neck, and the scent of her fruity shampoo and perfume fills my nose. Why does her skin have to smell so fucking good?

The desire for every inch of my flesh to meet with hers grips my stomach. I wonder if she would let me fuck her raw?

What the hell am I thinking? I never allow that kind of contact. Not that I'm worried about knocking women up. I know that's not a possibility because of the accident I had as a teenager. It's more for the fact I've lost count of how many sexual partners I've had.

I suck her nipple into my mouth. I bet Kitten's not like that. From the looks of her and how she rejected my initial advances, I'd say her numbers are pretty low. Maybe I can break my own rule just this once. A girl like her doesn't come along very often, and she'll probably say no anyhow, but it doesn't hurt to ask. This will be my only shot to have her.

"Are you on the pill?" I say between kisses as I get to know every inch of her skin. She's careful. That's a good sign.

"Yes," she says the words breathy.

"Have you been tested?" Her body stiffens below me.

Shit. I knew she'd never let me.

"Y—yes. Have you?"

I push myself up to gaze in her eyes. I want her to believe me when I answer. "Regularly and I never do anything without wearing a condom, not even blow jobs."

Her eyes search me. "Well, why would you want to break that rule with me?"

I swallow hard. Truth is sometimes harder than a lie. "You're different, and real. If I only get one night with you, I want to feel you, every inch of you."

I wait for her to laugh in my face and tell me hell no, but what she does shocks the shit out of me.

She nods and kisses my lips. "Tonight, I'm yours. Make love to me."

My heart bangs inside my chest. Mine. I've never had that with someone. Even if this is only an illusion created by my fucked up brain to feel love somehow, I'll take it—one night to feel normal and loved.

I push a loose strand of her auburn hair away from her cheek. There's a softness in her eyes I want to crawl inside and live in—if only for a little while.

I close my eyes and run my nose across her jaw line. Her mouth drifts open and I trace her bottom lip with my tongue. I wrap her in one of my arms and position myself between her thighs. My tip teases her entrance and slides against her pussy. She moans as soon as I make contact with her clit and it's nearly my undoing.

I grip her shoulder and with one quick motion, I'm buried inside her. "Damn. I didn't know what I was fucking missing."

"Ohhh," she whimpers while her face buries into my chest.

I pull back. "I'm not hurting you, am I?"

She bites her lip and shakes her head. "Don't stop."

Jesus. If she keeps looking at me with that mixture of innocence and lust I'm not going to make it long.

I thrust into her slowly a few more times while her hand slides down my back and then grabs my ass. "You feel so fucking amazing."

"It's different?"

I nod and pump into her again. "You have no idea."

There's no way she knows how different this experience is for me. Even all the times I'd fucked Sophie, it'd been just that—fucking. This feels completely new, like we are connected somehow.

My mouth hangs open as I quicken my pace. Sweat slicks both of us as I continue the steady rhythm.

Kitten clenches her thighs around my waist and digs her nails into my back. "Zach, oh god."

"Don't fight it. Let go." I watch her in awe as she falls apart below me, allowing complete vulnerability with me.

I suck a quick breath through my teeth and a string of curses fly from my mouth. This is over too fucking soon, but I can't help it. Sex has never felt this good before. Shudders ripple through my entire body when I find my own release and spill into her.

I kiss her softly once, to see what it would feel like to not be in a hurry to fuck someone to forget life for a while.

When I pull away, she smiles. "Are you always so sweet to the girls you bag?"

I cringe inside. I hate that she doesn't think she's special to me, but if I was an outsider looking at me I would think the same damn thing.

I shake my head. "Only you. Don't ask me why, either, because I don't know."

Her grin widens as she reaches up and strokes my cheek. "Then I like the idea I'm the only one who gets sweet kisses."

I raise an eyebrow. "Don't let that get out. I'm not really known for being *sweet*."

"Wouldn't want it to get out you actually have a heart, would we?"

Definitely not. When people find out you actually give a shit, that's when they fucking hurt you. I know that pain all too well and never want to go through that again.

I grab the nape of her neck and kiss her hungrily while trying to push the idea of taking my time with her out of my head. This girl has the capability of crushing me if I let things get out of control. That's the whole reason we have this one time hump arrangement—to get each other out of our systems and move the fuck on. We both know we aren't good together and this thing between us would never go long term anyway because I would fuck it up somehow.

I close my eyes and will my stupid brain to stop overthinking the situation. She's just another woman out to fuck a rock star so she can have a memory of how wild she was before she settles down in suburbia and pops out some spoiled-rotten children.

Exhausted, satisfied and spent I collapse on top of her. Her hair surrounds me and I inhale the scent of her into my nose. Instantly, I'm turned-on again. I was right—once isn't going to be enough. I already want more.

Fuck me. I'm in such deep shit.

Chapter 8

AUBREY

After hours of mind-blowing sex we lay in the darkness wrapped in each other's arms. He strokes the bare skin on my shoulder while I rest my head on his chest. I never expected such caring from him—multiple orgasms, sure, but never a connection. This almost feels like the start of a relationship, which I know is insane. We barely know each other.

The burning desire to get to know this complex man burns inside me. How can he be one way to the world, and yet hide this caring side of himself away?

I trace the tattoos on his defined chest with fingers, lingering awhile on the name over his heart. "What happened between you and the girl?" His arms tense around me and I instantly feel like I've stepped over some invisible line that's been drawn around him. Desperate to keep him from shutting me off again and becoming Riff, I backpedal. "You don't have to tell me. I was curious."

Zach sighs into my hair. "It's not what you think."

I turn and rest my chin on him so I can peer up at his face. "Oh?"

I'm dying to know more, but don't want to push.

He frowns under my gaze. "Hailey was my sister."

There's no mistaking the word *was* in that sentence. I can't even fathom the loss of a family member, let alone someone close, because it's not something I've been through. I imagine it's soul altering.

I'm quiet for a few minutes, allowing him time to explain further without any prompting from me. When he doesn't answer, I ask quietly, "What was she like?"

A sad smile fills his face. "She was amazing—my ornery, little tag-a-long. That kid followed me everywhere."

"So, she was your kid sister?"

He nods. "She was eight when she died."

How awful. Her life hadn't even begun and yet it was ripped away at such an early age.

I tilt my head. "How old where you?"

"Sixteen."

My heart crumbles a little. "That's so young to have to deal with something like that. What happened to her?"

Zach pulls his lips into a tight line and stares up at the ceiling, clearly fighting back emotion.

It's always on the news that most tragedies where a child dies, some sort of preventable negligence occurred. I want to ask so badly if that's what happened, but when I glance up at Zach for answers he grows still.

"Don't," he says. "Whatever you've got going through your mind, let's not even talk about it."

Instead of pushing the issue further, I back off and give the topic space. It's obvious from his change of mood that he still has issues dealing with her death, and who am I to push him to open up to me. After all, I am still just some woman he slept with. We barely know each other.

I sigh and return my head to his chest and study the contours of his abs. I have to accept this night for what it is. Just sex.

It's not long before my eyes grow heavy and I'm fast asleep.

RIFF

I lay awake and watch her sleep against me. She's so beautiful. Her pouty lips drift open and she breathes slowly. She's peaceful and it's amazing to watch someone completely relax when they sleep.

I've drifted in and out all night, but now that the sun's up, I know it'll be a matter of time before we walk out of this room and I never see her again. So I don't want to waste any more time sleeping.

It's been a long time since anyone has asked me about Hailey's tattoo. Even longer still since anyone has cared enough to try to pump me for details about her. I knew Kitten was different from all the other women I've been with. That's why I wanted her so much.

The ringtone on my cell plays throughout the quiet room. I snatch it off the nightstand and without looking at the caller ID, I answer, "Somebody better be dead."

A bitter laugh rolls through my earpiece and my stomach clenches. "You might as well call me that."

My jaw tenses. "What do you want, Dad? I told you to never call me."

He huffs into the phone. "I would be happy to never speak to your piece of shit ass again, but seeing as how there's no payment in my bank account yet, I figured I'd better call to make sure you haven't forgotten about your dear, old Dad."

I squeeze the phone in my hand. "Nice to know I'm your fucking meal ticket."

"You listen to me you little bastard. That money better be in my account today, or so help me—"

Blind rage overtakes me and makes me forget Aubrey's asleep on my chest as I shout, "Or you'll what? Beat my ass? Sorry old man, but that bridge has long been crossed and we won't be going back over it. You're lucky I send shit. One of these days I'm going to tell you to fuck off."

He laughs. "Idle threats, son. We both know you owe me, so get me my fucking money!"

Before I can get another word in, Dad hangs up on me.

Fucking asshole.

I would give anything to be able to cut him out of my life. He's an old, bitter man who loves to make me feel like a fuck-up every chance he gets.

Disgusted, I toss my phone back on the nightstand. My eyes shoot down to study Kitten. Not once has she made a move like she's awake, which is a small miracle from God considering I basically screamed in her ear.

My relationship with my father is something I don't want anyone to know about, let alone witness first hand. I hate the fact that the guys in the band know about my past at all, but I hate even more that Trip and Tyke were witness to it. I hate people's fucking sympathy more than anything in the world. I'm a piece of shit and deserve none. I deserve the hell I've been through.

Aubrey stirs in my arms, and I tense.

Shit. She probably did hear that after all.

She stretches her slender arms out and yawns before she peers up at me through those sexy, long lashes of hers. She smiles and then snuggles back into me. "Good morning."

Relief floods me. Surely if she heard that fight she'd be

asking me who I was talking too. I'm glad I don't have to give her some lame-ass lie to try to cover up who I am. I don't need her knowing I'm a fucked up mess.

"Mornin'. You hungry? I can order us up some room service before we head back to the bus, or maybe we can go another round while we still have some privacy?"

She bites her bottom lip after she runs her tongue across it. "I think another round is definitely called for before breakfast."

Aubrey rises up and presses her lips to mine.

I really do like the way this girl thinks.

As things start to get good, Aubrey's cell rings. What the fuck is with all the calls this morning?

She tries to pull away, but I only squeeze her in my arms tighter which causes her to giggle. "Zach, I have to get that. It could be Lanie."

"Make it quick." I hold her a second longer before letting her go.

Kitten answers on the fourth ring. "Hello?" Her tone is raspy and slow.

She listens for a few seconds to the person on the other end of the line, and I notice how adorable she is when she tries to concentrate. I lean in and nibble on her neck.

She giggles. "Stop, Riff."

The use of my stage name causes me to pause. All night long she's used my real name. Is she calling me that to impress whoever is on the other end of the line? My heart sinks a bit, but I know she has got the right idea. We can't get in too deep with one another if we only have this short time together.

I kiss a trail down her chest and suck a nipple in my mouth, trying to coax her off the phone and back into my bubble for a little while longer.

"Yes," she says, breathlessly.

I grin. That yes sounded more like it was for me, than whoever's on the phone.

Aubrey sighs. "Don't be mad. We'll be together all the time in about a week when you come home. Besides you have Noel to play with."

Ah, she's talking to Lanie. In that case she definitely needs to get off the phone. The skin on her stomach is so soft against my lips.

Aubrey giggles again when I dip my tongue into her belly button. "But it could be *just* like that if you'd let it."

"Why don't you hang up and let me fuck you again?" I mumble before I suck her clit into my mouth.

She grabs a handful of the sheet and grips it tight. "Um, gotta go, Lanie. Love you."

She ends the call and tosses her phone to the side. I

grin and nip her skin. Victory is mine. Now her full attention is mine.

I shove two fingers inside and begin to work her into a frenzy.

AUBREY

Zach's bike screams as we roll into the parking lot. He parks us beside the semi-trailer he got the motorcycle from last night.

I peel my arms from around him. "I think you have a death wish."

He chuckles. "I like life with a little edge is all. Besides, I didn't drive that fast."

I hop off the bike and rip the helmet off. "Well, it was fast enough to scare the shit out of me."

He grins and hooks an arm around my waist and pulls me into him. I straddle his right leg as he still sits on the bike. "What happened to my self-assured wild cat from last night? The one that was fearless?"

I wrap my arms around his neck, and curse myself for letting this thing between us feel so easy. A guy like him can break my heart if I get attached, which is the exact thing I'm trying to avoid from happening again.

I shrug. "I'm trying to wean her out of my system."

His eyes search mine. "That's too bad. I like her."

Him liking my wild side is exactly the reason I need to change it. He's too similar to all my other exes. They all used me until they were tired of me and tossed me aside like my feelings for them meant nothing. I don't want to ever be treated like that again, if that means reevaluating my taste in men, so-be-it.

A man like Zach will never settle down and I don't want to be over thirty and still trying to find a man that will be more than a baby-daddy to me. I need a man that's into a family for the long haul.

"Wait here while I make sure no one fucks up my bike," Zach says before kissing me on the cheek and jumping off the bike.

His black t-shirt and faded jeans cling to his sculpted body in the right spots as his strong arms clutch the handles to push the motorcycle to the end of the trailer.

Zach asks the road crew to stash his bike back on the trailer and I glance around the busy parking lot. Behind the scenes of a massive show like this is crazy. People are everywhere. I can't imagine for one second this crazy world being my life. I don't know how the guys deal with being surrounded by so many people all the time. It would drive me insane to never have any privacy.

A group of women, some of whom I recognize from

standing and waiting for the tour bus to arrive, approach Zach as he supervises the roadies with his bike. A tall, leggy blonde with an obvious paid-for rack caresses his shoulder. Hate twists in my gut when he doesn't immediately shove her hand away, knowing damn well I can see him.

My body jerks, willing me over to tell the chick to back off, but I instantly stop myself. What the hell am I thinking? He isn't mine. What we had last night isn't anything more than a one-night stand. I know that, but it doesn't stop the jealousy from reaching every nerve in my body when I see him with another women.

I do hold a small amount of satisfaction in knowing I was given permission to call him by his real name, though. Actually, now that I think about it, I probably shouldn't call him that. That implies we have a certain level of intimacy—one he doesn't share with the other women he takes to bed. While I don't want to be grouped with the rest of the women he usually sleeps with, I don't want him getting any ideas about what we share happening more than this weekend.

Maybe I should set shit straight now.

I approach Zach and the women all stare me down on the way. The blonde doesn't make a move to remove herself from his side, and he doesn't seem to mind her there.

"Hey, Riff. I'm going to try to find Lanie. I'll catch you later," I tell him with as much confidence as I can muster to show I'm cool with parting ways from him.

I turn on my heel, only to find myself halted with Zach's

arm around my wrist. "You're not going to wait on me?"

The blonde is no longer at his side, but she stands with her arms folded and her lips in an obvious pout behind him. Zach crinkles his brow as he waits on me to answer.

I stare into his green eyes for a second before my gaze flicks to the pack of groupies waiting on his attention. "No. You seem busy."

He shakes his head. "Don't be like that. You're not jealous, are you?"

I flinch. Am I that easy to read? "No, of course not. I just don't want to be in your way."

He cups my face and gives me a quick peck on the lips. "Kitten, you'd never be in my way. I wish you would stay, but if you insist on going inside without me…here. He reaches into his back pocket and pulls out a golden ticket. "The guys know this means you're with me and will get you access to all the areas I can be in. Don't lose it, because I'm not finished with you yet."

A thrill shoots through me at the idea of spending another night tangled up in his sheets. I smile up at him. "Okay, then. Find me later."

He gives me a genuine smile before kissing me hungrily right in front of the women standing beside us. After he's fully satisfied, he lets me go. "That'll tide me over for a little while."

He winks at me before he turns and heads into the

back of the trailer with the road crew.

I touch my slightly swollen lips with my fingertips and then notice the evil stares I'm receiving from the women he left me alone with. The urge to stick my tongue out at them and sing "Nana-nana-boo-boo" overwhelms me, but I know that will probably end up with me in a fight. So, I decide to take the classy route and turn and walk away.

Two nights with him doesn't constitute a relationship in any form, merely a man I enjoy having sex with and want to do again before we part ways.

Who the hell am I kidding? If this keeps up, my heart is going to be in some serious danger here. If I'm not careful, I'll be heading towards the same path I've sworn never to go down again.

Chapter 9

AUBREY

Backstage is absolutely insane. Lanie is back here somewhere. I have to find her in this madhouse. I spot her instantly in the crowd. Her beauty stands out everywhere. She has it in her mind that she's an average looking girl. She never pays attention to the way people look at her. Her flawless skin stands out in her tank top and cut off jean shorts as she does her best to fade into her surroundings and become invisible. She flips her long, brown hair over her shoulder as she turns and I catch her eye.

"Hey, girl!" I wrap her in my arms.

She grins. "Hey, yourself. Nice of you to finally come up for air long enough to visit me for a while."

I roll my eyes at her. "Don't hate because I know how to let loose and have a little fun."

"I bet he got you loose," she snickers.

I smack her arm. "Oh, my god. I can't believe you."

"So, how did it go?"

My eyes roll back in my head. "Riff is amazing. Best sex I've ever had."

"Riff, really? Usually cocky men can't deliver."

I shake my head. "This one can." I hold up six fingers.

She shakes her head. "You two are perfect for each other. You're both machines."

I laugh and give her a playful shove. "So you're telling me nothing happened with you and Noel last night? You two were pretty cozy on the way back." Lanie sighs dramatically, and I'm instantly thrown into a giggling fit that she's finally let her guard down with Noel. "I knew it! Tell me!"

Lanie holds her hands up in surrender. "Okay. Okay. Jeesh, get a grip. We kissed."

I raise my eyebrow. "A kiss? Was it like a polite peck or was it full on tongue I-want-your-body make-out?"

She frowns. "It definitely wasn't polite."

A kiss, really? That's all. "Lanie, god, sometimes I swear for someone so smart, you sometimes act like an idiot. You should be ecstatic right now. Reconnecting with your first love is something people dream about and you're getting that. I don't see why you don't just let loose and let it happen."

"But the job—"

"But, *nothing*. Don't make me give the 'jobs aren't everything' speech. Jobs don't keep you warm or make you feel sexy, but Noel Falcon totally can. Anyone can see the guy is crazy about you."

I don't know why she can't see that everything she's ever wanted is right in front of her. What I wouldn't give for a package of tattooed sexiness to be madly in love with me. Stuff like that only happens in fairy tales, and she's wasting her chance at pure happiness.

The wheels turn in Lanie's mind, I can see it all over her face. I stare at her expectantly. "Quit doing that."

She flinches. "Doing what?"

"Overthinking things. You'll never know until you let down your walls a little." I hate it when she gets so uptight she can't see past the wall she's built around herself.

She runs her fingers through her hair. "Why are you pushing this? You hated him before."

I shrug. She's right. When he called her a ball busting bitch to a crowd of twenty thousand people, I wanted to kill him, but I've seen a different side of him now. He was hurt before because she left him once. I can totally relate to having a broken heart. Mine's been stomped on more times then I care to admit. "Because you're my best friend, and I love you. I want you to be happy. Plus, he's not the asshole I thought he was."

She gives me a weak smile and then wraps her arms around me. It's good to see I'm getting through to her a little bit. She'll end up driving him away and then hating herself for it if she doesn't stop rejecting him.

"Hey now…" We both turn and find Riff staring at us. "Nobody gets this girl's lovin' but me."

I giggle like a giddy kid at Christmas when Riff grabs me up in a hug. "Riff!"

Lane rolls her eyes at us. "On that note, I'm out of here."

Riff sets me on my feet. "What was all that about?"

I shrug. "Lanie has the tendency to push good things away in her life. Sometimes she needs a little help seeing things clearly, is all."

He pulls his lips into a tight line. "Maybe not everyone feels like they deserve good things to happen to them."

"Not Lanie. She's a good person. She feels like Noel will crush her heart. She still loves him. I can tell."

He sighs. "Maybe it's best you not push them together."

I tilt my head. "Why? They obviously still love each other. What do you know?"

Riff opens his mouth, but quickly closes it, clearly deciding not to spill any details.

"Come on. What's going on?"

He shakes his head. "Forget it. It's not my place to say. All I can tell you is us rocker types aren't meant to be trusted."

That comment throws me off guard. "You can't all be bad."

"Yeah we can, and I'm probably the worst."

A lump builds in my throat. "Why would you say that to me, Riff?"

"I'm the guy women have fun with, not the one they settle down with. I'm no good for you, Kitten. Trust me. I'm a one man heart-wrecking crew," he says.

Any doubts that I had in my mind that we could ever be more than this weekend flies from my mind. It can't be spelled out for me any clearer. So, I need to get my game face back on and look at this for what it is—a purely physical fling.

RIFF

I feel like a douche bag of epic proportions the moment I basically tell Kitten I'm using her only for sex. She doesn't deserve that from me, but for now it's the best I can give her. She doesn't need to get her hopes up that we can be more, because we can't. I fuck things up too much. It's only a matter of time before I do something stupid and she ends up hating my ass.

This whole situation is fucking up my head. More than anything I wish I was a good guy, someone worthy of a girl like Kitten. The only thing I can hope for is that one day she'll find a man that can give her everything she deserves, like monogamy and children. I can't give her either one of those things.

I shake my head as I finish warming up, trying to forget my screwed up life. Music and sex are the only two things I've found that help me do that.

My fingers glide over the strings and I hit a sour note.

Trip slaps me on the back. "What's with you man? Couldn't get it up last night?"

"Fuck you, dude," I snap.

He holds his hands up in surrender. "Easy, I was joking. Chill the fuck out."

The tension leaves my shoulders. Trip's been my best friend a long time, and I know he didn't mean anything by it. "Sorry, bro. I'm a little edgy."

Trip rolls his eyes. "Not this Sophie shit again? I thought that hot, little redheaded friend of Lanie's was pulling you out of that slump."

"This has nothing to do with Sophie. Noel can have her sorry ass. I hope those two assholes are happy together. I hate that he's stringing Lanie along like this. She seems like a nice girl."

Trip raises his eyebrow so high it touches the bandanna he has tied around his head. "Are you catching feelings for the redhead?"

"What!? No. You know me better than that." Damn it. How the fuck would he figure that shit out? Am I catching feelings? Is that why I feel so crazy?

"If you say so, brother. What am I supposed to think? You never spend an entire night holed up in a hotel room with a chick. The way you were lookin' at her on the bus the other day, it was like you'd been shot by that little fucker in diapers with wings and arrows like in the cartoons. And now you're concerned about Lanie's feelings?"

I laugh. "Did you really just talk about Cupid like he's real?"

"Whatever. Make fun of me all you want. All I know is between you and Noel I don't know which one of you is chasing the tail harder."

I shake my head. "Aubrey's here to have a good time for the weekend. No one's catching feelings."

Trip smirks. "Yeah. You keep telling yourself that."

That smart-ass I-know-everything look he's got on his face isn't helping the situation. "A girl like her would never really be into a guy like me."

"You're never going to know until you try. It's okay to have feelings for someone, Riff."

"Not for me. She can do so much better than me. I know that. Why set myself up for a tragic ending."

Trip frowns. "I know this is hard to hear, but not every situation is going to end up like—"

I jump up from the amp I'm sitting on. "Don't even fucking say it."

"All I'm sayin' is—"

I set my guitar down and cut him off. "Quit trying to convince me I'm not poison. I'll ruin her, like I do everything else."

Trip opens his mouth to start on me again, but I stalk away before he has a chance. He's been trying to save my worthless ass for years and I wish he would stop and let me be miserable like I deserve. He calls my name a couple times, but I don't dare look back.

I make my way over to catering and grab a cold beer from the cooler. I twist off the lid and take a long pull. Trip has a way of getting under my skin like no one else.

Several of the opening acts and a slew of groupies sit around the room hanging out in small groups, chatting amongst themselves.

I rub my forehead and close my eyes. Sometimes I really hate the fact that it's hard to get a moments peace on the road. There's so much shit inside my head I need to work out in order to feel like I'm not losing my mind over a woman.

"What's wrong? Blue balls killing you?" Donovan says next to me with a smart-ass snicker.

My eyes snap open and instantly narrow. "You got a fucking problem with me, asshole? Say the word. I beg you. Give me one reason to drop your ass right here, right now."

Donovan shoves his blonde hair out of his eyes. "Easy, Romeo. I was merely asking for confirmation that you bagged that hot redhead last night since you cock-blocked me."

I fold my arms over my chest. "I did. What of it?"

He shrugs and then casually reaches down and grabs a beer. "Just curious. I would've loved to tap that. It looked tight."

Before I know what I've done, I draw back and blast him square in the face. Screams erupt all around me, but it feels like I'm moving in slow motion. Shock registers on Donovan's face, and then it twists in anger. Before he gets a chance to land a punch on me, I hit him again with as much force as I can.

Blood pours from his nose and I pull back ready to strike again, but I'm suddenly being yanked away.

Trip hooks my arm and drags me back. "What the fuck are you doing?'

I can't answer him, because honestly, I'm not sure what came over me. It's not like it's the first time he's razzed me about a woman, but the mention of him wanting to fuck my girl made my brain short circuit.

I shake my head. My girl? What the fuck is wrong with me? She isn't my girl. Why do these stupid, fucking thoughts keep rolling through me? This girl is driving me insane.

I take a deep breath. "I'm cool, man. You can let go."

Trip stares at me, while he decides if he can let go or not. After a couple seconds he loosens his grip on my arm. "You going to tell me what that was about?"

I throw my hands on my waist and try to slow my breathing. "He's just being his normal cocksucker self. What do you want me to say?"

He shakes his head. "I heard what he said. Why don't you admit it to yourself? You like that girl."

I open my mouth to protest his accusations, but Trip narrows his eyes. Fuck. I hate it when he tries to go Dr. Phil on my ass. "Even if I did, it can't happen."

"Why?"

"Because I can't let it, that's why!"

"Give people a little credit, Riff. You have to learn to let some in. You let me and Tyke in."

"Yeah, I let Noel in, too. See how that turned out, right. You and Tyke are the exception. You guys were there before —" I quickly cut myself off. It's too difficult to even bring up. I hate reliving the past and the fucked up shit I've done. It reminds me that I'm a dirt bag.

Trip sighs. "Noel is a fucker, I'll give you that, but I still don't believe he did it on purpose. He still swears he doesn't remember."

I rub the sides of my shaved head. "I'm so sick of Noel. I want all of that behind me."

"Then that's what you do." I stare at him quizzically. "You move on. Let that hate and anger go and focus on something good for a change. Like the red-head. She seems very positive if you ask me." I scowl and Trip laughs. "See! I knew it! You're catching feelings. Admit it and go after her."

That's the problem when you've been friends with someone since grade school. They know you too damn well. "Okay. Fine. I'll see where this thing goes."

Trip grins. "I should've been a shrink instead of a drummer."

I shove his shoulder. "That would've worked if you could read."

He laughs and then gives me the finger. "I would've just banged a geek and got her to do all my work. I would've found a way through."

I roll my eyes. "You are so messed up."

AUBREY

Standing on the side of the stage and watching the guys perform to a sold out crowd is amazing. This truly is the best seat in the house. Riff's guitar screams a sexy note as he wiggles his tongue at the crowd. My face heats as I allow my mind to drift back to all the amazing things he can do with that thing.

My cell buzzes in my pocket and I pull it out, hoping it's Lanie explaining where the hell she is. She was supposed to meet me over here so I wouldn't have to stand here alone like an idiot.

Lanie: *Sorry. Went on to Mom's I'll be back before we head out to say goodbye. Didn't figure you'd miss me since Riff seems like pretty good company. ;)*

A winky face, Lanie, really? I shake my head. She's a goofball, but she knows me too well.

I was supposed to go visit my folks tonight, too. That was the purpose for meeting up here in our home state, but it doesn't look like that's going to happen. I promised Riff one more night.

As soon as the set is over, the guys all head my way. Trip and Tyke hig-five me before heading out of sight.

Sweat lines every inch of Riff's skin as he approaches. He obviously gives everything he has in a show.

"You were amazing," I tell him as soon as he's close enough to hear.

"Thanks! It's a rush being out there."

I nod. "I can tell."

Noel approaches us. "You seen Lane?"

I shake my head. "No, but she did text me, telling me she already left for her Mom's house."

Noel furrows his brow. "She didn't wait on me? I was supposed to go with her."

I shrug. "I'm not sure what she's doing."

He runs his hands through his sweaty hair. "Okay, guys, catch you all later. I'm going to try and find her."

Riff watches his band mate retreat. "He's lost his mind."

"I think it's kind of sweet he's so into her."

He turns his piercing eyes on me. "You wouldn't think that if you knew the things I knew about him."

"What do you mean?"

Riff shakes his head. "Forget it. I shouldn't have said anything. Come on. I need a shower."

He grabs my hand and tries to tug me along with him, but I plant my feet firmly. "You can't say something like that and then blow it off. Lanie's my best friend. If he's going to hurt her, I want to know."

He sighs. "What Noel does is his business. I'm not getting in the middle of it."

"Are you saying you have secrets?"

Riff frowns and touches my cheek. "We all have secrets, Kitten. Even you. I'm not going to try to pretend that we know everything about each other, but it's a fact of life. No one discloses every piece of information about themselves to someone else. It's not human nature."

He's right. Everyone has something they don't want others to know. Just like the information I know about this charity project. It kills me I can't tell Lanie the truth and I'm thankful she hasn't brought it up to me since I've been here. I don't know if I could hide that from her once we're face to face.

"Something wrong?" he asks.

I shake my head. "Just thinking about how you're right."

A sad smile plays on his lips. "Come on. Enough lingering on life lessons. Let's go do something fun."

I raise an eyebrow. "What do you have in mind?"

Riff gives me that wicked grin he's famous for. "Something that ends with me inside you."

Oh dear God. Every hormone in my body nearly convulses at his words. That man knows exactly what to say to nearly cause me to lose my mind.

Chapter 10

RIFF

Cruising around the dark streets of Dallas on my bike with Aubrey wrapped around me feels like freedom. I love my job. The money's great and so are the chicks, but I never really feel at peace.

While I would love to spend another night locked away in my hotel room with her, I figure a little excitement is in order. I told Trip I'm going to see where this goes, so to show her that maybe I can be more than just sex to her, I'm taking her out.

We pass by a small bar with a neon light shining from the window. Perfect. We can grab a beer and chat and won't have to worry about fans or that fucker Donovan starting shit. I want some one-on-one time to see where this girl's head is.

I back my bike against the curb and throw down the kickstand. Aubrey hops off and yanks the helmet from her head while I readjust my backwards baseball cap.

I catch myself almost mesmerized by her as she runs her fingers through her hair. I don't remember feeling this way after I bagged a girl before. Ever. Usually, after the initial humping, they lose their allure. Not Aubrey. All I can think about when I look at her are ways to keep her around longer.

She throws her hands on her hips. "What exactly are we doing here?"

I stand and store the helmet. "I figured we could get a beer and get to know each other a little better."

The corners of her mouth turn up. "I thought that's what we did last night."

I shake my head and pull her against me. "Last night we fucked, and I still haven't gotten you out of my system, so I'm left with one alternative."

A blush washes over her cheeks. "What's that?"

I shrug. "To see if this thing between us can ever go anywhere."

"Riff…"

If she's about to give me the reasons why this can never work between us, I don't want to hear them. "Before you say anything, give me the weekend. We only have tonight and tomorrow, and if you end up hating my guts by the time you leave, then you never have to see me again."

Kitten pulls her lips into a tight line. "Okay, then."

"Yeah?" I hug her to me. "One more thing."

"What's that?"

"In public, around the band and the fans, I don't mind you calling me Riff, but everywhere else I want you to call me Zach." It's a weird request. The name she calls me shouldn't matter, but it does. If I'm going to step out of my comfort zone and see if this can go somewhere, than I want it to be as real as possible. I don't want her to like me for Riff, my stage persona and all that it entails. I want her to like me for Zach— the fucked up guy with loads of problems.

She'll probably be running for the hills this time tomorrow.

I lead her into the small bar. Her tiny hand fits perfectly in mine as I hold it causally at my side. The bar is dark, with only the light over the bar providing light around the room. A few older men sit with their shoulders slumped at the bar talking to the bartender. This is exactly the atmosphere I'm hoping for. Nice and secluded.

A fairly modern juke box plays an old-school country song as we make our way over to the bar.

The thirty-something bartender raises an eyebrow and shoves her brown hair over her shoulder. "IDs?"

It's been a long time since I'd been carded to drink. It's nice to know she's completely oblivious as to who I am.

After she's double-checked them, she asks, "What can I get you?"

I turn to Aubrey. "Ladies choice?"

She smiles. "Two *Budweisers*, please."

The bartender nods and meanders off to get our drinks. I lean against the bar as I wait with Aubrey. She's looking exceptionally beautiful tonight. Her long, red hair falls around her shoulders in loose waves and the green halter-top she's wearing accentuates her fantastic rack.

She grins at me when she catches me staring at her tits. "You see something you like?"

I laugh. "I'm trying to determine if it's your ass or your tits I like best. I'm usually a breast man, but your ass in those jeans…I literally want to bite it."

She giggles. "I think you already did once or twice last night."

I run my fingertips down the length of her arm. "And I can't wait to do it again."

Memories of last night flood me, and she's right. I do remember giving her love bites on that tasty, little booty. My dick twitches at the thought of getting her naked again and I reposition my legs.

I'm about to say screw talking and let's get back to fucking when the bartender hands us our beers. "That'll be seven fifty."

I pull out my wallet. "No tab in this place?"

The brunette shakes her head and glances down at my tattooed forearms. "Not to strangers."

If only I can tell her I can buy this place with the swipe of my debit card, but that would make me seem like an arrogant jackass, not to mention blow my cover.

I lay down two fifty dollar bills. "This should cover us for a while."

She picks them up and holds them up to the light as we turn and take a seat at the end of the bar. Kitten sits on one side of the corner and I on the opposite side so we can sort of face each other.

She takes a sip of her beer and stares at me expectantly. "So what do you want to know about me?"

I swallow hard. This is a totally new experience for me. The confidence I typically have falls away from me. "I, um, I don't know. How about we start with why you decided to give me a chance."

She picks at the label on her bottle. "I'm not really sure. It goes against everything I came down here to do."

I lean back in my chair. Interesting. "Exactly what were your intentions when you hooked up with me?"

She hooks a strand of hair behind her ear. "I'm almost embarrassed to say."

"I've already seen you naked. There's no shame between us anymore, Kitten. Spill."

She takes another sip and my stomach clenches. Whatever she's about to say is going to suck. I can tell by all the tension in her body.

After a couple long seconds, she sighs. "You're sort of my last hurrah."

I scrunch my brow. "What's that supposed to mean?"

"My mother has been on my case to quit going after your type."

I raise my pierced eyebrow. "*My typ*e?"

A blush creeps over her cheeks. "Yeah, you know. The *bad boy*. The *assholes*. Guys that are notorious for breaking hearts."

I hate the idea that there were jerks before me that couldn't see how amazing she is. Not saying that I'd be any better, but at least I recognize something special when it's in front of me. It makes me want to show her even more that I am worth a shot.

"So what changed your mind?" I ask.

She bites her lip and stares at me through those innocent eyes of hers. I hold my breath as I wait on her reply.

AUBREY

Zach's quest for answers takes me by surprise. I never imagined that he would ever be interested in more—seems like I'm definitely standing out to him.

He waits patiently for me to reply. I know I can make or break a relationship we might have with what I say.

I shrug. "I can't explain it. I feel like there's a connection between us…"

He frowns. "But? That sentence sounds like there's a *'but'* coming."

"My family is a little…uptight."

"What does your family have to do with us?"

My eyes drift from his pierced eyebrow to the bulging muscles in his tattooed forearms.

He stiffens. "Are you saying you're afraid of what they would think of me because of the way I look?"

I bite my lip. "It's not just your appearance. Your career…"

He tips his bottle up finishing his beer and then signals to the bartender for another. "I know you're too good for me. Trust me. I know this, but I think if you give me a chance. I'm great at charming moms."

I reach over and touch his hand. "I'm not saying this to be mean. I think you're an amazing person, but I've been hurt by men before. I've never really had a good relationship. My mom, she's been there after each heartbreak to help pick up the pieces. She's been telling me for years to find a nice guy—one that will love me and be there for me—to settle down with. After the last man I dated crushed me, I've decided she's right. If I want to be happy I think I need to change things."

He traces patterns on the back of my hand with his

finger. "So you want to hide the person you truly are? You think that will make you happy?"

I shrug. "It's better than being miserable all the time."

Neither of us says anything for a couple of moments. Being completely honest with someone is draining. I can't tell what he's thinking, but I can tell by the slight slump in his shoulders that he's disappointed. If we lived in the same city and he wasn't a famous rock star with temptations of other women in his face constantly, I might be more into the idea of having a relationship with him. But as it is, I can't go through heartbreak again. I might not make it through another.

"You're right," he says. "I'm probably not that guy you're looking for. I'm not the white picket fence kind of guy. Things between us would probably end eventually."

Even though this is basically what I said to him, it doesn't lessen the pain of rejection. I fight back my emotions and give him a casual smile. "Good. I'd still like to spend more time with you and end this thing as friends."

He pulls his lips into a tight line before he picks up his beer and clinks it to mine. "Friends it is."

Even though I'm getting exactly what I asked for, why do I have this pit of disappointment in my stomach?

"Well if this weekend is the end for us, I saw something a couple shops down I want to buy for you," he says with a wicked grin as he grabs my hand.

The look on his face tells me it's not a souvenir

keychain. "What is it?"

He shrugs. "Something I want you to keep an open mind to."

We leave the bar and head out into the cool Texas night air. Zach's long, guitar playing fingers wrap around mine as we walk hand in hand down the street past all the little shops. A glowing white sign with red letters catches my eye. It simply says *Naughty Land* on it.

I instantly giggle as he holds open the door for me. "A sex shop? Really?"

He bites his lip toying with his lip ring. "You seem to be down with the kinky sex last night, so I figure we get the right equipment this round."

Intrigued by him, I ask, "What do you have in mind?"

We step inside and my eyes widen. There's everything from battery-operated boyfriends to full on bondage beds lining every inch of this place. "Wow."

He steps behind me when I walk into a secluded aisle and places his hands on my bare shoulders. "Wow as in your down for some of this, or wow like you're scared to death of it?"

I shake my head. "I'm not scared."

"Then prove it," he growls in my ear. "Find something you want to try out and we'll buy it. Since this is my last time with you, I want to pull out all the stops and give you the fantasy fucking you've always dreamed of."

I swallow hard. His sexual forwardness in combination with the sight of all this stuff is enough to cause me to get a little wet.

He allows his fingers to trail down my arm and then down my waist before finally finding their way onto my ass. He squeezes it with enough force to let me know he means business as he grinds himself into me backside. "I want back inside you. Feel this? This is what you do to me."

The hard length of him presses into my back through his jeans. I lay my head back on his shoulder and let out a soft moan. The things this man does to me.

"That's it. Now keep this feeling in mind and go find us something to play with."

Before I can say anything else, he pulls away, leaving me panting. A cold rush of air fills the space against my back where his body used to be and reality sets in that I was so turned on for a moment I was just about ready to fuck him right here in this store.

I walk around the room and pass all the vibrators. I don't have any problems having an orgasm with Zach, so I don't feel like those will be exciting enough for us. The sex game boards don't interest me either, so I drift over towards the fetish section.

A black riding crop catches my attention and I think about how much Zach enjoyed being blindfolded last night and how something like this could be fun.

"You ever used one of these?" he asks, startling me.

I shake my head. "No, but it looks interesting."

"They can be fun if you know how to use them the right way."

"H—how…what's the right way?" Even I can hear the uncertainty in my voice.

He takes one off the rack. "I'll show you."

After he pays for the equipment and we ride back over to the hotel. We barely make it through the room door before we're all over each other. He kisses my lips and neck while he strips away all my clothes and then his own.

He pulls the crop out of the bag and rips it from the package. "Use this on me."

"I don't think I can," I whisper.

He places a finger under my chin. "You want to dominate. I saw it last night with the blindfold game."

"I failed miserably at that. I was thinking, maybe…" Gah! This is harder to ask for than I thought. "You could use it on me."

He bites his bottom lip and flicks the ring between his teeth. "You're so fucking sexy it hurts. Do you know that?" He kisses my lips. "Go bend over and put your elbows on the bed."

I make my way over to the bed and do what he asks. I feel a little self-conscious with my ass sticking in the air. "Like this?"

"Exactly like that." He gets behind me and rubs the curve of my ass before giving it a little swat with this bare hand. "I love how secretly naughty you are."

The contact stings a bit at first, but then an intense pleasure fills me. "Oooh."

He grabs me around the waist and leans over my back to whisper in my ear. "I knew you were a bad girl. You need a good spanking, don't you?"

I chew the inside of my lip, but don't answer unsure of what to say.

"If you want me to keep going you need to tell me you want this," he says roughly.

I don't want him to stop so I say it. "Spank me."

He growls as he kisses my shoulder and then pulls back to give me another little smack, only this time he uses the crop. It has more of a sting than his hand does. I whimper as he smacks me again.

"Do you like that?" he asks. "Do you want me to keep going?"

"Don't stop," is all I can manager to say as I bite my lip.

"Spread your legs more."

A couple minutes later he bends down behind me and flicks my clit with his tongue. His fingers slip inside me as he begins to work me up into a frenzy. My breathing quickens and a moan escapes my lips as I teeter right on the edge. Right before I do he stops and stands at my side. He wraps one arm around my waist as his hard cock pokes me in the belly.

He takes the crop and smacks it against my folds. At first it's gentle and then he quickens the pace and every nerve in my body starts vibrating.

"Yes! Oh, god, Zach!" I cry out as I have one of the most intense orgasms I've ever had.

While I'm still on my high, he flips me over onto the bed and pulls my hips towards him. He shoves his cock inside me and I grab handfuls of the comforter as he works his way deeper.

"You're so fucking wet," he rasps as he grabs my thighs and pounds into me.

My toes curl as his steady rhythm pushes me into a second orgasm. I grab his wrist and arch my back as I come hard a second time with him deep inside me.

He stares into my eyes. "That was the hottest thing I've ever seen."

Zach's eyes watch me intently as he licks his lips and works towards his own release. A shine of sweat covers his bare chest and face. His tattooed forearms bulge as he grips my legs tighter.

He closes his eyes. "Fuck!"

All the muscles in his body tighten as he comes while he's deep within me. This is one man that knows how to please a woman. I would love to keep him around longer because he has the power to make me feel so damn good, but I know too much of a good thing can also be bad.

****

We pull up to the parking lot where Big Bertha is waiting on his bike. The sun's nearly set, so I know it's getting late and almost time to say goodbye to Zach. The parking lot is a ghost town, a vast difference from when we were here last time after Black Falcon's show.

After the bike is parked we head inside the bus. I set my overnight bag down and look around the empty place. At first, I thought we were alone because I didn't see anyone around. I assume the twins are still out partying somewhere while Lanie and Noel are probably still at her mom's place. I set my bag down on the floor and pause the instant I hear a moan come from the bedroom.

"Oh my god!" I whisper harshly. "Should we leave? I don't want to interrupt if someone's back there."

Zach shakes his head. "The only person allowed to have chicks back there is Noel. We don't cross the boundary of sex in each other's beds. Sometimes it's weeks before our sheets get washed."

"Gross."

He shrugs. "I know. We might as well make ourselves comfortable."

He plops down in the love seat and tugs me down with him. Even though I know this isn't going anywhere, it feels nice to snuggle with him. I lay my head on his chest as he wraps his arms around me.

I close my eyes. "I'm going to miss this."

"Me too," he whispers into my hair before kissing the top of my head.

As I start to drift off, I hear the bedroom door open and then close. Lanie tip-toes down the hallway in what I imagine is Noel's shirt. A grin fills my face. I knew she was still in love with that man. I'm glad she's finally let herself feel something for him.

Lanie tilts her head and raises her eyebrows as she stares at Zach and me. I open my mouth to call her out, but she heads right into the kitchen and does her best to ignore me.

"Come on," Zach says as he stands and then pulls me up with him.

We take a few steps and sit back down on the bench seat at the table.

Lanie squats down and looks through the cabinets. The fabric from Noel's shirt is big enough that it hangs down over her thighs, but it still shows a ton of skin. She fidgets with the material while searching the shelves.

Zach smirks as he stands and reaches into the overhead cabinet next to the sink. He lets the door bang shut and chuckles when Lanie jumps at the sound. He sits next to me again with a package full of Oreos. Lanie eyeballs the blue package of cookies when he sets them on the table. I can practically see her mouth water from here.

"Make yourself useful and grab us some milk from the fridge," Zach says to Lanie. "I always keep it in there. The guys know better than to take my stuff."

She grabs the a gallon of two percent white milk and sets it on the counter before she searches for a couple of glasses.

"There should be some plastic cups on the top shelf, above the sink," Zach informs her while she pokes around in the cabinets.

There's only one cup left in the bag when she holds it up. Her smile deflates as she pours the milk into it and walks over to the table. She sets the cup down, and slides into the seat across from us.

He pushes the package across the table to her after handing me a cookie. "You don't want some milk, too?"

She shrugs and pulls out a cookie. "Only one cup."

Zach smiles and puts his cup in the middle of the table so we can all use it. "We can share it—no double dipping. I heard where your mouth's been."

I smack his arm and give her an apologetic smile.

"Sorry, Lanie, but you were kind of loud."

Her face flushes, like it never occurred to her that she's loud enough for anyone to hear her and Noel having sex.

Zach chuckles and dunks a cookie in the milk. "Nothing to be embarrassed about, it was fucking hot. Noel's one lucky son of a bitch."

I giggle and then he winks at Lanie, which only makes me laugh harder and nearly choke on my food.

She covers her face with her hand. "Oh, god."

Zach bites into his cookie. "You say that a lot, don't you?"

Lanie's head snaps up. "Can we please stop talking about this? It's not exactly the kind of conversation I should be having with you guys."

He shrugs. "You know, about the ticket thing, I'm sorry. You did try to blow me off. I didn't think you meant it. I thought it was your angle."

"My angle?"

Zach nods. "Most chicks play games with me. You weren't the first girl who tried to play the hard-to-get card with me. I figured you read one of my interviews where I said that turned me on."

She dips a cookie in the milk, too. "An interviewer actually asked what your turn-ons were?"

"You wouldn't believe some of the shit we get asked. Noel gets the worst of it, though, being the front man and all. People are constantly trying to dig things up on him, but he's good at keeping his life secret."

"It's not like Noel has a lot of dirt to find," Lanie answers a little defensively.

He raises his eyebrows. "How long has it been since you dated him?"

"A little over four years. Why?"

Zach looks away from her and takes out another cookie. "A lot can happen in four years, Lanie."

There he goes with that damn secret. I wish he would tell her what he's doing so she can deal with it before she gets in deep with him. Hopefully whatever he's hiding isn't a deal breaker.

She shrugs. "I'm sure Noel isn't intentionally hiding things from me. We all have our pasts and secrets we don't want people to know."

My stomach tenses as the secret I'm keeping from her crosses my mind. I'm still having serious doubts if I'm doing the right thing by hiding it from her.

Zach's eyes scan her face like things are clicking for him. "We most certainly do."

He pops the last Oreo in his mouth. His gaze never leaves Lanie. He's waiting for more questions, but she never asks and neither do I—even though it's killing me to find out.

Zach looks at me before standing beside the table and sticking his hand out to Lanie. "Truce?"

She smiles as his large fingers wrap around her hand. "Truce. I would like that. We should be friends since you and Aubrey…you know."

He glances over at me and wiggles his eyebrows. "Oh yeah, I know. Friends it is."

When Zach leaves the room, I turn in Lanie's direction. I smirk at her and she shakes her head. "Don't you shake your head at me, missy. I told you all about mine, now it's your turn to dish. It sounded like it was incredible!"

She pinches the bridge of her nose. "Aubrey…"

I hate when she does this to herself. I yank her hands away from her face. "Stop it. Don't be embarrassed. You had a good time—nothing wrong with that, Lanie. So, tell me, does he get his Sex-god title back now?"

She rolls her eyes and smiles.

I smack the tables and grin. "I knew it. That guy is sex on a stick."

I hang out with my best friend and my lover on the bus until it's ready to head to the next stop on the tour. We eat Oreos and tell jokes until it starts getting late and the twins make their way back onto the bus. This weekend was one of the best I've had in a long time. I don't want it to end, but I know I can't stay. I have a life, and a job waiting for me back in New York.

I rub my forehead as I take a look at my friend. I debate on telling her about Diana Swagger's plans and how Isaac is working on the charity.

"Something wrong?" Zach asks.

I glance over at him and smile. "No, everything is fine."

He wraps his arm around my shoulders as his eyes search my face. In the small amount of time I've spent with him he's shocked me. He's nothing like I expected. He's caring. It makes me wonder why he hasn't settled down and what he's hiding.

Tyke glances out the window. "Taxi's here."

He sighs and leans his forehead into my cheek. "I guess I should walk you out."

I nod. "I'd like that."

I stand and then lean down and wrap my best friend in a hug. "I'll see you soon. Love you."

She squeezes me tighter. "Love you, too."

Zach grabs my bag and takes me by the hand as I tell the rest of the band goodbye. My feet are heavy as I make my way down the steps. I hate goodbyes. I hate them even more when I'm not sure if I'm ever going to see someone again.

The cab driver hops out of the car and takes my bag

from Zach before popping open the truck.

Zach grabs both of my hands in his and we face each other. "So…this is it?"

I nod and fight back the sting in my eyes. "Yeah. I think so."

He glances down at the pavement beneath our feet. "Can I still message you since we're friends?"

A tear drips down my cheek as I smile. "I'd like that." Without thinking I throw my arms around his neck and breathe in his scent one last time. "I'm going to miss you."

He stiffens in my arms and hugs me tighter against him. "I'll miss you more."

Before I turn into a puddle right here on the ground, I shove myself away from him and hop in the cab. I never imagined saying goodbye to him would be so difficult. I press my hand onto the glass as I say goodbye.

My heart crushes as the driver pulls away, leaving Zach standing in the parking lot with his hands shoved in his pockets. There's a pained expression on his face and I fight back the sob that's threatening to expose how sad I am about leaving him. Our eyes lock, and we don't break out stare until the cab turns the corner and he's out of my sight forever.

Chapter 11

RIFF

My fingers tangle and I hit the wrong chord as Noel and Lanie pass by hand in hand. She grins up at him like he's perfect and he has the biggest smile on his face.

That shit isn't fucking fair. I want to out him so bad. Assholes like us don't deserve happiness.

Trip catches me staring as he twirls his drumstick in his fingers. He shakes his head. "Don't do it, dude. Nothing good will come out of you getting involved."

"I'm going to tell her."

Tyke looks up from his base. "Tell who, what?"

Trip looks at his brother. "Riff wants to tell Lanie about Sophie."

Tyke frowns. "I have to go with Trip on this one. Stay out of it."

"You guys don't get it." I go back to working the strings on my guitar.

They don't understand what it feels like to want something you can't have. They've never been through real emotional pain. I don't want Lanie to go through that if she doesn't have to. Sure, it'll hurt no matter when she finds out Noel's keeping a secret baby from her, but it'll hurt even more once she's got a ton of time invested in this relationship.

Noel approaches us as we get ready for our set. "Hey, guy. I've got some news."

"Oh, joy," I say, sarcasm thick in my voice.

He quickly cuts me a look before continuing. "I got a call to visit a sick kid out in Arizona for a charity."

"That's awesome, bro. When do you leave?" Tyke asks.

"Tonight, right after the show."

My wheels start to turn. "Is Lanie going with you?"

Noel shakes his head. "No. She's actually going to stay on the bus with you guys for the night. Can I trust you all to look after her?"

I roll my eyes. I know that little dig is a warning for me to stay away from her, but what he doesn't know is I'm not interested in her for that any more. It will, on the other hand, be the perfect opportunity to share with her a certain secret our fearless leader has been keeping from her.

Trip snickers. "You mean can you trust us not to try and

sleep with her? Yeah. I think we're all pretty clear she's your girl after all the times we've heard her scream your name."

Noel grins. "She does do that a lot."

I turn my back and try to block out the love fest over Noel's sex life going on behind me. That fucker doesn't even know how good he has it.

****

The crowd screams as I play the signature riff of our biggest hit song. I love this. The energy the fans throw out to us rocks me to the soul. There's nothing like being in the moment and having thirty thousand people sing the words to our songs in unison.

Noel brings the mic close to his lips. "This next song goes out to the girl who shredded my heart without hesitation back in high school. It's called *Ball Busting Bitch*, and Lanie, this one's for you."

I shake my head and laugh. He has balls, I'll give him that. I'm surprised he even uses that line in the show now that she's back. If I were Lanie I would throat punch him for talking shit about me to the world.

We play together in perfection. Noel hits every note and the rest of us play the shit out of our instruments. The guitar solo is my favorite part of this song. I love the way it screams like a scorned woman telling her lover to take a flying leap.

The song wraps up and I fling black guitar picks with our band name into the crowd. It's amazing to see the fans fight over something because one of us touched it. It really solidifies that we are actually pretty fucking cool.

I hand the roadies my guitar and head off the stage. On the other side of the amps stands a tall blonde in a skin-tight, black mini skirt. She grins at me and then twirls a piece of hair around her finger as I come within a couple feet of her.

I know what she wants, but I've kind of lost all interest in the band, gigs, and even chicks since Kitten left. I've not handed out one golden ticket since we hooked up because I experienced a connection with her. I'm actually starting to worry that she's ruined me for all other women.

The only time my dick gets hard now is when I think of her and our nights together.

I walk past the blonde and she grabs my arms as I pass by. "Riff, can I get your autograph?"

I sigh. "Sure. You have a pen?"

She bites her pouty, bottom lip. "I was hoping maybe you'd sign me in a more intimate place."

Typically I'd be all over this shit. She's practically begging for it and I know she'd do anything I want. Maybe even anal if I wanted.

I shake my head. "Not tonight. I've got other plans."

She studies me for a long moment. "Too bad. Can I go back to your bus anyhow? Maybe one of the other guys—"

I don't give her time to finish her sentence because I'm

not in the fucking mood. Trip and Tyke are perfectly capable of finding their own ass for the night. They don't need my help for that.

After grabbing some food and hanging out with the twins for a bit I head off to find some peace and quiet. I make it to the sanctuary of the bus. I gather some clean clothes and head into the shower. While I'm in there, the distinct sound of Lanie and Noel going at each other pours through the thin walls.

All the noises make me think of Kitten. I wonder what she's doing right now or who she's with. I haven't talk to her since we left Dallas. I've been tempted to message her, but stop myself every time. I don't want to seem like a weepy sap and beg her to be with me another night. She made it very clear I'm no good for her and that we should stay friends.

The only problem is we can never be friends. People don't keep daydreaming about fucking their friends.

I towel off and get dressed before making my way to the kitchen. Tyke and Trip are playing the *Xbox*, battling over gamer supremacy as I grab my Oreos and milk. The guys go at it as I enjoy my most relaxing snack. Watching the cookie dip into the milk reminds me of Hailey every time I do it.

God, I miss her. What I wouldn't give to have her back.

Before I get too swept up in my thoughts, Mike climbs inside the bus. "Where's Noel? I've been waiting nearly a half hour."

I grin. This is the perfect time to piss him off. "Let me go get him."

I bang on the bedroom door when I get to the end of the hall. I wait a couple seconds and when I don't hear any movement I fling open the door and barrel through.

My eyes widen as they land directly on Lanie's naked breasts. She screeches at the top of her lungs as she attempts to cover up her shirtless chest.

Noel protectively wraps his arms around her. "What the fuck, dude? I didn't say come in."

"Sorry, bro. Didn't know you were..." My eyes slide down her body and a slow grin spreads across my face. Busted. "...busy."

Noel's eyes narrow. "Well, now you know. So get the fuck out."

I glance over at Lanie's horrified face and then turn my attention back to Noel. "Just thought you would want to know your ride to the airport has been waiting for almost twenty-five minutes, but I can see you're busy. I'll tell them to piss off."

A heavy sigh leaves Noel's mouth. "Thanks, man. Tell them I'll be out in a second."

I raise my eyebrows and make a show of trying to be the non-asshole out of the two of us. "You sure? If I were you, I think I'd make them wait."

Noel's fingers roll into fists. "Yeah. Now get the fuck

out."

I close the door behind me after shrugging and mumbling, "You're the boss," under my breath.

Noel has absolutely no plans of telling Lanie about Sophie. He's going to ride this ocean of lies as long as he can. Well, I've got news for him, this shark is about to ruin his perfect wave.

AUBREY

I check my cell for the tenth time in the last hour. Isaac has me working overtime with him on Noel's charity since I came back from Texas. Markers and storyboards clutter his normal tidy office. I've never seen it in such disarray.

Isaac himself appears more casual. His suit jacket hangs on the back of his high-back chair and his white button up shirt has the top two buttons undone while his tie hangs loose. The sleeves are shoved to nearly his elbows, exposing his defined forearms.

He shoves his hand into his thick blonde hair and lets out a loud sigh. "I'm stumped. I think I need a change of scenery to get the brain firing again."

I collect my notepad from the chair beside me. "I think calling it a night is a good idea. I'm beat."

Isaac shoves his glasses up his nose. "I was thinking more like we should go get a drink somewhere."

I raise my eyebrows and alarms go off in my head, but I figure what the hell, "Sure."

"Great." He smiles. "Let's go."

We catch a cab over to the Flatiron Lounge. Isaac and some other big wigs at the firm like to frequent this place after work. I've heard some big deals have gone down in this place. The area is tight, like most spaces in New York, but the atmosphere is nice. The lights are turned down, but it's still bright enough to see everything clearly. Patrons sit closely at the bar and at small tables, talking amongst themselves.

The evening crowd is mostly dressed in clothes to go out. Women wear trendy cocktail dresses while the men still have dress shirts and slacks on. Isaac fits in perfectly, but me on the other hand could've used a shower and fresh clothes. My pencil skirt is wrinkled from hours of assisting my boss on the charity project that's supposed to belong to my best friend.

I frown. I need to talk to her about this soon. Things are spinning out of control quickly, and if I don't get some input from her now, this won't be her project at all.

"Something wrong?" Isaac asks while peering at me through his square, black framed glasses.

His blue eyes search mine and I debate telling him how bad I feel about keeping this from Lanie, but decide against it. I'm sure he's sick of hearing about this by now.

I smile. "No. Everything is fine."

He takes my hand and leads me to the bar. The small gesture surprises me, but I don't pull away. It's actually kind of nice.

We place our order—our hands still connected, and then take our drinks to the nearest open table. He lets go of me and sweeps his hand in front of him, indicating for me to sit first. I slide into the long couch and Isaac sits next to me. We face the bar, both sipping on our drinks. It feels a little awkward now that we're here together and held hands. I'm not sure if that even meant anything.

Isaac clears his throat. "Is this the first time you've been here?"

I nod. "Yes. It's nice though."

"I like it, too."

Another moment of awkward silence follows and I take a drink.

A couple at the end of the bar catches my attention. The man stands out among the suit wearing types with his black shirt and multiple ear piercings. I smile. He must be lost.

I bite my bottom lip as my thoughts drift back to Zach and how much he would stand out in a place like this too. It's only been a couple days since I saw him, and I know I said I only wanted friendship from him, but I miss him. The easy smile he wears when we're together—the never stagnant conversations. Things with him felt so easy, which is hard to explain because we don't really know a damn thing about each other. Well, other than every inch of each other's bodies.

"It's good to get out of the office. It really helps me to refocus when I'm stumped on a project to get some fresh air, so to speak," Isaac says as he leans back into the booth. "I'm glad you came with me."

I smile. "I'm glad you invited me."

I pause. Am I glad? I mean, this is the kind of man I said I needed to settle down with and I am completely flattered by his attention, but that doesn't stop the fact that two seconds ago I was thinking about how I actually missed another man.

Isaac raises his arm and rests it along the back of the booth behind me. "That's good news. You're a really hard one to read. I wasn't sure if you would agree to a date with me."

I raise an eyebrow and cross my legs in his direction. "I wasn't aware this was a date."

A bashful grin fills his handsome face. "I'd like it to be if that's okay with you."

He's a good man with a level head on his shoulders. He would be a stable choice and probably wouldn't hurt me like most guys I date. This should be a no-brainer. Why do I feel so hesitant?

Before I can think on it any longer, my cell vibrates on the table. "Sorry, let me grab this."

Lanie's text pops up on my screen. She's sad Noel's

leaving her for the night. I respond and tell her to get some much needed sleep while he's gone because I'm sure she's going to need her strength when he gets back.

My cell buzzes again and I roll my eyes. She always has to have the last word.

The moment my eyes scan my phone my breath hitches. An instant message from Riff pops onto my screen.

Riff: *Kitten, I miss you. What are you doing right now?*

Guilt floods through me while my gaze darts to Isaac. Zach misses me. That's got to count for something, right? Maybe he isn't the one-night stand kind of guy? Did I do the right thing blowing him off? I was only trying to protect myself from getting hurt, and yet I fear I made a bit of a mistake.

I wish I knew for certain we'd work out. I don't want to go through heartbreak of being dumped yet again. A man like Zach can't be trusted.

Isaac tilts his head. "You all right?"

I run my fingers through my hair and close my eyes. "Yeah. Totally fine."

The only way I'm going to get over the passion I felt in Zach's arms is to move on. Contact with each other will only scratch at the tiny opening of hurt I already feel. I need to end it.

Aubrey: *I'm on a date...*

Before I can toss my phone back on the table, it buzzes

again.

Riff: *Do you like him?*

I sigh as I reply.

Aubrey: *Too early to tell at this point.*

What's with the twenty questions he's throwing at me?

Riff: *I bet he can't make you scream his name out like I can.*

I shake my head.

Aubrey: *Friends don't talk to each other like this…*

Hopefully that reminds him of the little conversation we had at the bar.

Riff: *Fuck being friends, then. I want you.*

I feel a blush creep into my cheeks. He's knows exactly what to say in order to get to me. A forceful man that isn't afraid to go after what he wants is my biggest weakness. I guess it's why I'm always falling for the wrong type of man. Guys like that don't think about consequences or futures, which is why relationships with them never work, no matter how much I want them to.

Aubrey: *I can't…*

Riff: *Can't what?*

Aubrey: *Be with you.*

Before he has a chance to respond, I toss my phone

into my purse. Isaac stares at me expectantly, but I merely shrug. There's no way I'm going into the long sordid details of how my weekend fling wants more from me. Information about your sexual relationships getting out in the workplace is never a good scene. People are so judgmental and I don't want to be known as the office slut because I enjoy having a little fun from time to time.

Isaac opens his mouth to speak, but before he does I cut him off because he's so predictable I know exactly what he's going to say. "Everything's fine. It's Lanie. She's missing Noel."

He raises his eyebrows. "So she and Noel Falcon are…"

I sigh. Sometimes I let my loose lips get me into trouble, but the cat's out of the bag now. I might as well answer the best I can. "She knew Noel growing up. They were high school sweethearts. They're actually pretty, sickeningly-sweet."

"You don't think that's romantic? Reuniting with a first love can be powerful thing."

I grin. "That's actually one of the most romantic things I've ever heard a man say."

He twists his lips and fights back a smile. "I try."

I lean my elbow on the table and rest my cheek in my hand. Maybe there is something that can work about a nice guy. I can't even imagine what it would feel like to have someone love you back just as much as you love them. I gaze into his clear blue eyes and wonder if I can be truly happy with a man like him. Would I miss the wild nights? He doesn't look like he's the type to spice things up too much in bed.

But is that the trade off? Love of a solid man equals the loss of amazing sex?

Isaac leans in a bit. "I like you, Aubrey, and want the chance to get to know you better. Would you go out on a real date with me sometime? No strings attached, just dinner."

"Isn't that against some sort of company policy?"

He shrugs. "I'm sure it is since I'm your direct boss, but we can keep things between us for a while and see how things go."

He's right. The fact that he's my direct boss probably is a bad thing, but he doesn't seem too concerned about it. If we start down this path and things don't work I don't know what that'll mean for me, but I know that Isaac is a nice guy. He'd never try to start something if he wasn't sure we'd work out. He's too much of a planner to be spontaneous.

Dating him may be the change in my love life I need.

Chapter 12

RIFF

Aubrey's response that she can't be with me cuts deep. I fire back am instant message asking her *why*, but she doesn't answer. The urge to fling my phone across the bus fills every inch of me. Why didn't I see this coming? I'm a rotten bastard that deserves this misery, and I want to kick my own ass for allowing myself to feel things for this girl—to want more with her. She's genuine, and that's what I want.

Big Bertha rolls down the road, taking us to the next city on our tour. I hate being trapped on here at a time like this. More than anything I want to hop on my bike and drive for a few hours to try to clear my head.

I hate that I'm so fucked up that no one can stand to be around me long term.

"Fuck you, bitch. I got you!" Trip yells at the television as he smashes buttons on the game controller.

I shake my head. "What's with you guys and video

games?"

Tyke shrugs, but never removes his eyes from the screen as he fights his brother. "I could ask you the same thing about the Oreos."

My shoulders tense. Oreos are special to me because of my sister, but that's not something I share with anyone. The twins know all about my family and the trauma we went through, but that's only because they knew me when it all happened. What I wouldn't give to block out my past. It's too fucking painful to think about. I don't deserve to be alive, let alone have any happiness. Oreos and the happy memories of me and Hailey together tied to them are the only positives I allow myself.

When the game ends, Tyke gets up and grabs his notepad. "I've been working on some new lyrics. I want you guys to tell me what you think."

"I'm down," Trip says.

I close up the cookies and push them aside, eager to work on some music. After I grab my Gibson from the front of the bus, I sit down on the love seat glad to have something to occupy my mind.

"Okay, the beat goes a little something like this." Tyke slaps the table in front of him to a steady beat. "And I'm thinking the bass sounds raunchy."

He starts making low-pitched noises with his mouth while keeping time on the table. I close my eyes and allow the melody to fill me. It's a dirty beat and my fingers glide over the threads as the vision of the cords I need to play flood my brain.

Like every other time we write a song, I strum the first notes that come to mind. We play it through for a couple minutes and Trip sits down and takes over the drum beat and we start again, only this time I open my mouth sign the lyrics on Tyke's paper. The parts he still needs to write I improvise with a little humming.

"Through the rain cloud—there you were…hmmmm, hmmm, hmm," I sing.

Trip nods his head. "Yeah, I like it."

We run through it a few more times, each time getting it tuned finer. "It's great, man. The bones are solid."

Tykes grins. "Thanks, bro. You know how it is when I write. I never know until we start putting it together if it's going to work or not."

I roll my eyes—always the self-doubter. "I think you got something with this one."

We wrap up our jam session and Lanie opens the door and makes her way down the hallway. Her hair is a little frizzy from sleep and she squints at the bright lights.

I glance over at the clock. Damn. It's nearly four in the morning. She's probably pissed we woke her up.

"Hey, if it isn't sleeping beauty," Trip teases. "Lonely back there in the love shack?"

A blush creeps up into her cheeks as we all laugh. She squeezes in next to me on the love seat and lowers her chin to avoid our stares.

Trip and Tyke gravitate back to the *Xbox* to resume the game they were playing.

Trip looks over at Lanie and smirks. "Lanie, since he isn't here, you have to tell us what Noel was like when you guys dated before."

"Yeah," Tyke agrees, while adjusting the bandanna on his forehead. "We need dirt—the good stuff. Did he get the crap kicked out of him in school? We need ammo to torment him."

She shrugs. "Sorry, guys. There's isn't much to tell. Noel's pretty straight laced. He doesn't have many secrets."

"That *you* know of," I chime in.

Her head snaps toward me. "What's that supposed to mean? You keep alluding to some big thing Noel is keeping from me."

I shrug. She really doesn't have a fucking clue. Damn him. I knew it. "It means just that."

"Noel doesn't keep things from me. He doesn't like secrets between us."

"Well maybe you should—"

"Dude!" Trip cuts me off. "Now is not the time, man."

"You don't think she should know? I guarantee he hasn't told her. Look at her face." I point to Lanie. "She has no fucking clue what I'm talking about. I'm trying to look out for her. She's a nice girl and I don't want to see her get hurt."

Trip rubs his forehead. "I know. I know. But, it's not our place to tell her."

Lanie waves her hand. "Guys, I'm right here. Tell me what the fuck is going on."

I set my eyes on her. She really does look clueless, like she trusts him completely and it makes me feel pity for her. She has to know. I don't give a fuck who gets mad, least of all Noel. I've had enough of his shit. "Lanie…Noel has a girlfriend."

She furrows her brow. "What? No way! You guys are messing with me."

Tyke frowns, and I shake my head.

"I—I don't believe you. He wouldn't…No."

I toy with the hoop through my bottom lip. "It's true, Lanie. I'm sorry."

She clutches her chest. I can literally see her struggle for air to breathe. She gasps with her eyes wide and then turns pale.

Fuck. I'm not prepared for this big of a freak out.

Tyke drops to his knees in front of her and places of his hands on her shoulders. "Breathe, Lanie. You're white as snow."

There's a long pause as she processes the information and for a second I feel guilty for telling her, but know deep down it's the right thing. Hopefully, this pain will be like a band-aid. One quick rip and done.

She raises her head and questions, "How long?"

"How long what, Lanie?" Tyke asks.

"The girl. Has he been with her long?" Tyke looks to Trip then to me for an answer. He hates being wrapped up in drama of any kind. Guess it's up to me to field this one.

I roll my lips into a line, and this is harder to do than I thought. "Not long—only a few months."

"This whole time—why would he do this?"

"Because Noel Falcon is a selfish prick," I say. "He doesn't give a shit about anybody but himself."

She scrubs her fingers down her face. "Oh, god. I can't believe this."

I touch her shoulder gingerly. "I'm sorry, Lanie. He's a shit."

Her face twists and it's obvious she's fighting back tears. Her legs wobble as she pushes herself up from the seat.

"Lanie? Are you all right?" Tyke asks.

"I'm fine," she says before heading towards bedroom door, slamming it behind her.

As soon as she's gone Trip turns around and glares at me. "Jesus! What the fuck was that?"

I rub my forehead. I knew he'd be all over my ass. "Don't start. It had to be done, man."

"But I told you, nothing good would come of doing that."

My eyebrows crinkle. "Her knowing is good. Noel needs to take some responsibility for his actions. Someone needed to force his hand."

"And that had to be you? Don't you know how much shit this is going to stir up? We're already struggling to keep this band together as is. Do you want to fuck this all up on purpose for us?"

I shake my head. "No! I just…"

I stop myself from yelling out that Noel's a selfish prick and I'm done with that fucking asshole.

I sigh. "Look, I'll go talk to her, okay."

Trip glances at his brother and then back to me. "You better fix this, man. This band is my fucking life."

I shove up from the love seat and head towards the back of the bus. I knock softly on the door. I feel like a complete ass for saying anything now, but she needed to hear the truth.

When she doesn't answer, I open the door slowly. The mattress is bare and the sheets lay in a massive heap in the corner of the small room. She's a fucking tornado when she's pissed.

Her tear streaked face stares up at me, and I can see how torn up she is. Her shoulders sag as she pats the spot beside her on the bed.

I give her the best smile I can muster, but I know it's sad "You okay?"

She shakes her head, "Yes."

"That's not very convincing."

She sighs and her voice quivers. "I know, but what choice do I have?"

I tilt my head. "You have all the power here, Lanie. Noel screwed you over like he did to me. That's who he is. But you have the power to do what's best for you and get the hell away from him. I would if I could, but I'm kind of stuck here."

She snorts. "I know the feeling."

"Ah, yes, the job—I almost forgot about that. Well, I guess you and I are both screwed by him."

She turns toward me, clearly trying to figure me out. "You mean you'd leave this band if you could?"

I nod. She has no clue how much I wish I could be free of Noel and his bullshit. "In a heartbeat. I can hardly look at the guy without wanting to kick his ass. But, this band is my life. It's all I've ever known. I can't walk away, no matter how much I want to."

"I've noticed there's some tension between you two."

I laugh, but it has a bitter edge to it. "Yeah, well, when your best friend fucks your woman, you'll have that."

Her eyes widen. "Noel..."

"Yes," I answer her unspoken question. "His girlfriend is my ex, Sophie."

Lanie throws her hand over her mouth and darts out of the bedroom. The paper-thin walls in the bathroom don't muffle sound at all. I hear every heave as she loses all the contents of her stomach.

When Noel gets back, I'll have a fight on my hands—spilling this secret will not go over well.

Chapter 13

RIFF

Noel throws open the curtain to my bunk and lunges inside. "You fucking told her?"

"You can't have them both," I yell back the moment he grabs handfuls of my shirt. I knew this moment was coming as soon as I told her. "I won't let you do that to Sophie."

I hear Lanie's voice in the background. "Noel, stop!"

In a split second, Noel loses it. He yanks me from the bunk and throws me down on the hallway floor. I try to stand, but before I get the chance, Noel's on me, connecting a hard punch against my jaw.

I grunt and grab Noel into a tight headlock when he dips his head down. If it's one thing I know how to do well, it's fighting. Dad would come at me every time he got drunk, so it was learn to protect myself and fight back or get the shit kicked out of me.

Noel flings his arms wildly, his fists crack against my ribs and knocks the wind out of me for a second.

"Stop it!" Lanie yells again.

Trip and Tyke's curtains fly back and they jump out of

their bunks. The twins get in-between us and eventually yank us apart. My chest heaves as I taste metallic on the tip of my tongue. That fucker was going for blood.

We're both still red-faced determined to get at each other as he fight against Trip and Tyke.

"I can't believe you fucking told her!" Noel shouts while still in Trip's firm hold. "You need to mind your own damn business."

I laugh harshly. "Me? Mind my own business? You make it pretty hard to do when you're fucking my girlfriend behind my back!"

Noel's mouth drops open. "She came to me. I didn't go after her."

"And that makes it fucking okay? Jesus, Noel, you were my best friend—my brother and you still screwed me over. I'm not going to let you do that to Lanie."

"I was going to tell her!" Noel shouts with his arms spread wide.

"When? When were you going to tell her? After Sophie has the baby?"

Out of the corner of my eye I notice Lanie falls back against the wall. A baby isn't something I told her about. I figured if I told her about Sophie, Noel would fess up about knocking her up on his own. But in the heat of the moment, I said it to further piss him off.

Noel's body stills and his eyes snap to Lanie. She shakes her head under his stare and slowly backs away from him.

"Lane?" Noel says her name as heads back to the bedroom. "Lane, wait!"

She slams the door behind her and Noel instantly jerks his gaze at me. "This isn't over, motherfucker."

"It is for you," I snap back.

He glares at me for a second longer like he's debating on trying a round two with me, but he knows better. I'll fucking end him if he comes at me while I'm ready for him.

He shakes his head and heads after her.

"Come on, man. Let's head over to the hotel and chill out for a while." Trip pats my shoulder.

****

Trip walks me back to our floor in the hotel, keeping an extra eye that I don't turn around and charge the bus to go after Noel again.

"I can't believe he yanked you out of the bunk like that," Trip says.

I shrug. "I would've probably done the same thing. I basically ruined things between him and Lanie."

Trip shakes his head. "It was good you told her, though.

182

I hate keeping secrets from people."

I nod, but don't answer because I'm keeping things from Aubrey, too—things she may leave me for when she finds out.

"I'm gonna go toss my shit in my room and use the bathroom. I'll be right back."

I plop down in the chair next to the elevator. "I'll wait for you right here."

Thinking about Kitten makes me want to hear her voice.

AUBREY

The sound of *Maroon 5* from my cell phone wakes me up. I roll over and grab it from my nightstand. It's Lanie. Why is she calling so early in the morning?

I smile when I answer, "What's up, lucky girl? How's that fine man of yours?"

There's a long pause on the line before she says, "Not good."

As soon as the words leave her she's bawling into the phone. I sit up in bed, immediate concern rocks me. She's falling apart. Did she find out about Diana's plan to take the charity away from her?

I have to know what's going on. "Aw, baby cakes, tell

me what happened?"

She sniffs. "He's such an asshole."

A heavy breath leaves my lungs as relief washes through me. I'm sad she's hurt, but I'm glad it's not because of me and what I'm keeping from her. "Did he hurt you? I'll kill him if he laid a finger on you."

"Nothing like that. He's just..." She takes a deep breath. "Noel has a girlfriend, Aubrey."

"What!?" I screech. "What do you mean he has a girlfriend?"

"I guess he has for a while, but that's not the worst part."

"What can be any worse than that?"

"She's pregnant."

I gasp. "Like, with a baby?"

"Yes. She says it's Noel's."

"Oh, my god. Screw the job, Lanie. Run away as fast as you can from that freak show. Come home."

She's quiet for a second and then she calls out, "Just a minute."

"Who is that?" I question. It better not be Noel. He better thank his lucky stars I'm not there to punch him square in the balls.

There's a rustling noise on her end of the line like she's moving around. "It's probably just housekeeping." After a distinct sound of a deadbolt unlocking, I hear her say, "What are you doing here?"

Noel's deep voice rumbles and asks, "Can I come in?"

There's a thump as the door closes and then she sighs into the phone. "Aubrey, I'll have to call you back."

"Is it him?"

She whispers, "Yes."

I inhale deeply through my nose, trying to hold in my anger. "Tell him to fuck off, Lanie. You don't need to put up with his shit."

"I will. I promise."

"You call me back if you need me. Hear me?"

"Okay," is all she says before disconnecting our call.

I flop back against my pillow and rake my hair back from my forehead. What a mess. If only I could've seen this coming…

My lips twist. This is exactly what Zach was trying to warn me about. Why didn't he tell me or her for that matter? Just further proves why I can't date a guy like him. That whole bros before hoes mentality is sickening.

I open the message box to Zach and see the last message he left me.

Riff: *Why?*

I shake my head. There's so many reasons why I can't date him. This situation with Lanie doesn't help.

Aubrey: *Because men like you keep girlfriends on the side.*

I toss my phone back on the nightstand and head into the shower to get ready for work. I can't believe he didn't tell me what Noel was up to. Why make me try and guess?

I scrub vigorously in the shower, running through everything Zach ever said to me about Noel. There's nothing I can recall that screams Noel wasn't exactly single.

I know it's not Zach's fault that his friend is a douchebag, but he knew exactly what was going on. He had to. And he didn't tell me, or more importantly, Lanie.

I run a fluffy towel through my hair, sopping up the water as I walk back over to my cell. The blue message light flashes. I pick it up and touch the screen.

Riff: *Lanie called you?*

I roll my eyes.

Aubrey: *Of course she called me. We don't keep things from each other.*

After I hit send, I think about how that isn't exactly true either. I'm keeping something from her too, but I'm doing it to protect her, not out of selfish gain.

Riff: *Look, I'm the one who told her, okay? I was trying to help her. I told you I didn't think it was a good idea for them to be together.*

Aubrey: *You should've told me, so I could break it to her.*

Riff: *I struggled with it because it wasn't exactly my place to tell her and I didn't want you involved.*

I sigh. He's right. Noel should've manned-up and told her. Instead he kept it from her, causing her to be crushed.

Aubrey: *You're right. I'm sorry. I don't mean to lash out at you. Thank you for telling her.*

Riff: *It was the right thing to do.*

I smile.

Aubrey: *So noble…who knew?*

Riff: *I wouldn't go that far.*

Aubrey: *I would.*

Riff: *What's your cell number? I hate instant messaging.*

I tap my finger on the side of the phone. Where is this going? It's only going to torture both of us if we keep this up.

When I don't respond right away another message pops up.

Riff: *Come on, friends call each other.*

I nod in agreement. What the hell? He's right.

I fire my cell phone number into the message box and hit send. Two seconds later the phone rings showing an unknown number on the ID screen. What the hell did I get myself into?

RIFF

I haven't called a girl I liked since junior high school. They typically call me. The palm of my hand is clammy as I dial her number. I know she said friends only, but that doesn't work for me. I think about her way to damn much to leave it at that. I need more time with her. I'm not even sure why. I know that the weekend I spent with her was the first time I'd felt alive in a long time. I didn't dwell on past things I can't change as much. I even allow myself to picture what a life with her might be like. I don't want those kinds of feelings. I don't deserve to have them.

If I can spend more time with her, I know she'll eventually piss me off, and whatever this is that I'm feeling will go away. Then I can get back to being the fucking asshole everyone knows and loves.

She answers on the third ring. "Hello?"

"Hey. It's me," I reply.

"I'm glad you told her," she says instantly.

I let out a heavy sigh, relived she doesn't think I'm a

total dick. "I had to. It was eating away at me."

"Why? Because you didn't like Lanie being wronged?"

I shake my head. "That's part of it, but mainly it's because I think Noel is a gigantic douche."

"I thought you were friends?"

I laugh bitterly. "Definitely not friends."

"But you guys got along pretty well when I was there." I can hear the question in her voice. She wants the details about our beef.

"The girl Noel knocked up was sort-of my girlfriend."

She gasps. "Oh, Zach. I'm so sorry. No wonder you're pissed. You have every right to be. Were you with her long?"

"No, not long at all. We weren't even that serious, really. She was just a chick I kept around to…" I trail off. What will she think of me if I tell her Sophie was a random groupie that didn't annoy me too much, so I kept her around as my fuck-buddy for a couple months? She'll probably think less of me than she already does knowing I use women that way.

"Say no more. I get it. Regardless of what she was to you, Noel overstepped his bounds. I'd be livid if my friend did that to me." I tilt my head. She gets it. She's even saying my anger at him is acceptable.

"It's so nice for someone to be okay with me being pissed at him for a change."

"You mean the twins are okay with what he did to you?"

I shrug. "They aren't exactly okay with it, but they do think I need to let it go for the sake of the band."

She sighs into the phone. "You shouldn't allow anyone to walk all over you, Zach. You're too good of a person for that."

I raise my eyebrows. "No one's ever called me that before."

"What's that, good?"

"Yeah, *asshole*, *dick*, sure, I get those a lot, but never *good*. Most people end up hating me."

"You don't let them see the caring side of you that I know is in there."

"What makes you think I have a caring side?"

"Because I've seen it. The way you were with me...it was nice. I like Zach more than I like Riff."

I close my eyes. I should've never let my guard down with her. She shouldn't feel this way about me. I'm not a good person.

"You still there?"

I nod, knowing full well she can't see me, but I can't bring myself to say anything. My chest squeezes knowing Kitten doesn't think I'm an evil bastard. This is so not good. It only makes me want her more. Turns out she's too good of a

190

distraction from the hellhole that is my life. She's actually allowing me to believe there's hope for me, and hope is a dangerous thing to a rotten human being like me.

It's in that moment I decide I'm going to have her. I don't care what she said about being friends. I like how I feel with her. I'm a better person with her.

I'm going to have to make her see she wants me, too.

"So, tell me about this date you were on last night," I ask to totally change the subject off my less desirable qualities.

"It was okay. Nothing big—drinks with a friend."

I arch my pierced eyebrow. "Is he your friend like I'm your friend?"

She laughs. "Definitely not. At least not yet, anyhow."

Relief washes through me. I knew she wasn't like that with everyone. There's something about me that pulls her in and I need to figure out what it is.

"So you're saying you don't tie him up and visit sex shops with him yet? How did we move to that place so quickly? You used me for my body, didn't you?"

"And you didn't use me for mine?" She tries to be stern, but I can hear the smile in her voice.

"I will admit your tits are amazing."

"See!" she exclaims. "I knew it!"

I laugh. "Well it's not *just* your tits that I like."

"Your ass is pretty great, too."

"Uh-huh. I told you."

Looks like it's time to admit something real if I want her to take me seriously. "I also like your sense of humor, and you're cute as hell when you're feisty. And I like being with you."

"I like being with you, too…which is a problem."

"Only if you let it be. I like having fun with you."

She sighs. "Zach, I explained this in the bar. Our weekend together was great, probably one of the best times I've ever had with a man, but that kind of magic can't last. Soon, reality will set in. You'll be on the road. I'll be here in New York. Things will get complicated and this nice friendship we have now will be ruined."

The thought of what it'd be like being her friend crosses my mind. If by some miracle of God Lanie and Noel end up working things out, Aubrey will be around from time to time. I don't think I can handle seeing her, knowing that she's the one person who believes I'm a good person, while she's with someone else. I won't be able to deal. It'll drive me even crazier than I am right now.

"I want to complicate the hell out of our friendship, Kitten."

"You're only saying that because I'm saying no. You like a challenge. That's all this is."

"No," I say, "It's not. I want you because I *just* do. Like I told you, I can't explain why, I just know I do."

"Zach…" I can hear the waver in her voice. I nearly have her convinced to be mine.

As I wait on her reply, Trip's door springs open. Shit. He's the last person I need overhearing this conversation. He'll never let me live down that I have feelings for Aubrey. It's hard enough undergoing his speculations.

"Look, Aubrey, I want to finish this talk, but I have to go. I'll call you later, okay?"

"Okay. Talk to you soon."

I end the call and stuff the phone back in my pocket as Trip makes it to the end of the hallway.

Trip runs his fingers through his black hair and then slaps his baseball cap on backwards. "Who was that?"

I narrow my eyes. "No one. Why?"

He shrugs. "You seem weird, like all fidgety or something."

I square my shoulders. "I'm not fucking fidgety."

He smirks. "You forget how long I've knows your ass. You do fidget, especially when you're uncomfortable. So out with it? Was it your dad?"

"No? Why would you think it was him?"

"Because every time he calls you, you get this way—

out of sorts. It's like you don't know what to do with yourself. On one hand you want to hate him, but on the other you won't let yourself because you still believe his shitty life is your fault."

I pinch the bridge of my nose and count to three. I'm about three seconds from losing my cool on Trip and I don't want to fucking do that. I know he's trying to help me. "Leave it, man. You don't get it."

I turn to walk away from him feeling the sudden urge for space, but he grabs my arm, halting me. "I do fucking get it. I was there, remember? What happened to your sister—and your mom—wasn't your fault. You don't owe him shit. You have to cut him loose."

I roll my eyes and stare up at the ceiling. "I can't do that. It's my fault we don't have a family. He wouldn't have a drinking problem and could hold down a job if my mom were still around. Don't you see, his shitty life *is* my fault!"

Trip pulls his lips into a tight line and then lets go of my arm. "I hope one day you can see the truth. You're not the bad one in this situation. You were only a kid. Your dad needs *real* help, not financial help like you give him."

"Yeah, well, sometimes life is what it is, Trip. We're both fucked up in the head, and no amount of professional help is going to change that." I don't give him time to say anything because I don't want to fucking hear it.

To think a few minutes ago I was actually giving myself permission to have a little happiness. Sometimes reality's perfect timing socks me in the nuts with a reminder that I'm an asshole that doesn't deserve anything good.

I need to leave Aubrey alone, but I'm afraid at this point I can't. She's worked her way into my head, and I don't see any other way of getting her out other than letting her see the ugly side of me that sends her running for the fucking hills. We'll have to see how long I can hold out.

AUBREY

It's been a few days since I talked with Zach. I waited for his phone call that night, but my phone never rang. He was probably still drunk from the night before. That's the only explanation I have for him talking crazy about wanting a relationship.

I sigh as I grab the Black Falcon file from the drawer and open it up to work on sponsorship letters for the campaign like Isaac asked.

I glance across the hall at his open office door across from my desk. Since we had drinks the other night, he's left it wide open every day. It's almost like he's waiting on me to make the next move. While I would love to focus my undivided attention on his advances, my stupid heart won't let me. Somehow, I allowed a crazy, tatted-up rocker to get under my skin.

I promised myself the time I spent with him would be

the last of my wild days, not the beginnings of another guaranteed heartbreak.

The shrill ring of my desk phone breaks me out of my thoughts. "Yes, Mr. Walters."

Isaac chuckles into the phone. "That's not a good sign. I'm back to Mr. Walters."

Heat fills my cheeks. "I'm sorry. It seems more, I don't know, formal, I guess."

"Yes. I suppose it does. Do you mind bringing those sponsorship letters in as soon as you have them written up? I want to double check them before you send them out."

I raise my eyebrows. He doesn't think I'm capable of typing a letter? I'm a little put off he wants to check it like we're in the second grade, but what can I do? He is my boss. "Sure. No problem."

"Great. See you in a bit."

I shake my head and try to refocus on the document on my screen. The words flow, but not as easily as they did before he put the nugget of doubt in my brain that I might actually suck at this job.

When I'm finally finished printing the last one, I grab the stack and head into Isaac's office.

He's working away on his computer. His black-framed glasses perch on his nose as he stares intently at the work on the screen. The black suit-jacket is a stark contrast to the bright green tie he's wearing, but it works. It totally helps bring out the green in his eyes.

He smiles when he notices me in the doorway. Isaac leans back in his chair and rubs his hand over the back of his blonde head. "Come in. Have a seat."

I sit stiffly in the chair across from him after laying the letters on his desk. He inspects each letter one by one, carefully reading over my work right in front of me.

I try to relax a little, but every muscle in my body is clenched tight. It's hard being judged, especially by a man who wants to date me. The last thing I want is for him to think I'm a moron and question why he hired me in the first place.

I cross my ankles together and tug at my skirt while I wait on him to say something. The corner of his mouth twitches at one point and my heart squeezes for a second. "Something wrong?"

He glances up. "Oh, no. It's great."

My shoulders relax. "Okay good." I stand and hold my hand out to collect the papers from him. "How soon would you like me to send these to potential sponsors?"

He grimaces and pulls the papers away from my grasp. "Actually, I was thinking of rewriting these."

I tilt my head. "I thought you said they're great."

He bites his lip. "They are great…for a first try. You haven't quite hooked the reader with your sales points. The bones are there, but I need to spruce it up a little for you before you send them out."

"You don't think I'm capable of correcting my own work?"

He shakes his head. "No. no. You misunderstand. I want your work to shine."

I frown. "Yeah, but if you fix it, it won't be my work anymore. It'll be yours, Isaac. Lying about my skills and sleeping with my boss is not how I intend on moving up in this company."

He stands and motions with his hands for me to keep my voice down and then he points towards the open door. "Look. It's not like that, okay. I see how bright you are. You're a hard worker and someday you'll do big things on your own. I'm trying to help you get to the next level faster."

"I don't want to move on any faster than I'm ready for."

"Is that why you haven't named a date when we can go out again?"

My stomach clenches. "I want to take things slow, okay. I have the habit of moving too fast in relationships and always wind up getting hurt. I want to change that. I want to start taking things slowly. I'm tired of all the flings. I want to find someone who is real and genuine—someone who loves me for me."

Isaac steps around the desk and closes the door. He turns to face me once we are trapped inside alone. He takes a step toward me then takes my hand. "Well, maybe I can be that for you. I like you, Aubrey. I want to see where this goes. I'm a patient man. I'll give you time to see that maybe we can be more if you let it."

I stare down at our fingers twined together and think about how it feels nice, but it's missing that spark—the one filled with excitement. I'm attracted to Isaac, but the chemistry between us feels forced. It doesn't feel natural. Maybe this is how it is when you settle for something you don't really want. I know deep down my heart craves Zach, but he's too unpredictable. He'll only hurt me. Isaac is the safe way to go, but my feelings for him won't be instant. "I think I'm going to need lots of time.

He nods as I glance up at his face. "That, I can give you."

We stand still for a few more seconds, waiting on the other to make a move. Finally, he says, "Guess we should get back to work. I'll have these edited and back to you by the end of the day."

I smile as he lets go of my hand. "Thank you."

I rush out of the room, needing space to figure out what the hell just happened in there. One minute we're talking about work, the next minute he's trying to figure out our relationship.

I rub my forehead. A rush of pain hits me between the eyes. I haven't had a stress headache since my last week of finals in college.

I pull open my bottom desk drawer and open my purse to look for the *Tylenol*. I notice a little blue message light flick on my phone, indicating a message. I tap my screen. There's a missed call and a message from Zach.

I lean back in my chair and play the message. He has about the worst timing in the world.

"Aubrey, hi, it's me. I know I fucked up by not calling you. It's what I always do—fuck things up. I won't blame you if you tell me to go jump into traffic or something, but I would really like a chance to apologize. Call me back when you get this."

My teeth pinch the inside of my lip between them. This is exactly what a relationship with him would be like—constant fighting and breaking up. I don't want that. I've been through those enough already.

I throw my phone back inside my purse and slam the drawer shut. My co-worker, Sadie, at the next desk over whips her head in my direction wearing a scowl on her face.

I throw my hands up. "Sorry."

Sadie rolls her eyes and turns back to her computer. God I miss Lanie at times like this. Most of these people are stuck up asshats. She helped liven this place up a little. I haven't heard much from her over the past few days—not since Noel cornered her into staying because she's contracted to stay on the tour.

I need to call her and check in—make sure everything

is okay with her.

I turn my attention back to my computer and an instant message pops up from Zach.

Zach: *You around?*

He's persistent when he wants to be. Too bad he isn't consistent on his follow through. I was so close to giving into him and trying a relationship with him against my better judgment. It's actually a great thing he blew me off the way he did. I got to see his true colors early.

I close the message box and log off the site completely. No more distractions. No more going down the bad boy path. Hopefully, if I ignore him he'll give up and move on.

Two seconds after opening my work email, my cell chimes and buzzes with a new message. I roll my eyes.

I hope that my theory that he'll walk away easily proves true.

Chapter 14

RIFF

I've never been one to basically stalk a woman until she talks to me, but the fact that Kitten is ignoring me cuts right through me. I should've called. I know that. Not calling was a dick move on my part, and I feel like an asshole, but there's nothing I can do about that now, other than apologize. I was seriously trying to distance myself from her, but I only made it three fucking days.

I ring her cell one more time, since I've put myself on a pattern alternating my method of attempting communication with her every thirty minutes. None of my instant messages, texts, or calls are answered.

"Are you going to be on your phone all fucking night?" Trip whines next to me as we walk through the parking lot back to Big Bertha. "I want to go find some chicks."

"I have to keep trying until she answers," I snap as yet another attempt goes straight to her voicemail.

"I know I told you to try with her, dude, but if she's ignoring you it's a sign that you need to move on."

"Why is she mad?" Tyke questions from the other side of Trip.

I sigh and stuff my phone in my pocket. "I basically begged her to give a relationship with me a shot, promised to call her back, and I didn't."

Trip jerks his thumb in my direction as he explains to his brother, "This dumbass tries to call the girl three days later, but then gets crazy when she won't answer any of his messages."

Tyke shakes his head. "Tough break, Riff. Maybe you should forget about her."

I shake my head. "I can't."

"Why not?" Trip asks. "What is it about that girl that you like so much?"

My mind flashes to the first night I saw Aubrey. She was the most beautiful thing I'd ever seen, and when she shoved me away from her, I was a goner. I had to have her. It didn't help she made me work for it a little first, that only drove me more. But the true clincher wasn't even the kinky sex we had. It was the moment when she said I was a good person. She didn't make me feel worthless like almost every other goddamn person in my life. There's no way I'm telling these two that, though. Trip is already bad enough with his psychobabble bullshit.

Trip grips my shoulder. "Look. What you need is to get your mind off her. Come out with me and Tyke, find a hot chick and bang her. That's all you really need, dude—a good lay. Maybe that'll help you let her go."

I shrug his hand off. "I don't want to let her go."

He yanks my shoulder, halting me from storming off. "If she doesn't want you, then you have to. That's how this shit works."

I grind my teeth together. It isn't like I don't know that already. I hate it when he makes so much logical fucking sense. There's an ounce of hope left in me that she's not done with me yet.

I glance from Trip to Tyke. "Fine we'll go out, but I'm not in the mood to score chicks."

Tyke sighs. "Well you'll be an awesome wingman tonight."

I roll my eyes. "Please, like you two need my help to rope in the pu-tang."

We all laugh in unison as we make to the door of Big Bertha. Trip and Tyke skid to a stop at the top of the steps in front me. What the fuck?

I shove around them and instantly freeze, too. What the hell is she doing here?

Sophie stands in the middle of the bus, looking as flawless as ever in her long, blonde ponytail that sits high on her head. Her porcelain skin has a slight redness on her cheeks, no doubt a side effect of the little baby bump she's sporting.

I clench my jaw tight. Why is she here?

Trip clears his throat. "Should we leave? Looks serious in here."

Noel shakes his head as he glares at Mike and Sophie. "No. Stay. You're just in time to hear some secret Sophie's been keeping."

Trip pulls himself up on the counter, making himself comfortable, and Tyke leans next to him while pulling his lips into a tight line. Trip leans forward and places his elbows on his thighs. He's ready to jump in and mediate the situation if need be, I'm sure. His ass loves drama.

I flex my jaw muscles as I step into Sophie's direct view. This is my chance to get some fucking answers. "How many more secrets can she possibly have?"

She doesn't even bother to acknowledge me as I walk to the other side of the counter where the twins are.

Mike frowns at Lanie and then flicks his eyes back to Sophie. Agony is the only emotion I can read on Mike's face.

Sophie locks her gaze on the couple in front of her. Lanie's small hand squeezes Noel's arm in a sign of support.

Sophie sighs like she's totally put out. "The baby doesn't belong to Noel."

My fingers curl into fists.

Noel yells, "WHAT?" at the exact same time I do.

Mike stands beside Sophie and threads his fingers through hers. "It's mine."

Noel's hands fly into his hair, and he grabs handfuls of it in his fingers. He paces back and forth with his eyes closed.

He whips his head towards me, and his eyebrows shoot up. He wasn't lying. This entire time he was telling me the fucking truth and I made his life a living hell every chance I got. Guilt fills every inch of me.

"Told you I never fucked your girl," Noel says to me. "I would never do that shit to you!"

Rage fills me causing my lips to twist and my nostrils flair. Who the fuck does she think she is? Does she even know how much fucking pain and hurt she's caused this band with her selfish fucking ways? Does she even care? When I can no longer keep from lashing out at her, I shout, "You fucking slut!"

My words echo in my ears as I turn and storm off the bus. The pavement's solid under my boots as I head towards the back of the bus. I rub my face, wishing I could rub away all of my frustration.

I lean back against Big Bertha and tilt my head towards the sky. I can't believe it. This entire time Noel and I have been fighting for no reason while that asshole Mike let us have at each other. Pure, unadulterated anger flows through my veins and I crunch my hands into fists. That douche needs to be taught a lesson. He fucking played us all.

I shove myself away from the bus before I round the corner and run smack into Noel.

Noel takes a step back. "Easy, buddy, where you off to?"

I take a deep breath through my nose and try to side step him. "Get out of the way."

He shakes his head. "I can't do that. You and your fucking temper need to cool it. Let it go, man. Those lying fuckers deserve each other. They aren't worth it."

I throw my hands out towards the bus. "How can you be so fucking calm about this? Don't you want to beat his ass?"

"I'm not saying I'm not pissed. I'm fucking livid with them. But…now that the truth is out I can get my life back. We can be friends again. Lane won't hate me anymore. I can be happy again."

I nod. I know exactly how he feels. I'd give anything to feel like that. "You're right. It's all working out for you."

I shove my hands deep in my jean pockets and stalk off to the nearest bar to text Aubrey some more.

AUBREY

Way too early in the morning my phone rings again. Damn that boy. Hasn't he ever heard of giving a girl a little space? I grab my phone. It'll probably be best if I shut it off. I don't have to be at work today and I prefer to sleep in on my days off.

The second I turn it off, I hear my front door knob rattle. I sit up and gasp, thinking quick of what to grab to stop a burglar. New York is famous for apartment robberies. I tiptoe through my bedroom and into the front room in the dark. Once I glance around and make sure no one has gained entry to my apartment, I rush to the front door.

I slam my body against the wooden door. "I'm calling the cops!"

"Aubrey, it's me," Lanie says from the other side of the door.

What's she doing back already? She's not due back here for a couple more days.

I click the deadbolt and fling the door open. "What's going on? You all right?"

She shakes her head as she wheels her suitcase inside the apartment. "No. It was too much. I had to get away from there."

I scrunch my brow. "Did something else happen?"

"Sophie showed up."

"As in the pregnant chick?"

She nods and then flops down on the couch. "It's not Noel's baby."

My heart pounds against my rib cage as I sit next to her. "Does that mean it's…"

I swallow hard as I think about the possibility that this baby is Zach's child. I don't want a relationship with him, but the realization that it will never be an option stings. Why does this news feel so crushing on my heart?

"It's not Riff's either if that's what you're thinking. The baby belongs to their bodyguard, Mike."

"How do you know that?"

Lanie shrugs. "Riff can't have children."

I tilt my head. "What makes you say that?"

She stares at me dumbfounded. "I figured telling someone that you're sterile might come up before you do the deed."

My mouth drops open. No wonder he was okay having sex with me without a condom. He knew there was no way he could knock me up. It also explains why Sophie would try to pin a baby on another man in the band. She was probably hoping to get some cash out of the situation.

I lean back against the couch. "Do you know why he's sterile?"

She pulls her lips into a tight line. "Something about some sort of accident…that's all I know."

"Was his sister involved?"

She shakes her head. "I really don't know. Why do you ask?"

Things click in my head. The moment we started talking about Hailey, Zach completely shut down. I'm beginning to think there's a lot more to that story than he led on.

I know he doesn't have a great relationship with his father. I overheard them yelling at one another over money on the phone the morning after I'd slept with him.

"You okay?"

I shake away my thoughts. "Yeah, why?"

"I don't know, you look…distracted, like you figured something out."

I nod. "I think I did."

Zach's definitely got some secrets, like he was implying. If only I knew what he's hiding.

****

Monday morning Isaac stops at my desk. He's particularly dashing in his pinstriped suit and matching tie. Every blond hair on his head lays perfectly groomed, while he smiles his dazzling, white smile at me.

"Good morning, Isaac. I have those memos you asked for all ready." I hand him a file with all the letters I typed since he likes to double check my work.

"Thanks. Say, I hear Lanie Vance is back today. Still

didn't get any details from her?" he asks.

I shake my head. "No, but I do know that she's worked on some things and has a proposal for the marketing campaign all drawn out."

He grimaces. "I already turned the proposal into Diana last week."

"Why? I thought you wanted her input?"

"I did, but there was no time. Diana wanted it from me, so I worked it up with you and presented it to her."

I rub my forehead. Great. I am the world's worst friend. Lanie's going to walk into Diana's office with hope and optimism and she's going to be crushed. I look down at my watch. I have a few minutes before she's due to report to Diana. Better late than never, right?

"Where are you going?" Isaac asks as I rush past him.

"Something I should've done to begin with."

I make it to the elevator as it opens. Lanie stands there in her blue blouse and pencil skirt with her project folder in her hand.

"Oh, thank God." I shove her back in the elevator and press the lobby button.

Her eyes widen. "Aubrey, what the hell are you doing?"

I hold myself up against the wall as I try to catch my breath after hurrying down the hall. "I'm sorry, Lanie. I'm a shitty friend, and I should've told you earlier, but Diana has had my boss Isaac working on Black Falcon's account behind your back."

Her eyes narrow. "She what?"

"I'm sorry. I don't know much more than that, but I can't allow you to walk into a meeting with Diana blind."

She sighs. "How long have you known?"

My lips turn down. "Before Dallas."

"*Before* Dallas? Are you freaking kidding me right now? You knew about this and didn't tell me? Why?" Her gestures are wild. She's pissed. She only ever gets that way when she's livid.

"I didn't tell you because I didn't want you to walk out on the opportunity to be something in this company. It's your dream to be here. But, the main reason was because I know you're in love with Noel. I wanted to give you time to figure out your feelings for him and admit to yourself that you love him."

Her shoulders sag and tears fill her eyes. "I do love him, but I think I've ruined everything. I ran out on him...again. He's never going to forgive me."

I wrap my arms around her. "He loves you. He'll forgive you. And I'm sorry I didn't tell you. I wanted to, but I didn't want you to get angry and walk out on your job here and out on a chance to be happy with Noel. Please don't hate me."

"I could never hate you," she says and then squeezes

me tighter. "You're my best friend and I love you. You were only trying to do what you thought was right."

I pull back as the elevator doors open to the lobby. "Thank you. Now…" I punch the twentieth floor button. "Go have your meeting with Diana and kill it. Make her love your ideas!"

She explains all of her ideas for the project on our ride up. They're pretty amazing and I hope Diana gives her a chance. Lanie's a smart cookie.

My mind keeps drifting back to the physical pain I saw when Lanie talked about ruining her relationship with Noel. I owe her and I have to see if I can help fix things.

Chapter 15

RIFF

I lie in my hotel bed and stare up at the ceiling. It's nearly two in the afternoon, and yet I haven't found motivation to get out of this bed. Trip and Tyke went out solo last night. Noel headed to his room right after the show and so did I. We've gone from partying, womanizing maniacs to pathetic saps because the women who we want don't want us back.

My cell phone buzzes on the bed beside me. I grab it and then look down at the number on the screen. My heart pauses for a beat.

"Hello?" Aubrey doesn't answer on her end of the line. Fuck! Did she butt-dial me? "Are you there?"

"Hey. Yeah. I'm here," she answers quietly.

"I'm glad you called, I wanted to say I'm sorry for not calling you back that night. I know how that looks, and I apologize." Whether she accepts it or not, it feels good to get it off my chest. "Relationships aren't something I'm used to doing, so I'm afraid I'm not very good at them."

She sighs into the phone. "I'm sorry too for not giving you a chance to explain yourself. I don't want to get hurt."

My stomach clenches. "That's exactly why I distanced

myself. I'm not a good person, Kitten. You deserve better than me."

"How do you know that? I could be the biggest bitch you've ever met."

"No you're not. I've spent enough time with you to know you're exactly the opposite."

"Zach…I'm not a very good person either. I set out to use you."

A sharp pain around my heart only hurts for a second. "I know, but you cared more about me in those two days than any other woman I've ever been with."

"I'm sure that's not true."

I pinch the bridge of my nose. "My own mother didn't even care enough about me to ask how I felt about my sister's death, yet you tried."

It sounds worse when I say the things that play through my mind out loud, but it's true. Mom hated me until the day she died. It was hard enough dealing with what I did without having my own family loathe me.

Aubrey's quiet for a few moments and I wonder if I've freaked her out with all my self-hate. Finally, she says, "That's terrible you had to not only deal with the loss of your sister, but a strained relationship with your parents. I don't understand how she could've been so cold to you knowing you were only sixteen years old. Did they not realize you'd be hurting, too?"

This is the part I never want to talk about. But, seeing as how I've already opened myself up to her and she's still talking to me, I figure what the hell? She might as well judge me for the real me fully. One of the biggest things in any relationship is trust. I need to be able to trust that she's okay with the real me, evil parts and all.

I swallow hard. "She did that because she blamed me."

"Why would she blame you?" Aubrey's voice is calm, like she's not sure what she got herself into.

It's too much, too soon. I have to back off so I don't freak her out any more than I already have. "It's really not a big deal. It was a long time ago. I'm over it."

Another awkward pause on her end indicates to me she's getting scared off. I start to open my mouth to apologize for dropping all my emotional baggage shit on her, but quickly shut it when she starts speaking again. "I am actually calling for a favor."

I raise my eyebrow. "So this call wasn't just about us?"

She clears her throat. "No, but I'm glad we talked. I like that you've opened up to me."

"I'm waiting for the day when you figure out what a piece of shit I really am and tell me to fuck off for good."

"Zach...I really wish you didn't think so poorly of yourself. You're an awesome person and friend. I mean, you warned Lanie about the baby situation. I wish you could see what I see."

"What do you see?" Is it too much to hope that I may actually have a shot with this woman?

"A good person, like I told you before."

It's been a long time since someone other than Trip believed in me so much, and it feels fucking awesome. If it weren't for Trip over the past few years, I probably wouldn't be alive. I want things to work with Aubrey. I need her around. I'll do anything to prove to her that I'll treat her right.

"So what's the favor you needed from me?"

"I want to get Noel and Lanie back together. She's miserable without him. Do you think you can arrange a time for them to meet up?"

I rest my hand on my bare chest and close my eyes. I still feel like total shit for not believing Noel and not seeing through Sophie's lies. Helping Aubrey arrange a meeting for them is the least I can do to start making it up to him. "We're playing a small bar in Columbus tomorrow night called the *A&R Music Bar*. A crowd of only three hundred—a completely acoustic set. She can get to us easily. I'll hook her up with a pass." I smile. "Tell her it will be under Long-Dick Dong."

Kitten laughs. "Any particular reason for the name other than..."

I smile and then flick my lip ring over my teeth. "I knew you liked me for my body."

"Well...It is pretty nice."

I raise my pierced eyebrow. "Nice? Maybe I gave you the wrong impression last time. Why don't you let me come visit you while Lanie's away and show you how un-nice I can be."

"I think I like the sound of that."

The thought alone of being buried deep inside her makes my cock throb. As soon as the Columbus show is over, we're scheduled for a break and I know exactly where I'm heading.

AUBREY

I sit on Lanie's bed and watch her fold the last of her shirts and stuff into her suitcase. The remnants of the story she told me yesterday still hold fresh in my mind. "I can't believe you quit!"

She smiles as she tosses another shirt into the bag. "Believe it. That woman's a tyrant."

I poke my bottom lip out. Even though I know her telling the owner of our company to stuff it was the right thing to do, I still don't want her to leave. "You sure you can't stay here? There are a thousand other jobs in this city other than marketing."

Lanie zips up her suitcase. "I love marketing. That's where my heart lies. It sucks that I can't stay here with you, but going back home will be good. Mom misses me like crazy, and I can find a job in Houston or something." She sets her bag on the floor and pulls up the handle until it clicks. "I think I'm all set."

I step around the bed and wrap my arms around her neck. Lanie leans into me and sniffs. I close my eyes. I hate that she's leaving, but I know this is right for her and her life. I rub her back and try to reassure her. "It's going to be okay, sweetie. You and Noel can finally have your happily ever after."

She squeezes me tight. "I don't know if we can. The entire time we've been fighting over him getting a girl pregnant, he asked me not to leave him—to let him show me I wasn't second to him. Then at the first sign of a problem in our relationship, I ran. I don't know if he'll forgive me for walking away from him a second time."

I pat the back of her head. She still doesn't see that man can never stay mad at her. "Sure he will. True love can get through anything. You'll see." I pull back and wipe away a couple fallen tears. "Go on, before I decide to hold you hostage here."

She frowns. "You sure you're going to be all right by yourself?"

I sniff and then smile, hoping to lighten the mood. "Are you kidding? Now I can have all the wild sex parties I want with you gone. Maybe I can even get Riff to visit."

She rolls her eyes. "I'll tell him you miss his…"

I smack her arm. "Don't you dare tell him that, no matter how true it is. That boy has one giant—"

She shoves her index fingers in her ears. "La! La! La! La! Not listening to you!"

I laugh. "Go on smartass, before you miss your flight. Riff says the pass to get into the V.I.P show for tonight will be at the door under Long-Dick Dong?"

She shakes her head. "Those guys really love giving that pseudonym. I'm so glad to hear he and Noel are working things out since Mike finally told them the truth."

I sigh. "Me too. I can't believe that bitch would do that to them. Doesn't she know she nearly destroyed one of the greatest rock bands ever?"

"Love makes people do insane things, Aubrey. Look at me. I'm traveling cross-country to apologize to a man I'm not even sure wants me anymore. He's not called once in the last couple days since he learned the truth. This is probably a mistake."

I push her long, brown hair over her shoulder. "The only mistake when it comes to love, is not going for it."

As I say those words I realize that's some pretty sound advice and wonder why I've been too stupid to take it myself.

****

The next couple of days drag on without Lanie. Sure, I

missed her before, but I knew she was coming back so it wasn't as bad. Now, with her gone for good, I'm completely alone in this big city, with only my co-workers who don't speak to me much.

"Hey, Aubrey. You got a second?" Isaac asks from his doorway.

I nod. "Sure."

I pick up my notepad and head into his office behind him. Isaac sits in the chair opposite his desk and gestures for me to take the one next to him. I look down at the legal pad in my hand. Something tells me I really didn't need this.

Isaac clears his throat. "I wanted to check in with you and see if you've thought about what we talked about the other day?"

I twist my lips. "I'm not sure I follow you."

"About us?"

I tense a little in my seat as it suddenly clicks I'm kind of playing two men. I'm not a woman that does that, at least, not intentionally. Things with Zach have gotten more complicated since I went out and grabbed a drink with Isaac and stated trying out the idea of dating him.

How can I tell Isaac I'm just not that into him without making things tense for me here at work?

I sigh. "Right now isn't a good time for me to date anyone."

He rubs his chin and glances down at the floor. "Fair enough. I hope we can still remain friends?"

I smile. "Friends it is."

He thrusts his hand out to me and I give it a firm couple of shakes after I stand. "Guess we should get back to work then."

Isaac frowns as I let go and turn towards the door. I feel terrible for hurting his feelings, but it's better than leading him on more when my heart isn't fully in it.

I halt mid-step the moment my eyes land on my desk chair. Zach sits in it, with his long legs stretched out and his hands behind his head. His full lips pull into a slow grin the moment our eyes meet. I allow my eyes to rake over him. The dark jeans fit snuggly around his powerful thighs and his hair pokes up at the ceiling in true Riff style. He looks just as good as I remembered.

I glance around and notice all my female co-workers watching us intently. I'm sure their curious what this tattooed man is doing making himself at home in my seat.

"What are you doing here?" I whisper harshly as I walk over to him.

He shrugs with his head still propped up. "I had a little time off, so I decided to come see my favorite girl."

I walk over to my desk and throw my paper and pen down. "And you decided to come here while I'm working. Why didn't you text me and let me know that you were coming?"

"I didn't want to give you a chance to tell me not to come. Once I was in the cab, I told the driver to bring me here."

I glance nervously over my shoulder. All I need is for Isaac to see me with another man after I told him I didn't want to date anyone right now. "Where are you staying? After work I'll come visit you."

He wiggles his eyebrows. "I planned on staying with you since I know Lanie isn't there."

Great. "Zach, I don't think that's a good idea."

He shrugs again. "Okay then, I'll sit here with you until you get off work and you can come help me find a hotel. It's nearly four, so you won't be much longer, right?"

I run my hand through my hair. I hate being bullied into situations. "All right, fine. If you promise to go right now so I don't get into trouble with my boss, you can stay with me."

Zach's grin gets even wider as he stands. "Where do you live?"

I snatch a scrap piece of paper off my desk and write down my address. "I'll meet you there at five fifteen."

He takes the paper from me. "How will I get in?"

I walk around him and open my bottom desk drawer. After retrieving my keys from my purse, I hand them to Zach. "Go ahead and make yourself at home until I get there and leave it unlocked for me. I have the feeling we'll need to have a little chat about the boundaries of our friendship."

He pushes himself up from the chair and stands before me. We're so close I can feel heat radiating from his body. He pushes a strand of my hair off my cheek and my breath catches. "We certainly do." I swallow hard as he steps back and grabs his bag off the floor. "I'll see you later."

As soon as he's out of sight I plop down in my chair and rub my temples. I remember he mentioned coming to New York last time we spoke on the phone, but I thought he was joking. I'm not angry he's here or anything. I don't like being caught off guard, especially where I work.

I sigh. Will I ever be able to figure this man out?

Chapter 16

RIFF

Okay, so surprising her didn't go exactly like I'd planned. I wasn't expecting a Hollywood sap where she runs into my arms in happy tears, but I was at least expecting a smile. It was like she was embarrassed I was there, which stung a little. I know I'm not exactly clean-cut, but I'm not horrid or anything. Maybe she's more uptight than I thought.

"Go on up, sir," Aubrey's doorman says after he calls her to confirm I'm allowed in. I guess all the tattoos make me seem a little intimidating and untrustworthy.

Once I'm on the correct floor I track down her apartment number and then let myself in with the key. I pull my sunglasses off my face, glancing around the small space. The kitchen and living room are practically in the same room, which is typical for places in the city. There's a large brown couch in the middle of the room and three blue doors to my right. I set my bag inside and shut the door behind me.

It smells nice in here, like some sort of apple scent. I

can totally tell this is a girl's place. I haven't stayed in a place that's had a woman's touch in a long time.

My ringtone echoes around the room. I pull the phone out of my pocket.

Shit. A call from him is never good.

"Yeah?" I say into the receiver after hitting talk.

"Don't yeah me you little shit. I'm your father. You give me some respect when I talk to you," he slurs into the phone.

I clench my fist. "What do you want?"

"I need more money."

Fuck me. "You went through thirty thousand dollars in less than two weeks?"

He laughs bitterly into the phone. "Well, since I have to take care of all the bills by myself since your mother isn't here that chump change you call a paycheck you send doesn't last long."

I rub my forehead vigorously. "Do you have any idea how much fucking money that is? What did you spend it on?"

"I spent a weekend in Vegas. Next time I'm going on vacation you need to send me more money."

"I'm not sending you anymore," I growl.

"You will send me more money or I'll—"

"You'll what?" I fire back. "There's nothing you can do

to me. Not anymore. Your threats of beating my ass no longer scare me. I've done nothing to you!"

"Other than kill my wife and daughter! You're a murdering son of a bitch, Zachary! You owe me money because you took away my life. If you hadn't done what you did they'd both still be alive. How do you expect me to deal with all this and work? I can't and it's your fault. That's why you send me the goddamn money."

Tears burn my eyes, but I refuse to let them fall. "Fine. I'll send you two million dollars and then we're fucking done. Forever. You get me? Totally forget my fucking number."

"No problem. Send me the money and you'll never hear from me again." His voice almost sounds giddy and it makes me sick to my stomach.

How can he be so excited to exploit their deaths? It's fucking sick.

"Great. I'll have my accountant wire it to your account," I say and then hang up the phone.

Two million dollars is a small price to pay if he keeps him off my back.

Anger pulses through my veins. I raise my foot and shove the small brown coffee table across the room. It crashes into another small stand holding a lamp and it falls to the floor shattering against the hardwood floor.

I lean back against the wall and slide down it. It's times like these I wish I was dead, too. Sometimes life is too fucking hard and I can't even deal. I stretch my legs out in front of me and stare up at the white ceiling.

Why did my life have to turn out this way? I never imagined as a kid I would end up like this—a broken piece of a man. No one ever says when they grow up they want to be known as the reason their mom and sister died.

The tears I've been trying so hard to hold back drip down my face. I hug my knees into my chest and rest my forehead on them.

The deadbolt clicks and I jerk my head up as the door opens. My heart stops in my chest the moment Aubrey comes into view.

Fuck.

She's the last person I ever wanted to see me in one of these states. She'll never want to be with me if she sees how unstable I am with my emotions.

I flick the tears off my cheeks and quickly stand up as she takes inventory of the destroyed room. "Hey. I'm sorry about the mess. I'll totally clean it up and replace all the broken stuff."

She glances at my face and then touches my cheek with her fingertips, whipping away a residual tear. "What happened? Are you okay?"

I nod. "Yeah. It's fine. I was on the phone with my dad. He has a way of getting under my skin."

She frowns. "Is it about money again?"

I flinch. So she wasn't asleep through that phone call after all. "You heard that?"

"Yes, but I didn't mean to, so I pretended to be asleep so you wouldn't feel awkward or feel like you had to explain yourself to me. I was just some girl you slept with."

I cup her face in my hands. "You were never that to me. I can't explain it, but right from the start, I knew you were special. There's something about you that pulls me in. No matter how much I try to force myself to stay away from you, I can't. I'm no good for you. I know that, but damn it, I can't stop myself from wanting you."

Kitten bites her lip. "Then don't."

The overwhelming need to have her at that moment crashes over me and I crush my lips against hers. She opens her mouth enough for my tongue to slide in—the silky-smoothness of our wet tongues sliding together my makes my dick throb. It reminds me so much of what being inside her without a condom feels like.

I growl into her mouth as I grab the waistband of her skirt and yank her flush against my body. "I fucking want you."

She pushes me back against the wall and wraps her arms around my neck. I love it when she's forceful. Our tongues mingle together while I slide my hand under her shirt. The shear fabric of her bra is all that separates my hand from one of my most favorite parts of her body. I untuck her blouse and begin undoing the tiny white buttons. Once it's all open I slip my fingers inside her shirt and peel it off her body.

Her bra is nearly see-through. I rub my thumb over her chest. The nipple becomes rigid beneath my hand. I dip my finger inside the cup of her bra and pull the fabric down, revealing her full breast. I bend down and take her nipple into my mouth, playfully biting it. She throws her head back and moans, causing my dick to jerk hard inside my jeans.

Her skin blazes against my lips as I kiss a path back up to her mouth. All of my fingers find their way into her hair and I yank her head back a little as I kiss her hungrily. The material of my black t-shirt strains as she yanks a handful in her fists and kisses me back with just as much force. This rougher sex turns me on more than anything. I like the battle for control. A woman who knows what she wants is always fucking sexy.

I reach behind her and unhook her bra before pulling it off and tossing it to the floor.

I walk her backwards towards the couch, and when the back of her knees hit it, I lay her down.

The need to have her skin on mine zings through me, causing me to practically rip my shirt off my body in order to get it over my head. Aubrey peers up at me with her almond-shaped eyes while her chest heaves. I tug at the zipper on the side of her skirt and slide it, along with her panties, down her legs.

She starts to kick off her red stilettos, but I grab her ankle and shake my head. "Leave those on."

Rock My Bed

I toss her clothes to the floor and stare down at her naked perfection. Her red hair and pumps only increase her sexiness factor. I wrap my hand around her right ankle and lift it to my lips. I kiss and lick my way to her inner thigh and she squirms beneath me as I slide a knee against her other leg on the couch.

I throw her leg over my shoulder and bend down at the waist. The tip of my index finger flicks over her clit a few times before it moves inside her. I trace her folds with my tongue before I wiggle it over her sweet spot.

Within a couple minutes her back starts arching—I love that she's so receptive. It makes it really hard to hold back my urge to drive into her.

"Oh, god," she whimpers while grabbing a hold of my ear with her hand, holding me firmly in place. "Yes!"

As soon as her legs stop shaking I grab her hips and yank her towards me. I shove my jeans and underwear down and kick them across the room in my excitement to have her again.

I grab the base of my cock and swirl it around her entrance a few times before sliding it inside her. It's so warm and inviting. I squeeze my eyes shut and focus on how fucking good it feels. "Your pussy is so nice and wet for me. I've missed this so fucking much."

I lean down and run my nose along her jaw line. The intense scent of fruity shampoo and a light perfume fill my nose. Every nerve inside me is consumed with her presence.

I pull my hips back and then thrust them again, stretching every inch of her around my dick as I go in deeper. Her legs relax and open even wider on the next pump and I can almost get my entire length inside her, but it's still too tight to push the entire cock in. "Shit, Kitten. You're so fucking tight."

I drag my lips across the flesh of her neck. Her head drifts to the side and a moan escapes those red, pouty lips. She's getting close again already. I increase my pace and allow my hips to smack into her thighs. When her eyes close, I lean up and continue to pump into her. I slide my hand down her belly until it finds the top of her pussy. I flick my thumb across her clit and her entire body jerks while she gasps.

"Fucking come for me," I growl as I pump harder while the heel of her shoe digs into my ass.

The urge to taste her rages inside me, so I snake my tongue out and lick her earlobe before nibbling on it. Kitten grabs my face with both hands and crushes her lips against mine.

A growl rumbles in my chest as the need to claim her pushes through me. "Tell me you're mine. Tell me you want me."

She peers up at me through sex-hazed eyes and says, "I want to be with you. I think I have since that first night."

I kiss her with as much force as I can without hurting her. Knowing that she's finally admitted she wants me too makes this the best fuck I've ever had. I bury my face in her shoulder and wrap her tight in my arms and I pound into her, searching for my own release.

"Zach," she breathes my name and it's my undoing.

My breath comes out in ragged spurts as my cock tenses then blasts her full as I release into her. The way I feel about this girl is crazy. This crazy connection is odd to me and I can't quite wrap my head around it. It's like she genuinely cares for me, and that's something from a woman I've never had.

I collapse on top of her. "I don't think I'm ever going to get enough of that."

She runs her hand down my back. "That's good, considering I just committed to you."

I lean up on my elbow so I can look into her eyes. "You're serious about that?"

Kitten bites her lip. "Weren't you?"

I pin her gaze with mine. "You have no idea how much I've wanted this. I'm a little afraid."

"Of what?" she whispers.

"Of disappointing you," I admit.

She licks her lips and places her palm on my cheek. "Be real with me and let me in and you won't."

I give her a sad smile. She has no idea what she's asking for. "I'll try."

"That's all I ask."

My heart squeezes as I lean down and kiss her lips. For the first time ever I find myself sleeping with someone who's committed to me and it feels fucking amazing.

AUBREY

After one last kiss, I push myself away from the couch and out of Zach's arms. I can't believe we defined our relationship into more. It's crazy. Never in a million years would I have ever believed Riff of Black Falcon would be the man to crave and commit to a relationship with me.

"Where are you going?" Zach grabs my wrist.

I turn and smile at him. "I'm going to take a shower."

"Okay don't be too long." He smirks as he smacks my bare ass.

I giggle as I head towards the bathroom and stop short of the shattered lamp that's still lying on the floor. His father triggers instant rage in him. I'm not sure why Zach owes his father money, but whatever the reason, it seems to tear him up every time he calls.

"I'll clean all that up," Zach says behind me as he places both hands on my shoulders. "I swear I'll replace everything I broke."

I nod and pat his hand. "Okay."

I want to bombard him with questions but I know it's too soon. Someone like Zach cannot be pushed.

His warm lips place a light kiss on the side of my neck. "I promise."

After my shower I come out of the bathroom to find my apartment clean. You would never know a wrathful hurricane came through here. The aroma of some sort of mouthwatering food fills the apartment and I find myself drawn towards it. Zach's stands in the kitchen over my stove stirring a steaming pot.

It's an odd sight, really. One of the world's hardest rockers appearing all domesticated in my kitchen, cooking dinner, no less. His rough exterior of all the tattoos makes me think more of Ozzy Osbourne than Martha Stewart. All he's missing is a polka-dotted apron.

He glances up and smiles when catches me watching him intently. "I figured you might be hungry after working all day."

"I'm starving," I say as I sit on the stool at the bar and watch him work.

Zach sticks a fork into the pot and brings one of the spaghetti noodles up the side and cuts it in two. "This was how my mom taught me to check if the noodles were cooked thoroughly. If they cut apart with ease, they're done."

"Good tip. I wish I knew how to cook."

He places a strainer in my sink. "Maybe I can teach you

all my mad skills. Mom taught me a ton of helpful little tips before she passed."

That's the first time I'd ever heard Zach talk fondly about his mother and that makes me curious about her. "Can I ask you something?"

He grabs the pot handles with some dishtowels and carries it over to the sink to strain the water off the noodles. "Shoot."

I swallow hard, knowing this might not be a place he wants to go with me yet. "What happened to her?"

He pauses for the briefest second and then shakes the rest of the noodles out of the pot. "She killed herself soon after Hailey died."

I gasp and grab my chest. "I'm so sorry. That had to be hard on you."

He nods as he carries the pot full of strained noodles back to the stove and dumps the simmering red sauce over the noodles and begins to stir. "It was. Losing them both so close was almost more than I could bear. I almost didn't make it myself. It was a very dark time in my life."

I lean my elbow up on the counter. "What brought you out of it?"

He opens the cabinets searching for plates. "Trip mainly, and Tyke. Music—the way I could lose myself in it. It helped me forget how shitty my life was, still does to this day."

"Are things still bad for you now?" I wonder out loud.

Zach shrugs as he fills two plates full. "It's getting better, or at least right now it feels like it is."

I smile as he sets a plate of spaghetti in front of me. "Thank you. It looks amazing. I have to say this is a first for me."

He sits beside me. "What is?"

"A man has never cooked for me before. You're full of surprises."

He winks at me, like there's more up his sleeve before taking a bite of food. "Sorry there's no meat in it. You didn't have any hamburger. Tomorrow I'll go shopping for us and cook for you while I'm here. Hopefully I can teach you a thing or two."

"I'd like that." I twirl a noodle around my fork and pop it into my mouth. "Mmmm. This is so good."

He grins. "I'm glad you like it."

The question of what's happened in his past still lingers on my mind. If his mother killed herself over the grief of the loss of her daughter, why does Zach's father blame him for their deaths? Suicide is a personal choice kind of thing. It isn't like Zach made her do that. Something about the whole situation doesn't add up and while he's being so sharing I might as well try to figure out the mystery behind this man.

"Can I ask you something else?" I ask quietly.

Zach takes a drink of his water and says, "You can ask me anything you want and I'll try to be as honest as I can with you."

"It's about your sister…" He freezes up again at the mention of bringing up his sister again. I'm starting to see the pattern with that every time I ask something about her. It's almost as if he's afraid to talk about her. "What happened to her?"

He sets his glass on the bar in front of us. "She died in a car crash."

At first I think those kinds of tragic accidents happen every day. I still don't see how Zach's dad blames him for any of this.

Zach traces patterns in the condensation on the glass and I worry he's shutting down again until he opens his mouth and continues. "There was a guy in my high school—a real know-it-all type jackass, and he kept taunting me with his flashy new Mustang. I always tried my best to ignore petty bullshit like that, but this guy was able to get under my skin like no other. He talked so much shit everyday about how his car would smoke my Camaro in a race, that one day it finally got to me."

This is not the story I was expecting from him and I'm perplexed on where he's going with this. "So what happened?"

He sighs. "I told him I'd race him after school to get him to shut the fuck up."

I crunch my brow. "How did that involve Hailey?"

He stares down at the counter and takes a deep breath. "I was responsible for driving Hailey home from school. Instead of making her wait at a playground or something while I raced, I kept her in the car with me." He frowns. "I thought she was safer with me than alone at a park. There's so many weirdo creeps. I didn't want one to come along and take my eight year old sister, you know."

My heart leaps up into my throat as everything starts clicking. Hailey's death. The fact Zach's sterile. "There was a crash?"

He nods. "It was a two lane road. An oncoming car forced me off the road and I hit an embankment and the car flipped us about five times. I broke an arm and fractured my pelvis. Doctors said I was lucky to even be alive because I was so mangled. Most of the damage was on Hailey's side, though. She was gone on impact and it was all my fault." He sucks in a deep breath and he starts choking up. "I never meant to hurt her."

I rub his back and place my chin on his shoulder as my heart aches to comfort him. "I'm sorry."

Zach wipes away a fallen tear. "Thank you, but I don't deserve sympathy. I should've died, too."

"You were just a kid," I say softly. "Kids make bad choices, doesn't mean you don't have the right to grieve."

"But it's my fault she's dead. I'll never be able to forgive

239

myself for what I did. My parents never did. I killed their baby." He sniffs.

"Don't say that. It was an accident," I try to ease his burden.

He shakes his head. "My own mother said that at my trial. She told the court to punish me to the fullest extent of the law for killing her baby."

I gasp and clutch my chest. "You went to jail over this, too?"

"Juvenile prison and my license was suspended until I was twenty five, but I think they let me off light. I deserve to still be rotting in that jail cell."

"It was an accident, Zach. You didn't mean to hurt her. You have to learn to forgive yourself," I say.

"I don't think I ever will. The best I can hope for is little moments of forgetting, like my time with you." He stares into my eyes. "When I'm with you, I don't feel as shitty about my life. You give me hope that I can maybe one day be a better person."

I place my hand on his arm. "You're already a good person. You have a good heart. I know that. You need to know it, too."

He sets his hand on mine that still rests on his forearm. "I'm trying, but deep down I think I know I don't deserve anything good."

Rock My Bed

I stand and wrap my arms around his neck. He squeezes me around the waist in a tight embrace and we hold each other, connecting without words.

This man is far more complex than I thought. I'm glad he trusts me enough to tell me his story, but I get the feeling that he hasn't known real love in a long time, and that explains so much. It answers the question on why he's never settled down even though he's got a good heart.

I'm going to show him that he's capable of giving and receiving love. He deserves to know he can.

Chapter 17

RIFF

I put away all the groceries I bought from the local shop. I'm excited. Before I leave in the next couple days, I'm going to teach Aubrey how to cook one of Mom's specialties, chicken and noodles. Granted we aren't making the noodles from scratch like Mom did, but these frozen ones will work out nicely.

Waiting on Aubrey to get back from work is more difficult than I thought. I filled my days with sleeping or shopping while she's at work, not the most glamorous tour break I've ever had, but it's been the most rewarding. Our connection keeps getting better, even after day four with her—I'm still not annoyed. Matter of fact it's the opposite. I want to spend every second with her, which is so unlike me.

I begged her to blow off the rest of the week and spend all her time with me, but she's too responsible for that. Center Stage is a huge advertising firm, and she explained how she's lucky she even has a foot in the door considering how competitive it is to even get an internship there, let alone a job.

She's a secretary to some young, hot-shot type. From the way Aubrey described him, he sounds like an uptight pain in the ass.

I could never work for a douche like that without telling him to shove his memo corrections up his ass.

I plop down on the couch in the living room after all the stuff is stored and flip on the television. Some afternoon celebrity tabloid show pops up on the screen. It catches my eye immediately because Noel and Lanie's faces fill the screen in a kiss while a jagged line cuts down part of the screen and shows Sophie walking with her head down. The words home wrecker flashes and my fingers tighten around the remote.

These fucking tabloid shows never get their shit straight. The shit they tell the world is half-truths at best.

A text message chimes into my phone. I grin as I read Aubrey's words. "Miss you. Be there in a few minutes."

Never in a million years did I ever figure I would feel like this. For once in my miserable life I don't feel like a completely evil being all the time. And Aubrey didn't go running for the hills when I came clean about my past, which was a relief. I don't know what I would've done if I'd lost this feeling so soon after getting a taste of what happiness feels like.

The door opens and Aubrey steps through it. Her auburn hair styled into loose waves over her shoulders stand out against her gray sweater-dress. Even after eight hours of work she still looks amazing.

"Hey," she says with a smile. Her bright green eyes focus on me as she sets her bag down and plops down next to me on the couch and snuggles into my side. "I missed you."

I comb my fingers down her silky hair and then kiss her forehead. I don't even want to think about how much I'll miss her when I head back out on tour. I know distance is the true test of all relationships.

"Do you want a break from cooking tonight?"

I pull back and she peers up at me through her sexy, long eyelashes. "Why? Are you tired of my cooking already?"

She shakes her head. "No. I thought maybe you wanted to take a break and we can go out to eat."

I shrug. "I'm okay with cooking, but if you want to go out, we can do that, too."

"There's a place around the corner that I love—really low key, and has my favorite pizza in the whole world."

"Sounds good, Kitten. Anything you want."

She kisses my cheek. "I'm going to go get ready."

An hour later, she comes out of her room in jeans, a black top, and tall heels. She stops and grins as she does a little turn so I can check out her entire outfit. The black blouse dips down so low I can see the small of her back. "Jesus. Are you sure you want to go out. I'm sporting a half-wood just looking at you."

She grins. "Then this is perfect. I like making you wait

because I don't think you're used to that."

I stand and wrap my arms around her, pressing myself against her. "I'm not used to anything like you." A blush floods her cheeks. "I like that you can't hide emotions. Your fair skin gives you away every time."

She giggles and kisses my lips. "I'm glad I stand out."

"You have no idea how much."

The restaurant is tiny, almost to the point that if I weren't aware of it, I would've never found it. Ten small, two-person tables fill the dimly lit dining area and the rest of the space is brick ovens and kitchen. Customers picking up carryout orders stream in and out of the door in constant revolution. The heavenly aroma of melted cheese and simmering sauce surrounds us as we take out seats.

"It smells good," I say.

Kitten smiles as she opens the sticky menu. "That's because it's awesome. Once you try it, you'll see."

The dark-haired waitress wearing a red and white checkered apron pops over to our table. "What'll it be?"

"I'll have a Coke," Aubrey answers.

"Make that two," I add.

The server yanks a green notepad from her apron pocket and cracks her gum. "Do you know what kind of pizza you want?"

I glance over at Kitten. "I can eat anything, so order whatever you like."

"We'll have a pepperoni with extra cheese, please."

The waitress scribbles the order down and says, "It'll be out in a few."

The girl scurries off in the direction of the kitchen and once she's out of earshot I turn towards Aubrey. "Did you have a good day at work?"

She shrugs. "Same old same, you know. I did get to type up a couple memos for the Black Falcon account, so at least I was allowed to think about you all day."

I bite my lip and rake my eyes over her. The idea of her having dirty thoughts about me all day at work is nearly enough to make me say fuck the pizza. "What exactly was I doing in these daydreams?"

She giggles. "Lots of things…"

Her words trail off and that only excites me more. "Care to elaborate? I hope it's kinky. You know I like it when you're like that."

As she opens her mouth to speak, her eyes widen as she glances over my shoulder. I turn to find a guy wearing a yellow, polo shirt and pressed khakis at my left. The shirt nearly matches the color of his perfectly styled hair. He reminds me of Hailey's perfectly plastic *Ken* doll only with glasses.

"Hey, Aubrey. I didn't know you frequented this place," Ken doll says while completely overlooking the fact that I'm sitting right here.

Kitten sits a little straighter in her chair. "It's one of my favorites. Isaac, this is my…" She gestures to me but trails off unsure of what to call me.

Things click. This is Isaac, as in her douche bag of a boss that grates on her nerves. I stick my hand out to the dude. "Boyfriend. Riff. What's up, bro."

I'm not sure whose eyebrows raise higher, Kitten or Issac's when I proclaim our relationship status for the first time to a stranger. I want people to know she's taken. Might as well start with her boss, because I can see the way he's looking at her. This fucker needs to know to keep his dick in his pants.

He grips my hand and gives it a firm shake. "Good to meet you. I actually work at Center Stage. I've had a hand in helping out with your charity project alongside Lanie Vance. I didn't know you knew Aubrey personally."

His eyes flick over to Aubrey's face and she merely shrugs under his gaze like she's been caught in something. "It never came up."

Isaac's eyes never leave her and instantly I feel a surge to protect what's mine come over me. I need to get rid of this joker before I lose my cool. "Okay, well, good to meet you. She'll see you at work then."

Aubrey flinches at the sudden short tone of my voice

and then turns back to her boss with an apologetic smile. "I'll see you tomorrow, Isaac."

Isaac stands there for a moment like he's debating something before he nods. "Tomorrow it is, then."

The minute he walks away Aubrey turns towards me with a frown. "Why did you do that?"

I lean in further towards her. "Because I saw the way that Ken doll looked at you. I want him to know up front that he can't have you."

She squares her shoulders. "I'm perfectly capable of handling things on my own, and don't call him that."

"What? *A Ken doll*?"

"Yes!" she snaps. "It's rude."

I lean in. "Have you not seen the guy? He looks Barbie's fake fucking boyfriend. Too perfect to be real."

She rolls her eyes. "He does not, besides he won't try anything if he knows I'm with someone. He's not that type of man."

I shake my head. "Sometimes guys need a little more deterrent than a polite no from a woman for the message to sink in that she's not interested. Take us for example. That first night in the hall, your mouth said no, but your body said yes. I'm keeping things clear in this case. You're mine, Kitten. You said so yourself. Now it's time the world knew."

Admitting my feelings about claiming her out loud

makes me seem a little cavemanish but I don't give a shit. I want her. The thought of another man thinking about fucking her is enough to drive me over the edge.

I wait for her to be pissed and tell me that I don't own her and all that crap that I've seen women spout when their men try to control them, but Aubrey does quite the opposite. She smiles.

"I hope you know that goes two ways." She eyes me carefully. "If we're exclusive then that means no other women for you."

I lean back in the chair and lick my lips. "Kitten, there's no other woman on this planet that can compete with you, so I don't think that's going to be a problem."

Her smile grows wider and I can't wait to prove to her that I am worthy of her trust because, after all, isn't that the foundation to a good relationship?

AUBREY

I watch Zach throw the last of his things in a duffel bag. "I can't believe you have to go back already."

My heart sinks at the thought of not being with him every day. Believe it or not, in a week I've grown used to having him here all the time.

He walks around the bed and pulls me up by both hands. "Come with me."

I throw my arms around his neck and squeeze against him. "I can't. I have my job here and all."

He sighs and rests his forehead against mine. "I know. I wish you'd quit and come on the road with me. I like having you with me."

"That would be better than anything in the world, but I've worked so hard for this degree and it's the best company in the field. I can't give that up."

He nods. "I know, but it doesn't make the pain of leaving you here hurt any less."

I rub the back of his head and the stubble scratches my fingertips. "I feel the same way. But like you said, we're only an airplane ride apart. Maybe I can come to you on weekends or something."

"I'll take whatever you can give me." He leans in and presses his lips to mine.

A crushing weight sits on my chest knowing this will be the last kiss I get from him in a while. I close my eyes, but it doesn't stop the burn that's taking them over. Squeezing them tighter doesn't work either. It merely forces a tear out of the corner of my eye.

"Don't cry," he whispers, "I'll see you again before you know it."

Rock My Bed

The call button on my apartment rings as someone buzzes the apartment entrance. "That's your ride."

I fist his t-shirt in my hands and kiss his lips with as much force as I can muster. This week has been perfect and I'm scared to let him go. I don't want this feeling to end, and I'm afraid that if we try this long-distance thing it isn't going to work out. They never do.

"I have to go." He gives me one last peck. "I'll call you when I board the plane."

I nod and pull my hands away from his shirt. I wonder if he feels this, too? The uncertainly of what lies ahead for us?

I sniff and do my best to hide the overwhelming emotion I feel building inside of me. The brightest smile I can afford to show fills my face as he steps back.

"This isn't goodbye. It's more like an I'll see you later, okay?"

"Okay," I answer softly.

He grabs his bag, takes one last look at me and then heads out of the bedroom. The minute the front door clicks shut, I fall back against my pillow and allow the breakdown I've been holding back to break free.

Never in a million years did I believe that kiss backstage with a sweaty, Mohawked rock star would lead to a connection like this. This is one curveball in life I wasn't expecting.

Michelle A. Valentine

Chapter 18

RIFF

I step onto the bus and Trip elbows his brother while they both sit on the love seat playing their video game. They both grin at me from ear to ear and it's fucking annoying. "What?"

Tyke winks at Trip. "Have a good week off? We missed you at home."

"Yeah, Riff. Where did you go last week, huh?" Trip asks.

I head towards my bunk and plop my bag inside my foxhole. They've obviously already figured it out, so I might as well admit where I was and get their merciless teasing over with now. "You all know exactly where I've been, so cut the shit and let's get this over with."

Trip and Tyke both howl with laughter. I roll my eyes and roll my hand, telling them to get it all out now.

"I never thought I'd see the day when Riff Oliver falls for a girl," Tyke says.

"I knew it was coming. It's about time this stubborn asshole admits he's capable of feelings," Trip adds. "I'm happy for you, bro. So tell us, is she walking funny?"

"You guys are idiots. I don't know how I've put up with

you two this long," I answer as I shake my head and totally avoid his question.

"Because we're the only ones crazy enough to put up with your moody ass," Trip says.

I open my mouth to answer, but quickly shut it, knowing he's probably right.

"She's not coming on the bus with us too is she?" Tyke asks while pounding away on the remote.

I crunch my brow. "So what if she does?"

"Relax, dude. It'll be tight is all. Noel is bringing Lanie back on the bus with him. Two chicks on this bus with us, hogging the bathroom all the time and complaining about our filth, might be more than the rest of us can take," Trip clarifies.

"I thought Lanie was going to her mom's place?" Maybe he's planning to keep her with him. I wouldn't blame him if he did. I'd keep Aubrey here if I could.

Tyke shakes his head. "Noel called earlier and said that she's staying for a while."

All this talk about girlfriends on the bus makes me miss my Kitten. I pull out my cell and dial her number.

"Hey," she says into the phone. "I wasn't expecting to hear from you until tonight."

I cradle the phone between my ear and shoulder as I grab my Oreos and a cup of milk. "Guess I couldn't wait. So what are you up to?"

I sit at the table and fill her in about the details of my flight home as I stack my cookies on the table. The twins instantly shut up and go busy themselves with restocking the kitchen once their game ends.

Noel walks in with Lanie under his arm. She stretches up on her toes and kisses his cheek before heading towards the bedroom to settle in. Noel grins as he watches her down the hall.

I sigh. Seeing shit like that isn't going to help me to get over missing Kitten.

Aubrey starts explaining the plot of some movie she watched on television as Tyke hands Noel a beer from across the island and distracts me from my private conversation. "Good break? I see that sappy grin."

It's hard not to listen to Noel and Tyke talk too since they're practically standing next to me and aren't exactly quiet when they speak.

Noel twists off the cap. "Don't hate."

Tyke holds his palm hands up. "I'm not. It's going to be weird around here with both you and Riff settled down and all."

Noel chokes on his drink and quickly wipes his mouth. "Riff?" I grin as shock registers on his face. "With who?"

Tyke gives him a pointed look. "Lane's friend, Aubrey. Who else?"

His eyebrows rise. "Reallllly? Wow. I thought they just

hooked up."

Tyke shrugs. "Apparently he spent the entire break with her in New York, and he's been on the phone with her now for the last hour."

"Huh," he says while he shakes his head.

It's official my world is officially changing and everyone around me knows it.

"Zach? You still there?" Aubrey questions on the other end of the line.

I readjust in my seat. "Sorry, I'm still here. The guys are all coming in. Looks like Lane's staying on the bus with us for a while."

"That's great. She and Noel need some time together to finish reconnecting."

I sigh. "It'd be better if you were here."

"I'm hoping soon. I can take a half day off work on a Friday and fly out to you for the weekend sometime this month. I don't think I can go an entire month without seeing you," she says.

I know it's twisted to enjoy someone's misery, but I kind of like the idea that she's missing me. It makes me feel almost downright giddy.

I try to frown as I say, "Soon," but I don't think I succeed because even I can hear the smile in my voice.

Rock My Bed

I roll my eyes. I've actually turned into one of those pussy-whipped pansies I always make fun of. Good god. What's this girl doing to me?

****

After three weeks of constant texting and emails I don't know how much longer I can go without seeing Kitten. This distance thing is killer. I'd give anything to be able to hold her in my arms all night like I did back at her apartment.

The catering area backstage at this show is pretty small. The room holds two round tables with four seats at each. Part of the road crew for Black Falcon fill one table, while the other is populated by Striker and Donovan from Embrace the Darkness. I roll my eyes and head to their table. I'd prefer to stay away from these two assholes, but I'm not going to let them bully me out of a seat to eat my dinner.

I sit down and open my silverware packet and pill out a plastic knife to butter my roll. The two men look up at me as I sit down without asking permission. Striker tucks a strand of his black hair behind his ear and relaxes, while Donovan smirks next to him.

Striker eyes me as I prep my food. "Hey, mate. How's it going?"

His British accent is so strong at times it's hard to understand him.

"Good. You?" I return pleasantries before I take a bite of food.

"Not bad. Say…" He leans in on his elbow. "I heard that little dish, Lanie Vance is staying on with Noel. Is that true, then?"

I swallow hard. "You better be careful with that. Noel's not messing around when it comes to her. He's serious about her. I suggest you stay away from her if you know what's good for you."

Both men laugh and my fingers curl into fists.

"Right, well, I don't think I'll be taking lessons in love from the likes of you. No offense, mate, but you don't exactly have longevity with the ladies," Striker says.

Donovan shakes his head next to him. "I don't know. He's seems attached to the red-head he's been fucking—tries to fight me every time I tried to get a piece of that action."

"Watch it, dick." Anger rages through me and I fantasize about punching this dick square in the throat.

Donovan throws his hands up in surrender. "Easy. Take it easy. She's yours. I fucking get that. It doesn't mean I still don't think she's hot as fuck, because let's face it. She is."

I uncurl my fingers and they throb as the blood begins to flow back into them. He's right. Kitten is a sexy woman. I noticed her beauty right away, so I imagine the rest of the male and half the female population does, too. First it was Donovan, then that pencil-dick boss of hers and I'm sure they won't be the last.

I need to figure out a way to cool all my emotional shit

before she gets tired of my bullshit.

I shrug causally. "She is, and I plan on keeping her all to myself for a very long time."

"Blimey," Striker says. "Are you telling me the biggest player I know is settling down?"

"It's time, man. She's the one."

It's a lot easier than I thought to admit my feelings. Maybe it's because Aubrey makes me feel so different, that it feels natural to want to be a different person—a better one.

Still, I don't want to push this level of calm anymore. If I stay here much longer I may rip their heads off. I finish my plate and stand before taking off towards the bus.

A string of groupies line the parking lot. They instantly paw at me the moment I'm within reach. Normally I would be eyeing one to hand a golden ticket to, but I have absolutely no desire for random sex. I only crave realness and that's something only one woman in the entire world has ever given me. There's no way I would break the little bit of trust we've built on a random fling.

AUBREY

My cell rings while I'm at work and I curse myself for not muting my ringer here. If someone's personal cell goes off with a music ringtone these people love to hand out dirty looks like candy.

I yank it out of my purse and answer Lanie's call. "What's up? Can I call you back in a bit?"

"This will only take a second," she says in a rush. "My mother fell and broke her leg."

I gasp. "Oh my god. Is she okay?"

"I hope so. I'm on my way to Texas as we speak to find out what's going on and take care of her. Quitting my job couldn't have worked out better since I would've probably been fired for taking time off anyhow."

"Fate has a strange way of pointing us in the directional path of our life. That's for sure."

She sighs. "Isn't that the truth? I'll call you when I find out more about her."

"Okay. Love you," I tell her.

"Love you, too." She ends the call and I throw the phone back in my purse.

Isaac pokes his head out of his office. "Hey, Aubrey. You got a second before we head out for the weekend?"

I nod and pick up my paper and pen. "Sure."

I walk into Isaac's office and he's already back at his desk. "Close the door, would you?" He gestures for me to take a seat across from him after we're shut inside together. I pick up my pen ready to take notes. "You won't need that."

I tilt my head as my confusion shows through my body language. "Okay?"

"I've been meaning to ask you how you and Riff are doing?"

I stiffen. Oh shit. Are we seriously going to do this? "We're good. Thanks."

He taps his chin. "How long have you been seeing him?"

I bite my lip. "A few weeks."

He nods like it answers some unspoken question of his. "We're you seeing him when we went out for drinks?"

I shake my head. "No. Not at that point."

"Things seem serious between the two of you. Are they?"

"They're definitely moving in that direction, I think."

He leans in on the desk. "You know, Aubrey. Men like Riff usually don't hang around long term. I would hate for you to get hurt."

"I appreciate your concern, but I think I'm capable of managing my own love life. If that's all…"

I turn to walk out of the door, but his voice stops me. "Aubrey, I won't hold this against you once things end with him. I would still very much like that date with you."

I don't reply to that. How can I? He basically said my worst fear out loud—that Zach would break my heart like all the others before him. I pray that he's wrong and our connection is strong enough to make a real go out of this relationship.

Chapter 19

RIFF

We roll on towards the next city on our tour as Noel carries luggage from the back bedroom to the front of the bus and drops it near the steps. Tyke and I sit at the table eating breakfast, while Trip stands at the island finishing a bowl of cereal.

I eyeball the bag before turning my gaze on him. "What the fuck is that?"

He shrugs apologetically. "I have to go, man."

"Go where?" Trip asks wiping milk from his lip after slurping down what's left in his bowl.

"He's going to Texas to be with Lane," I answer, knowing that because that's exactly what I would do if I were him.

"What about the rest of our shows?" Tyke asks with a frown on his face.

"We'll have to cancel or postpone them, I suppose." We all stare at Noel like he's lost his fucking mind. "Guys I'm sorry, but she needs me for a week or so. Her mom broke her leg, and she's sick. I have to go."

I flex my jaw muscle. As much as I want to be with Kitten, I would never screw people that depend on us. "Fine. If you want to disappoint all the fans because you're being selfish —"

"Selfish? This is the first time in my life I'm thinking of others." Noel meets each one of our stares individually. "I love her, guys. I have to be there when she needs me. I would really appreciate a little understanding on this."

After a couple tense moments of silence, I rub my chin. "I guess pushing back the dates a couple weeks wouldn't kill anybody." Trip and Tyke nodded in agreement. "I'll work on having them change the dates. It won't be easy, and will be a total pain in my ass, but I'll do it. Go take care of things."

A grin creeps up on Noel's face. "Thanks guys, I'll owe you one."

Secretly I know I'm the one who should be thanking him because he granted me the freedom to head off and see my girl.

AUBREY

The intercom by my apartment door buzzes as I sit down to watch a movie. I get up and press the button to answer.

"Good evening, Miss Jenson. Zach Oliver is here to see you," Barney, my doorman, says.

My heart races in my chest. Zach is here? He didn't even call to tell me. To say I'm shocked is an understatement. "Send him up."

I dash over to a mirror to fluff my hair up a bit and reapply some lip-gloss. I finish the last minute makeup touches as Zach knocks on the door. I fly over and yank it open.

A wide grin covers his face the moment he sees me. He looks amazing in his red t-shirt, faded jeans and boots. I practically leap at him and throw my arms around his neck.

Strong arms wrap around my waist as he lifts me into the air. "God. I've missed you."

The scent of him is amazing. It's like some sort of spicy soap. "I can't believe you're here! Why didn't you tell me you were coming?"

My toes touch the ground as he sets me down. "I wanted to surprise you."

I press my lips to his. "Well you succeeded. I've never been more surprised in my life."

He laughs. "Then my mission is complete."

I grab him by the hand after he lets me go and reaches down for his bag. "How did you manage this?"

We sit down on the couch with me practically on his lap. "Lanie's been sick the last couple days and is having a hard time helping her mom after surgery. We cancelled some tour dates so Noel could fly to be with her, and I'm taking full advantage of my time off."

I snuggle into his side. "I'm glad you're here. I've been practically starving since you've been gone."

He kisses the top of my head. "I know the feeling. I've been sexually frustrated since I saw you last."

I smack his arm playfully. "I meant food, but I've been a little hungry in that department too."

Zach threads his fingers into my hair and tilts my head up until we're practically nose to nose. "I think I can fix that on both accounts."

The firmness of his lips against mine is just as I remember. They're assured and know exactly what they want and I find an odd comfort in that. My fingers wrap around the nape of his neck as I hold him against me.

Our kisses deepen and Zach scoops me into his arms and carries me off into the bedroom where I'm sure one of my hungers is about to be thoroughly satisfied.

****

Rock My Bed

After being locked away in my apartment for nearly twenty-four hours, we decide it's time to come up for air. The bar a couple blocks away from apartment hosts a variety of patrons. There are the uptight suits along with the everyday working class heroes.

Zach leads me inside the dimly lit establishment by the hand. A long bar fills most of the space and is the focal point of the room. People mill about with their drinks chatting amongst one another as we pass by.

A couple women stare at Zach a little too long for my liking as we pass by them. I squeeze his hand a little tighter as he stays oblivious to their attentions. Deep down I know I need to get used to the idea of women lusting after my man. He is a famous rock star, after all, but it's so easy to forget that when we spend most of our time alone in my tiny apartment.

Zach walks up to the counter and orders us a couple beers while I take in our surroundings. The women that were checking Zach out earlier saunter over to us with their eyes focused on him. I might as well be invisible.

The leggy brunette taps him on the shoulder. "You're Riff, right?"

He gazes down at the two women and then turns his attention back to the bar. "Yeah, I am."

The short blonde nudges her friend to speak again. "Can we get your autograph?"

"Sure," he says without looking at them. "Do you have a

pen?"

The blonde shakes her head. "Not on us. We were hoping you'd take us to your room so we can show you a little double fan appreciation."

"Ew," I say out loud and the girls whip their heads in my direction and nearly shoot daggers at me with their eyes.

Zach turns and rolls his eyes. "I don't think so."

The dark-haired girl whines, "What a letdown. I thought you slept with your fans. You're famous for handing out fuck tickets."

"Things change. I won't be doing that shit anymore." He glances at me and smiles. "I'm a one woman man kind of guy now."

"Ugh. Come on, Trixie. We'll find another rich playmate for the night," Blondie says to her friend before linking their arms and sauntering off in their epically short skirts.

Zach hands me my beer. "Sorry about that. Sleeping around is kind of my trademark."

I sigh. "I know. It's why I originally agreed to our first night together, remember."

He nods. "Ah, that's right. I was supposed to be your last hoorah before you were going to settle down with someone like that fuck-stick of a boss of yours."

I cringe as he correlates the idea of Isaac and me together. "You're right about him, you know."

He takes a sip of his drink. "What do you mean?"

"About Isaac…he did…does want something more with me," I admit. "He's told me so."

"I told you. My fuck radar is never wrong. I could tell he wanted in your panties the minute he approached our table at the pizza place. He was practically drooling over you."

I shrug. "Don't worry. I told him we're together."

Zach furrows his brow. "He made another pass at you after I told him you were mine?"

I nod. "He basically told me he'd be waiting for when we didn't work out and that he wouldn't hold dating you against me."

Zach's jaw muscle works under his skin. "I'm going to kill that motherfucker."

I place my hand on his chest. "Forget him. He's not worth getting angry about. Isaac and I will never happen."

"What if I fuck things up? I can't shake the feeling that deep down I don't deserve you and I'm going to fuck us up somehow."

I shake my head and cup his cheek, forcing him to look at me. "I know you won't."

"You don't know that." He stares into my eyes, searching for some kind of answer.

My pulse pounds in my ears as I'm about to take a

huge chance. "I do because I love you and I think you love me, too."

Zach closes his eyes and takes a deep breath. I wait anxiously on him to respond—to admit he feels the same way. Instead, he grabs my hand and leads us out of the bar back towards the apartment, never answering. My heart completely sinks and I get the distinct feeling I've pushed him away.

Chapter 20

RIFF

I lay awake and watch Kitten sleep. When she told me she loves me back at the bar I froze up. The logical thing would've been for me to admit that I think I feel that way, too, but instead I panicked and brought her back here where I could have sex and clear my head a little bit.

I mean, I know I feel something for her. I'd be lying to myself if I didn't admit that, but I also know that I'm not ready for something so monumental. Telling someone you love them is huge. It changes things. I don't want to say it then find myself knee-deep in groupies fucking their brains out a week later because I decide I'm not ready to be committed that fully.

In order to be fair to her, I need to leave her alone while I sort out this fucked up mess in my head. Accepting someone's love is just as big of a deal as admitting that you love them back. The last thing I want to do in this world is hurt this beautiful creature lying next to me.

I move her arm off my chest and creep across the hardwood floor to my things. I dress quickly and toss all my stuff back into my bag.

Aubrey rolls over in bed and I freeze. A few seconds later she snuggles back into her pillow and I know the coast is clear. I grab my boots and tip toe into the hall.

I know I owe her more than sneaking out like we had a cheap one-night stand, but I can't face her. I can't admit that she deserves so much better than me.

I close the door behind me and slip on my boots before riding the elevator to the lobby. Before I leave, I stop and instruct the door man to ring her apartment and let her know that I left her apartment door unlocked. I can't in good faith leave her without knowing she's safe.

I slip the doorman a hundred dollar bill and slap on my ball cap before heading out into the rainy night.

****

The calls start around midnight. I assume the doorman woke her up and now she's freaking because she's seen all my shits gone. Kitten dials my phone repeatedly and guilt washes through me as I shut the phone off while I wait to board the plane to Kentucky. Trip and Tyke are already at the place we share there while we're on this break.

I text Trip and tell him I'll be there about two in the morning.

Trip: *What the fuck, dude? Something happen between you and Aubrey?*

Rock My Bed

Riff: *Explain later.*

I type that in and hit send, knowing full well I have no intentions of explaining anything. Trip doesn't need to know all my fucking business.

Three hours later, I'm pulling my rental car up to my house. It's nearly five thousand square foot and plenty big enough for me and the twins to live in. We each have our own wing with separate living rooms and bedrooms, so it's like apartments with a communal kitchen and living area for parties.

Eve, our grandmotherly, live-in housekeeper opens the front door as I shut off the headlights. She's the best cook in the world, but the nosiest old woman I know, and we affectionately call her our housemother. I grab my bag from the passenger seat and head into the house.

"Trip says you was comin' home tonight. Says you're having problems with some girl?" Eve questions in her thick southern accent as I give her a hug hello.

I kiss the top of her gray head. "It's nothing."

"Sounded serious according to Trip. He's done filled me in all about this Aubrey girl when I made supper last night."

I roll my eyes. "Of course he did."

"So tell me, sugar. You think this 'en is the one?"

I sigh and sling my bag over my shoulder. "I think she is, but I'm afraid I'll hurt her in the end, so I left before things get to serious."

Eve frowns, deepening the wrinkles around her mouth. "Baby, you can't let things like that hold you back from true love. If I'd been afraid of love, I would've never had forty long years with my Bernie. God rest his soul."

I know she's trying to make me feel better, but right now all I want to do is sleep. I place my hand on her shoulder and give it a gentle pat. "I'm going to hit the hay, Eve. I'll see you in the morning."

I walk back to my room and glance around. It's just as I left it. My king-sized bed sits in the middle with a gray comforter and matching pillows. All my books and records neatly line the bookcase on the far end of the room by my computer. I don't spend much time in here, so I haven't really personalized it too much. The only picture I have in here is on my nightstand of Hailey and Mom. Up until now, they were the only people that mattered to me other than my bandmates. Aubrey has done a number of fucking with my head and stirring up emotions in me that I don't like facing.

I flop onto my bed and close my eyes and let sleep take me away from everything.

****

Trip kicks the edge of my bed. "Get up, jackass. I'm tired of you mopping around her like a lazy alcoholic. Eve's says she's not going to bring your meals in here anymore, so you better get up and get ready to be fucking social."

I toss a pillow at him and pull the blankets over my head. "Fuck you, dude. Leave me alone."

He yanks my covers off. "You've been locked up in here three days now drinking yourself into oblivion. You need to fix this shit."

"I can't!" Why doesn't he let me be?

"You can! Here." He tosses my cell onto the bed next to me. "Call her."

"No."

He folds his arms. "Do it or I'm dragging your ass into the shower myself and hosing that stink off you."

"God!" I snatch the phone up and search out her number. "You're annoying as fuck."

Trip smirks but doesn't make a move to leave until he hears Aubrey answer.

"Hey," I say. "It's me."

Satisfied with himself, Trip laughs as he shuts my door on his way out and I flip him the finger.

"What happened to you? Did you leave because of what I said in the bar?"

"Yes," I answer honestly. "I'm not ready for that."

She sighs into the phone. "I get that. I really do, but you should've told me that instead of sneaking out in the middle of the night so you didn't have to face me like a coward."

She's right. Leaving like that was the biggest pussy move in the world to pull. If I were man enough, I would've stayed and told her how I felt instead of doing what I did.

"You're right and I'm sorry for that. You deserve better. Actually you deserve better than me period. That's why I left."

"When you say shit like that it's crazy. I hate when you talk down about yourself like this. Your parents fucked you up. You are capable of love, Zach. You have to open up and let me in. You can't keep blaming yourself for your mom and sister's death."

"They have nothing to do with the way I feel about you," I growl. "I'm no good for you."

"Don't say that," she cries.

"I'm not, Aubrey. I always ruin everything and hurt the people I love most. If I let myself love you, I'll let you down. I know it, and that will fucking kill me. I'm barely holding on to a string as it is. I can't take one more person that I love hating me. I don't think I'll make it."

"That'll never happen."

I rub my forehead. She's not going to give up unless I make her. "It already has."

"What do you mean?" she questions.

"I've moved on, okay. I found a couple chicks last night and brought them back to my place so I can forget about you and how you fucked with my head."

She's quiet for a moment and then I hear her sniff on the other line. I pull the phone away from my mouth and stare up at the ceiling cursing myself for being an evil bastard and making her cry.

"So, like I said. I'm no good. It's best we split now before I actually feel something for you. We're no good for each other."

"Okay," she answers with a shaky voice before she hangs up on me. I throw my cell against the wall, watching it shatter into a million tiny pieces, and hating every inch of myself.

AUBREY

The last few days I've thrown myself into my work. With Lanie gone I find myself working and sleeping with not much else in between.

I have nothing else here in the city. Not even my long-distance rocker any more. I should've listened to my head instead of following my dumbass heart and falling in love with a man I knew was trouble right from the start.

The phone on my desk rings and I glance down to see Isaac's name. "Yes, sir?"

"Do you have lunch plans?" he asks.

"No. Why?"

"I want to take you to lunch. We'll leave at noon. I have a few things to discuss with you."

"Okay, fine. I'll be ready." It's not uncommon for us to eat lunch together to work on a project that needs out right away, but it is kind of odd that he wants to take me out.

Nearly the second we hang up my cell in the desk drawer rings. I really need to remember to start silencing this stupid thing while I'm at work. "Hello?"

"Hey, girl!" Lanie says. "How are you?"

I sigh. "I've been better, but you sound downright chipper."

"Aw, Sweetie. What's wrong?" she asks concern thick in her voice.

"Riff's done with me." A tear falls down my cheek and I quickly wipe it away so my coworkers don't see it. It's harder than I thought to admit that out loud.

"What? I've seen the way he is with you. I find it hard to believe he can move on so quickly."

I sniff. "He told me he brought two girls home last night so he can move on."

She lets a heavy breath waft into the phone. "Why would he do that?"

Rock My Bed

"Because I told him I loved him and he wasn't ready to be that serious with me."

"So he goes and fucks two random groupies?" Lanie shrieks. "I don't believe it."

"Believe it. He told me so himself." I pause and take a deep breath. "We're over."

Lanie sighs. "That's too bad, because you two still have to walk down the aisle together in my wedding."

My eyes widen. "You and Noel are getting married?"

She giggles. "We are, and sooner rather than later. I'm flying you down this weekend for a dress fitting."

"Wow. In four days? That's soon. So when is this wedding?"

"In the weekend after this one."

"What's the rush?"

"No rush. We want to do this. It's the right thing for us, you know."

I smile, completely happy that my best friend is finally marrying the man she's loved for so long. "Where's the wedding going to be?"

"Here at Mom's house—out on the dock."

"Awww. That's so romantic. It's almost like bringing your love full circle."

"It totally is," she answers and I can hear the smile in her voice.

We talk a little while longer about wedding plans and my flight arrangements for the weekend before Isaac pops out of his office. I glance down at the clock. It's time for lunch already.

"I have to go. I'll see you Friday night," I say into the phone.

"See you soon. And Aubrey, don't worry about Riff. He'll come around."

"Okay," is all I can say because while I understand love is a new thing for him and something that probably scares the shit out of him, I don't think I can forget that he slept with other women so soon after being with me. The best thing to do is forget about him like he has me.

I grab my purse and follow Isaac into the elevator.

He presses the lobby button and glances at my face. "You okay?"

"I'm fine," I answer with a smile.

Isaac steps toward me and tentatively touches my cheek. "Is it him that you're shedding tears for? If it is, you shouldn't. He doesn't deserve you."

Even though I know it's wrong, I lean into his palm and close my eyes. It's nice to have comfort from someone.

He cradles my head in his hands. "I would never wrong

you. Ever."

I open my eyes and stare into his clear blue eyes. There's sympathy and caring in them, which is something in my current state I desperately want. I grab the back of his head and bring his lips down to mine trying to block out the pain Zach left in his wake.

Isaac freezes at first and then starts moving his lips with mine while we ride the elevator down. He gives me one final peck and then pulls back. "I've been waiting on that for a long time. You'll be happy with me, Aubrey. I swear it."

I smile. I don't exactly feel the same way, but maybe eventually I will.

****

The plane touches down in Houston and I quickly make my way through the airport looking for Lanie in baggage claim as we planned. I stop dead in my tracks when my gaze lands on Zach holding a small sign that reads "Kitten."

I roll my eyes and grab my bag off the carousel before I approach him. "What are you doing here?"

He smiles. "No hello? You mean, you aren't happy to see me?"

I shake my head. "Are you really that dense? Where's Lanie?"

He shrugs his broad shoulders. "She was busy."

"Of course she was," I mumble. Lanie always wants to

fix things or play matchmaker, which is the exact reason I didn't tell her about my very first kiss with Zach in the first place.

He grabs the suitcase out of my hand. "Let me carry that."

I jerk it away. "I've got it. I don't need your help."

Zach narrows his eyes and takes the bag out of my hand with force. "Can't we be friends at least?"

I yank back, refusing to let go. "No we can't. There's no such thing as *just* friends between us Zach and I refuse to be another slut you can toss away after you're done."

He opens his mouth to say something but quickly shuts it and shakes his head. "You're right. Maybe it's best we not even talk."

I stumble back a bit after he releases the handle of my luggage and gives me full control. "Fine by me."

He turns and calls over his shoulder, "Come on, then. Our new bodyguard, Kyle, is waiting in the loading area."

Without any more words I follow him outside to the black Escalade. He loads my bag into the back and I hop into the back seat and slide over, leaving the door open. Zach comes by and shuts my door with a little more force than necessary before taking the passenger seat next to Kyle.

I bite my lip. Now, I'm the one who is getting the cold shoulder? I didn't do a damn thing to him. What gives him the right to treat me this way?

The entire trip to Lanie's family home, Zach and Kyle talk amongst themselves up front, completely ignoring me, which is exactly what I asked for. So why do I feel this crushing weight sitting on my chest?

This is going to be a long weekend if this is how it's going to be.

Lanie scrambles out the door the moment we pull in and jumps into the SUV. Her slender arms wrap me into a hug as she tackles me into the seat. "Easy, there!"

She pulls away and flicks her gaze towards Zach. "Why are you back here by yourself?"

I frown. "I think it's better this way."

Zach snorts and gets out, slamming the door behind him.

She shoves my hair over my shoulders and shakes her head. "You two are some of the most stubborn people I've ever met."

After a long day of getting fitted for my bridesmaid dress, the entire group loads up to head to a local club for some drinks. Who knew so much went into planning a fifteen minute ceremony. We need to blow off a little steam and relax.

The club is packed. Bodies gyrate on the dance floor beneath spinning lights while the hypnotic beats the most recent top forty hits assaults my ears.

Trip elbows Tyke as a group of girls walk by and smile at them. They instantly take off after the girls in short skirts as Lanie and I slide into a round booth with Noel and Zach.

A waitress in a tank top and booty shorts comes to the table to get our drink orders. She flips her blond hair over her shoulder and doesn't try to hide the fuck-me eyes she's shooting at Zach. We all order alcohol of some type with the exception of Lanie who orders a water.

I furrow my brow at her the moment the waitress leaves. "You okay?"

She nods and smiles. "Never better."

I eye her suspiciously as I turn my attention back over to the twins out on the dance floor with a few women. She never turns down a drink, especially at a bar. As my thoughts wonder to the possibility that she may be pregnant, Trip makes me giggle as he lifts a girls skirt and smacks her ass in front of every person in the club. "He's crazy."

Noel grins. "He's loving all the attention since Riff and I are off the market."

I glance over to Riff, curious why Noel would say that? Isn't he back to banging every chick in sight?

Riff catches my stare and quickly leans forward, making a show of grabbing the girl standing next to him wearing a tube top and tugging her into his lap. "Speak for yourself, buddy. I'm a free man. You're the one about to be strapped to the old ball and chain."

Rock My Bed

My lips pull into a tight line and I fight back tears as Zach makes a show of whispering into the girl's ear. I understand he wants to move on, but he doesn't have to shove it down my throat. If that's how it's going to be, I'll play dirty right back. I'm tired of assholes walking all over me. I want to show him I can move on, too.

I flip my hair and turn towards Lanie and say loud enough for everyone to head, "I forgot to tell you I'm seeing someone and he's going to be my date at your wedding."

Her green eyes widen and her lips form the letter 'O.' "Who?"

"Yeah, who?" Zach adds in from the other side of me, but I can't see his face.

I lean back so I can catch his reaction this time. "Isaac. You remember him…*Riff*. You met him at the pizza place."

I know calling him by his stage name got his attention as well as the shocking news that I'm dating one man I know he loathes because his eyebrows instantly shoot up. "Your douchebag boss?"

I narrow my eyes at him. "Don't call him that. He's sweet."

"How many times have you been out with him?" I fight the urge to tell him everyday since the day we ended things to piss him off. In reality it's only been a three times, but I'm not going to tell him that.

I glare at him. "That's none of your business."

"The hell it's not!"

I shake my head. "I think it's pretty clear that we're even less than friends now, so I don't have to tell you a damn thing. Lanie, let's dance. Excuse us, Noel."

Noel howls with laughter as he slides around and lets us out. "I'm really starting to like this girl. She's not afraid to dish it right back to him," he tells Lanie before he kisses her lips.

Lanie melts into him, and before she changes her mind about dancing, I pull her into crowd. Amongst the writhing bodies, we shake our hips to the beat of the music. I try to push the thoughts of Riff with other women out of my mind and try to focus on the beat of the music.

"If you're trying to push his buttons and make him jealous, I think it's working," Lanie says after she glances at the table where Noel and Zach are.

I shrug. "That wasn't my plan when I came here, but if he's going to shove the fact that he's out with other women in my face then I'm going to dish it right back at him."

She nods. "Good plan. He's been miserable, you know. I think this show is for your benefit. Trip told me that Riff's been holed up in his room depressed since he came back from New York. I don't think he's been with other women."

"He has. He told me so." I shake my head. "I don't know why he's trying to punish me?"

Lanie grabs my arms. "I don't think he knows what the

hell he's doing. He's fighting his feelings for you tooth and nail for some reason. I know he still cares about you. Noel says he's never acted this way with any other woman. You've done something that's grabbed his attention."

I run my hand through my hair, frustrated at the entire situation. If he cares for me why run away? Why sleep with other women? It exhausts me even trying to figure it out. I glance back at the table and the girl is gone, but Zach watches me intently as he presses his bottle to his lips and throws back the last of his beer. His hungry eyes rake over me, but I refuse to let me use me for sex. I'm done with those kinds of random relationships. I'm ready for something real.

Chapter 21

RIFF

The rest of the weekend passes by quickly. Aubrey and I never really talked. I didn't help the situation out much when I flirted with every single girl I could in front of her. It's a childish game to play, but I want her to be okay with moving on even if it kills me inside. I need her to hate me.

"I like this one." Noel points to the plain black tux on the mannequin.

The middle-aged saleswoman nods and the black bun on the back of her head bounces. "Excellent choice, Mr. Falcon. It's very traditional."

"I like it, too," Lanie agrees.

"Okay, then. Mr. Falcon let's do you first. Follow me back to the dressing area so we can get you sized up. Riff, honey, you'll be next."

I smile as they leave the room, leaving Lanie and me alone in the front of the store. I finger a few shirts and try to pretend I don't feel a hole boring into me from her heated stare. I know she's pissed about how I treated her friend this weekend. I offered to go with her to the airport this morning, but both Aubrey and Lanie told me no in unison.

"You're an idiot, you know," she says to me.

I know exactly what she's referring to, but pretend I'm clueless. "Why's that?"

She walks over and stands next to me, trying to gain my full attention. "Because you're going to drive her right into that guys arms. If you aren't careful, you really are going to lose her."

I peer down at her. "What makes you think I want her?"

She laughs. "Come on. We all know it. It's you that can't admit your own feelings about her."

I sigh and go back to looking at shirts. "You're her best friend. Aren't you supposed to protect her from assholes like me?"

She shakes her head. "Not when the asshole is in love with her."

"I don't want to hurt her," I whisper.

Lanie places her small hand on top of mine that's resting on the rack. "Then stop what you're doing, because I know she loves you, too. If you keep fighting it, both of you are going to end up miserable and hating each other."

I swallow hard. It's not my intention to ever hurt her but that's exactly what I'm doing by trying to push her away. It kills me to know I'm hurting her.

Noel comes out wearing the tux he picked out and runs his hand through his thick, dark hair. "What do you think?

Lanie squeals the moment she sees him and rushes into his arms. "You look hot, baby."

I turn away as their make-out session commences.

My thoughts drift to my time with Kitten and how happy I felt when I was with her. She's the best thing that's ever happened to me and Lanie's right. I'm an idiot for throwing it away. I need to make this right with her. I still want her, but I'm afraid she'll tell me to take a flying leap because I lied to her about already sleeping with other people. I don't care if she's slept with that fucking Ken doll of a boss of hers. It doesn't matter. If she did, I know she probably only did it because of the lie I told her.

AUBREY

I can't believe this is the weekend my best friend gets married. It feels surreal to me. I can only imagine what it's like for her to finally marry the man she's loved for so long.

The minute my plane lands I turn on my cell phone and a text from Isaac pops up on the screen.

Isaac: *My flight lands tomorrow at ten in the morning.*

Thank you for asking me to be your date to the wedding.

I smile. He's so well mannered and the complete opposite of Zach.

I lay my head back against the seat. After last weekend, I don't look forward to seeing him again. It's hard enough knowing we have to walk down the aisle without killing each other at the wedding. Why did Noel have to pick him as the best man?

Aubrey: *See you then.*

Coming down the escalator to baggage claim, I immediately spot Zach standing with his little sign waiting for me again.

Great. This is going to be another fun weekend.

Why am I not surprised to see him? I'm beginning to think he's getting some sick thrill by torturing me. And why would Lanie allow it? I know she's busy, but couldn't she send one of the twins instead?

Zach tugs his ball cap low on his forehead and a places a pair of dark sunglasses over the bill. I hate the fact that even though I'm pissed at him for hurting me, I still think he looks good in his jeans and form-fitting black t-shirt.

Zach grabs my bag from my hand and says, "It's good to see you."

I stare at him with narrowed eyes. "Don't!" I snap at him. "After last weekend I'm over you."

A pained look overtakes his face as I turn on my heel to head for the exit.

I only make it one step before he grabs my wrist and stops me in my tracks. "Look, I was a jackass last weekend. You don't deserve to be treated that way. I'm sorry."

His eyes seem sincere, but his apology doesn't make me feel any better or make me forget what he's done. "I will accept your apology so we can get through this weekend, but it still doesn't change anything between us. You sleep with other women and shove it in my face to hurt me on purpose."

He takes his sunglasses off and rests them over top of his hat and leans into my face. "So, what if I have? You're fucking your boss! Don't you think that hurts me?"

I try to yank my arm free, because all I want to do is smack his face. The harder I yank the tighter his grip gets. "Let go of me!"

Zach shakes his head. "What is this? You get to hate me all you want, but when I mention you're doing the exact same thing you get pissed!"

"It's not the same thing," I huff, knowing that simple kisses are as far as I've been with Isaac.

He pulls me into him and forces me to look him in the eye. "Are you fucking him?"

I want to hurt him, like he hurt me so I refuse to give him a straight answer. "That's none of your business."

"It is my business! Now tell me!" One last jerk and my arm's free. I rub my wrist as I stay silent and gaze up at his face. His eyes never leave mine. It's almost as if he's studying me while his jaw works under his skin, trying to get the truth out of me. "Are you sleeping with him?"

I fold my arms. There's no way I'm going to make this easy on him. "You left me, remember! Why aren't you happy about this? It's what you wanted."

He drops my bag and grabs me by the shoulders. "Because you're mine! Can't you see that? I still want you and I know you want me too."

I gasp and my mouth drops open. Why would he say this to me now? Is it because I'm dating Isaac and he can't have me now? Well, too bad. I'm not going to let him play around with my heart anymore. "You told me to move on, so that's what I did. Get over it!"

He shakes his head. "I don't believe you! You still want me. I can see it in your eyes. People don't just walk away from a connection like the one we have. I'm going to make you admit that to yourself by the end of this weekend."

Before I have a chance to reply, he crushes his lips to mine. I melt into him, forgetting what we were even fighting about to begin with as I focus on is him. Both legs beneath me wobble and I wrap my arms around his neck and hold him close.

Damn my stupid body for reacting to him like this.

He pulls back and smirks. "See. Don't forget I know what turns you on and how you like it a little rough. You're going to want me to do more than kiss you. I promise you that."

My lips tingle as he bends down and picks up the bag and starts toward the exit. What the hell just happened here? I'm never going to figure this man out.

****

Sitting at the Mexican restaurant next to Zach reminds me of the first night we spent together when I met up with them in Dallas. The waiter drops off some chips and salsa at the table while a Spanish song plays overhead.

I shake my head as I my mind drifts back to how I felt him up that first night we were together. It was at the table just like this while I sat across from my best friend in nearly the same circumstance.

My cell buzzes and I look at the screen.

Riff: *Feel like being naughty again during dinner?*

My head whips in his direction and Zach grins and winks at me. Damn it. How did you know exactly what I was thinking? Well, I got news for him—fat chance of that happening again.

Aubrey: *You're an asshole.*

He chuckles as he reads my text.

Riff: *Maybe so, but I'm one that you still have feelings for.*

I shake my head.

Riff: *Yes you do. You know you miss me being inside you. Admit it so we can stop playing these stupid games and be together.*

I squirm in my seat as I read his words. He knows talking dirty to me gets to me. He's seen how I react to it when we had sex, but I can't let it affect me now. I refuse to let him have any sort of power over me.

I huff and toss my phone back into my purse unwilling to play along with his game. My heart is not a plaything. I don't want it crushed yet again by him when he decides he doesn't want it anymore. I'm tired of being treated like that. I want a man that really wants me and means it. I'm not settling for anything less than that anymore.

Chapter 22

AUBREY

I bite my thumbnail as I wait for Isaac to get off the plane. Images of how awkward this weekend is going to be with Riff and Isaac in the same room flip through my head. I hope Riff keeps his cool and doesn't do something crazy like I know he's capable of when he gets angry. Poor Isaac wouldn't stand a chance against his rage.

Isaac comes into view carrying a small, black bag and a suit bag in the same hand. He's dressed casually in khakis and a blue polo shirt with his hair styled in its traditional fashion. He pushes his black-framed glasses up his nose and gives me a small wave.

He wraps his free arm around my shoulders and pulls me into him. "I've missed you."

I squeeze him back and pat his back. "It's good to see you. Did you have a good flight?"

"It was fine," he answers as I take him by the hand and lead him towards the exit.

Things between us still feel forced and unnatural. It

takes a lot of work to keep a conversation rolling between us, but I'm not ready to give up on making this relationship work.

We walk to the short term parking section of the lot and he follows me to Lanie's car.

"A rental?" he questions.

I unlock the doors. "It's Lanie's. She let me borrow it to come pick you up."

"Ah," is all he replies.

We ride in silence on the highway. Like I said, conversation doesn't come easy between us, which is odd because we work together. There should be a million things to talk about between us.

Tired of the silence, I crank up the radio. The beat of a pop tune plays through the speakers filling the cab with a little noise as we drive to Lanie's house.

"What exactly are the plans for the night?" Isaac asks as he turns the radio back down.

"We're decorating the dock and tent for the wedding tomorrow. Then we have a rehearsal dinner at some Italian place."

He nods. "It's odd to have a wedding on a Sunday, don't you think?"

I shrug. "Not really. What's it matter what day they get married on?"

"It doesn't, I guess. I would think that most people would stick with a traditional Saturday wedding."

I twist my lips as I evaluate his tone that seems a little snippy and judgmental. "Lanie and Noel are anything but traditional, so why should their wedding be?"

"Touche," he replies.

Every inch of the driveway is full of delivery people when I pull in, forcing me into the side yard. Through the windshield I watch Zach direct a man with a bunch of flowers down towards the dock where the actual ceremony will take place. He glances over at the car and catches me staring at him and grins. It's not just any grin either. It's the one where he practically devours me with his eyes and makes things a little uncomfortable considering I'm dating another man.

I open the door and hop out of the car. He's not going to give up even though Isaac is here. He really does have some nerve.

Isaac steps out of the car and opens the back door to retrieve his things. "It's beautiful out here. Where did you say we are again?"

"Cedar Creek Lake. Lanie grew up here. Noel's family actually lives right next door, so we are all staying here for the night."

He rests his hands on the top of the car and stares at me. "Are you sure everyone's okay with me staying here?" His eyes flick in Zach's direction. "No one's pissed are they?"

I shake my head, knowing full well that Zach doesn't like him being here, but Isaac doesn't need to know that. "You're fine."

On our way into the house, Zach steps directly in our path. "What's up lovebirds? Did you have a good flight, Ken—" I cut him with a stare and he quickly corrects himself. "Isaac."

I roll my eyes and try to sidestep him. "Don't pay any attention to him," I tell Isaac as I grab his arm.

"Oh, come on. Don't be that way. I'm trying to be nice," Zach says as he moves out of my way.

"You're an asshole," I call over my shoulder as I lead Isaac into the house.

Once we're out of earshot, Isaac says, "Are you sure it's over between the two of you?"

I shake my head. "So over. He's the biggest man-whore in the band. I can never be with someone like him long term."

He wraps his arm around my shoulders and pulls me into his side. "Good because I don't want to get my heart crushed if you haven't truly moved on."

I tense at his words. That's a feeling I know all too well and I hate the idea of having someone's heart teetering in my own hands. I don't want to hurt him.

****

The Italian restaurant Lanie picked for her rehearsal dinner is loud with the hustle and bustle of the busy wait staff working their way around keeping dinner guests happy. The white table linens and candles add an elegant touch to the room. Noel rented out the entire restaurant so the band could celebrate in private.

Trip sulks in his chair, bummed by the prospect of not having any random chicks around until Noel's older cousin in her forties starts giving him the old fuck-eye.

"Dude, she so wants me. I'm going to Cougar land tonight," Trip tells Zach who is sitting between us. "That chick wants my nuts. Look at how she licks her lips when I look over."

Riff and I both glance over at the next table and watch the busty, bleach-blond do exactly what Trip said the moment he looks over. Zach and I both laugh at the same time.

"Did you see that!" Trip exclaims. "I'm hitting that tonight!"

"Have fun with that, bro," Zach says.

"Maybe she has a daughter or something and we can get them to take us back to their place," Trip says.

Zach shakes his head. "Better rope Tyke into your plans, because I don't get down like that anymore." His gaze shifts to me. "I've got something much better in mind."

I swallow hard and try to calm my nerves under his heated stare.

"I don't think I was supposed to bring this present to the

rehearsal dinner," Isaac says breaking my attention away from Zach's intense stare. Isaac stuffs the box he carried in with him between his feet.

"I'm being nosey, but what did you get them?" I ask.

"A crystal vase. I know it's not much and they probably don't need anything, but I figured it's the thought, right?"

I lean over and kiss his lips, trying to ignore the fact that Zach's right beside me. "It's very sweet."

"Rolls," Riff says while practically shoving the breadbasket in my face.

I shove it away with my hand. "I'm fine. Thanks."

He sits the basket back on the table. "I wanted to make sure you didn't miss out since you seemed pretty busy and all."

I fight the overwhelming urge to reach over and smack him in the face and then scream, "What do you want from me?"

When I can't take looking at Zach a second longer, I slide my chair back and stand without warning.

Isaac peers up at me concerned. "You all right?"

"I'm fine. Just need to use the ladies' room."

I storm off in the direction of the restroom and shove the door open. I throw my purse down on the counter and lean against it as I fight back the crazy, mixed-up emotions I feel inside. One minute he likes me...the next he doesn't. His psycho mood swings are giving me whiplash.

I stare at myself in the mirror, wondering what happened to the levelheaded girl I was a short time ago. Feeling this way is the very thing I wanted to protect myself from, and yet here I stand, miserable that the man I really want didn't want me back. When I offered him my heart, he crushed it in the palm of his hand like it meant nothing to him. I refuse to let him do it to me again.

I sigh. Why couldn't he tell me he loved me back when I told him in the bar? Why now when I'm trying to move on and give Isaac a chance. He's making me feel like the villain in this situation.

The lock on the door clicks behind me and I see Zach step into view through the mirror. "What are you doing in here? You aren't done torturing me yet?"

He shoves his hands into his jean pockets and nods. "I deserve that. I'm sorry for how I've been acting. It's childish and I really don't have a good excuse other than seeing you with him is driving me bat shit crazy."

I turn to face him. "How do you think I felt when you said you were with those two women and then pulled the girl into your lap at the bar? Do you think this is easy for me? I'm trying to move on like you told me to do, but I can't with you always making things so difficult for me!"

He takes a couple steps and wraps his fingers around my upper arms. "I'm sorry, all right. I'd take it all back if I could. I don't mean to hurt you, Kitten. I fucking love you and I don't know how to handle it."

Shock registers on his face as he realizes what he's said to me. He rubs his face and takes a deep breath before looking me square in the eye. "I love you."

"You love me?" I whisper. "Why did you wait until now to tell me?"

He bites his lower lip. "I thought I was doing you a favor by pushing you away. As much as I hate to admit it, a guy like Isaac would be a much better choice than a piece of shit like me. I wish I could give you every part of me, but I'm so fucking broken that I'm not sure where to start."

I place my hand over his heart. "Start by giving me this. All I ever ask is that you love me back just as much as I love you."

"What if I can't? I don't know how to love someone."

Tears fill my eyes and when I blink the warm, salty liquid flows down my cheeks. "You can. You already have. You love your mom and Hailey. I see it every time you talk about them, what they meant to you. I want you to let me in. I love being with you. I love the way you make me feel. I do want to be with you, but I'm afraid you'll crush my heart."

"I swear I'll never hurt you again. I'll spend the rest of my life proving how much I love you if you let me." He cups my cheeks in his hands. "I love you, Aubrey. I think I have from the moment you first turned me down."

I smile at him and wrap my arms around him. It's crazy and us together makes absolutely zero sense, but I can't fight the feelings I have for him. "I love you, too."

I close my eyes and focus on how good he makes me feel. It would absolutely crush me at this point if this doesn't work out again, but I can't worry about that, because right now I know he's being sincere.

He kisses me like he's never kissed me before. It's like he needs me to breath. He grabs my hips and hoists me up on the counter. "Thank god you picked a dress to wear tonight. This would be a lot harder in if not."

He reaches up my skirt and yanks my underwear down before sliding them the rest of the way off my body. There's no time wasted as he circles my clit with the tip of his finger in a forceful rhythm. I bite my lip and throw my head back as I moan from the sheer pleasure of his touch. I've missed being with him so much.

Within a minute my eyes roll back and my entire body shakes as I come hard against his hand.

I gasp as I come down from the high. All the time we've spent learning each other's bodies comes in handy during a quickie like this.

Zach unzips his pants and shoves them along with his boxers down to his thighs before he grabs the base of his shaft and guides it into me. A long moans flies from his mouth as it pushes his cock all the way in.

"Oh, god," I cry as softly as I can while he plunges into me.

We hold each other's gaze and I chew on my bottom lip. Zach leans over and nips my ear, grazing his teeth along my skin. "I love you."

"I love you, too," I breathe.

He grips my hips harder as he drives into me desperate to find his release. Small beads of sweat form on his brow as he works his way deeper inside me. I can't peel my eyes away from his face as he rocks into me again and again in a steady rhythm.

Long strands of my ponytail come loose and cascade around my shoulders. I can only imagine what a mess my hair must be after this.

He wraps his arms around me and I arch my back against his hands. To make him come faster I clench my muscles around his cock and hold them as tight as I can.

"Fuck, Kitten."

Both of his hands find their way into my hair after he pulls the elastic band from it, allowing it to fall around my shoulders. I wrap my fingers around the edge of the counter and brace myself as he picks up speed.

"You're so fucking sexy," he says against my lips. "Shit."

His entire body tenses under my touch. I squeeze my legs around him as he lets out a string of curses as he releases inside me, groaning so loud I'm sure the entire wedding party heard us.

He kisses my face all over. "You're fucking amazing, Aubrey. Every time keeps getting better. I promise I'll love you until the day I die."

I kiss his lips and rest my forehead against his. "What am I going to do about Isaac?"

He rubs my back. "Tell him you're with me and he needs to go home."

I shake my head. "I can't be rude to him. He's my boss I still have to deal with him."

He kisses my neck. "Fuck that job. I want you to stay with me all the time anyway."

"I didn't work hard for my degree to flush my first job opportunity down the damn toilet. Can we play it cool for this weekend and I'll let him down gently Monday."

He sighs. "We can do that, but if I see his lips touch you, I'll rip them off his face."

"You're impossible," I say.

After a few last kisses I slip on my panties and try to fix my disheveled hair. We leave the bathroom together while still adjusting our clothes and I freeze in my tracks. Isaac waits down the hall from the bathroom with the gift he had at the table in his hands, waiting for us to come out. The moment our eyes connect, he starts shaking his head and turns on his heel.

Instantly, I feel like total shit because I know what it's like to want someone who doesn't fully want you back. I always swore I would never be that person, yet here I am doing the exact thing I hate.

"Isaac?" I call his name as he blasts through the door to the parking lot.

He marches out towards the car, but doesn't stop as I keep calling his name. When he reaches Lanie's car he jerks on the locked door handle a few times before yelling, "Fuck," loud enough for the entire state of Texas to hear him.

I touch his arm. "Will you give me a chance to explain?"

He jerks away from my touch. "Jesus. How could you do this to me? Why did you ask me to come down here if you still have a thing going with him? I ask you point blank and you told me there was nothing going on."

Tears well in my eyes and my entire body shakes. The look on his face crushes my heart as I realize this game Riff and I played has finally caught up with me and is affecting someone else. I never meant to hurt Isaac and right now the harsh words from his beautiful lips are deserved.

I drop my head, unwilling to face him. I deserve his cruelty, so I don't defend myself.

The wedding gift he'd bought for Noel and Lane slams into the ground at my feet, tearing open. The crystal vases inside the box shatters upon impact and shards of glass litter the parking lot.

"How long Aubrey? How long have you been sleeping Riff behind my back? Did this go on last weekend, too?"

I lift my chin and find Isaac's usually delightful blue eyes dark and narrowed. There's no excuse for me to be crying other then the guilt I feel as the tears glide down my cheeks. "I—I'm sss…orry." My words are a weak stutter, but I suddenly have no control of the panic wrecking havoc on my body.

He shakes his head. "Sorry? You're sorry. That's the best you can do? You lead me on for nearly two weeks and all you offer is a half-assed apology." He throws his hands out. "And that's only because you got caught! What? Were you planning on stringing me along until he got tired of you? Because you know he will. You told me yourself he's the biggest manwhore in the band. What makes you think you'll be any different? That you mean anything to him?"

This is the most angry I've ever seen Isaac and it's hard for me to witness the nicest man I've ever known lose his head right in front of my eyes. The one thing I never wanted to happen did. I've ruined this relationship, but I love Zach. I can't fight my feelings for him.

"I don't know what else I can say," I whisper, still at a loss.

"There's nothing you can say. People at the office were right to gossip about you and call you a fucking whore." His words tear at my heart and I bury my face in my hands.

"That's enough!" Zach's voice cuts across the lot and I suck in a quick breath. "Don't you say another goddamn word to her or so help me…"

Isaac laughs. "So help you what? She's *my* date. I can say what ever the fuck I want to her, so butt out!"

"She is mine," Zach growls as he steps between Isaac and me. "And she's been *mine* long before you ever came into the fucking picture. She's only with you because I couldn't get my shit together. You were a distraction."

Isaac's eyes narrow. "Whatever. You're probably right. She's not worth it anyhow."

Without warning, Zach draws back and blasts Isaac square in the nose with his fist, shattering Isaac's glasses. Isaac grabs his face as blood pours from his nose while shock registers on his face. "Don't you ever talk about her like that again you son-of-a-bitch."

"Not a problem." Isaac's watering eyes flick to mine. "Aubrey, you're fired. Don't bother coming back to the office. I don't ever want to see your face again. I'll have your personal belongings shipped to you."

I nod as the realization I've lost more than my companionship with Isaac hits me hard and tears flood down my face.

Zach watches me cry and he growls, "Shut the fuck up and leave already you fucking Ken doll want-to-be or I'll make sure you never speak another word to her or anyone else ever again."

Isaac shakes his head and throws his hands up in surrender, clearly not wanting to test Zach's threat.

The tension in Zach's drawn fists relaxes as Isaac heeds his warning and walks away. Tears keep falling as I hate myself for being an awful person, but know deep down being with Zach is the right thing to do.

"Don't cry." Zach pulls me into a tight hug, wrapping his strong, tattooed arms around my small waist. "I'm sorry you had to go through that."

I sniff. "Me too, but if that's the price I have to pay to be with you, I'd do it all over again."

"I want you to know, I meant what I said earlier. I love you with every inch of my broken soul. I know it's a mess, but I'm giving you all the pieces, hoping you can make sense of it. I love you, Kitten." He kisses my lips and warmth surrounds my entire body and a sense of security flows through me as we stay wrapped in one another's arms.

Chapter 23

AUBREY

I fluff out Lanie's wedding dress as we stand in her kitchen waiting for the signal it's time for her to walk down the aisle. Her dress is bell shaped, showing off her naturally tiny waist and slim arms. The side of the dress has black designs in the tulle and looks very befitting for a rocker wedding.

This is the most beautiful I've ever seen her. She's practically glowing.

"I wish they'd hurry up. I'm starting to sweat," Lanie complains as she fans herself with her hand to keep the newly applied makeup from melting off.

I lift an eyebrow because I think the temperature is perfectly fine. "It's not hot in here. You're nervous."

She shrugs. "It could be, I guess. I'm thinking it's because my hormones are all out of whack."

What dumb luck. "Oh, damn. Did you start your period? That will so suck for the honeymoon."

She shakes her head and giggles. "I won't be having another one of those for a long time."

My eyes widen as a grins spreads across my face. "You're pregnant? I knew it!"

"Shhhh!" She laughs. "Yes! But no one knows except for our parents and now you."

"Oh, my god!" I wrap my arms around her and squeeze her tight. "I'm so happy for you. I've been having the feeling you were. No wonder you wanted to rush this wedding along."

Lanie steps back and pats her flat stomach. "Who knew I would be the one having a shot-gun wedding."

To say I'm stunned is an understatement, but I'm still ecstatic that everything is finally working out for them. I know she'll be a great mother.

A throat clears behind me and I turn around.

Noel's father and Zach walk into the kitchen together both sporting black tuxedos. Zach is dapper with his hair styled into a short all-black Mohawk to match his outfit. His eyes rake over me and linger on my chest a few seconds too long before we lock eyes.

He lets out a low whistle. "You two look amazing. Lanie, Noel is going to lose his shit when he sees you." He leans in and gives Lanie a peck on the cheek. "I'm really happy for you guys. You're perfect for each other."

Lanie smiles and touches his arm. "Thank you, Riff."

Zach steps back and wraps his arm around my shoulders, tucking me into his side.

Noel's father takes his turn hugging Lanie and whispers into her ear. I think it's sweet of Noel's father to walk Lanie down the aisle since her own father had passed away last year. I know she would give anything to have him here today.

Mr. Falcon pulls back and kisses her other cheek. "You're father would've loved to be here."

A tear leaks from her eye as she quickly grabs a tissue from off the counter and blots her face. "I miss him so much."

"I know you do, kid," he tells her.

Emotions flood me and a lump in my throat builds but I swallow it back to keep her from turning into a complete mess five minutes before she says her vows.

Lanie smiles at Zach and me with tears still in her eyes. "I'm glad you two have finally come to your senses and stopped all this craziness and admitted you have feelings for each other. It's good to see that you're finally together."

I laugh and try to lighten her mood. "You're just happy we're not going to make your wedding all tense."

"That, too."

Zach clears his throat again. "They sent us in here because they're ready to start."

Lanie raises her eyebrows and smiles so wide I can nearly see all of her teeth. "Let's do this."

"Shall we?" Zach pokes his elbow out towards me.

I tuck my arm through his and stare down at my black bridesmaid dress as I make sure everything is in order before he opens the door and leads us through. The humid evening air of the Texas summer blasts into me as we walk down the hill to the dock and I'm glad I chose an up-do for this event. The sun set in the horizon is the perfect backdrop to make the ceremony magically. Candles flicker all around, providing light while accentuating romance. The sound of Noel's voice signing a pre-recorded acoustic version *Faithfully* covers the landscape as it plays through the surrounding speakers.

Nearly one hundred wedding guests line the flower covered path at the bottom of the hill. The dock was too narrow for all the guests to sit on, so the wedding planner set up most of the white folding chairs on the grass just before the entrance to the dock.

Trip and Tyke grin at me from the dock entrance, manning their positions as ushers to make sure we don't trip and bust our faces walking over the threshold. Tyke's blond hair is styled back off his face while Trips shaggy, black hair falls into his, making his green eyes really stand out. It's the first time I've ever seen Trip without something covering the top of his head. If I didn't know better, I would think there's a real gentleman inside that tux.

White and red roses line every inch of the wood railing all the way to the end of the dock. A small landing sits at the end, allowing enough chairs for Lanie's and Noel's immediate family an intimate seat at the union. A beautiful floral archway filled with more roses creates a backdrop for the ceremony with Noel in his traditional black tux standing underneath it. The pastor stands next to Noel with a Bible in his hand ready to officiate the ceremony.

Zach places his free hand on top of my hand that's looped through his arm while we walk slowly down the dock. "I can't wait to do this with you someday."

I swallow hard and my eyes grow wide. Something so romantic coming from him takes me back.

Zach chuckles as he takes in my shocked expression. "I mean, way in the future, of course."

A light breeze scoots across the lake and blows my dress around my feet as I peer up at him and smile.

The thought of being with him forever causes my heart to pause for a split second. While we're nowhere near being ready to make such a huge leap together, it's nice to know he's taking our relationship seriously this round.

At the end of the dock, we part ways, and Zach claps Noel on the shoulder as he stands next to him.

I settle into my spot, and the wedding march begins to play. Everyone stands and turns around, directing their line of sight to the top of the hill.

Lanie makes her way down the path in her breathtaking gown, clutching Mr. Falcon's arm tight. The wedding guests all gasp and let out a collective "aww," as she comes further into sight. Her mom sits a couple feet away from me in a wheelchair with her injured leg in a cast straining her neck to get a better look. She blots her eyes and lets out a quiet sob as she takes in how beautiful her little girl looks.

Noel's face lights up as he refolds his hands in front of him while he anxiously waits for Lanie to join him by his side. I smile, knowing he's perfect for her.

Riff catches my eye and mouths, "I love you," to me.

The caring part of him is what pulled me in. I knew it was in there, and it's my job as the woman in his life to help him explore it. I grin at the thought of how special those tender words are coming from him before mouthing it back.

When Lanie makes it to the end of the aisle, Mr. Falcon gently unfolds her hand from around his forearm and guides her hand into the crook of Noel's arm.

Noel's gaze never leaves Lanie's face. It's in that moment I truly see how much love he has for her. While their relationship has had a rocky path to get to this happy point, kind of like Zach and me. Things for them will work out because they love each other, and as they say, love conquers all.

Lanie hands me her bouquet and joins hands with Noel.

"Dearly beloved. We are gathered here together in the presence of family, friends and loved ones to unite Noel Falcon and Lanie Vance in holy matrimony…"The pastor proceeds with the ceremony while my best friend stares into the eyes of the man she loves.

A tear wells up in my eye and before I know it, I'm batting them away like crazy. I'm happy for her, but it also saddens me to know that our friendship will now change. We're growing up and she and Noel are starting a family of their own.

Noel grins as he answers, "I do."

The same vows are directed to Lanie and she half laughs while crying as she answers, "I do."

The pastor points his gaze at Zach. "The rings?"

Zach fishes them from the inside pocket of his tux and places them in the pastor's outstretched hand.

The rings are held up for the crowd to see as he says, "The rings you chose are made of one of the strongest, and most precious minerals our earth has to offer. These rings will withstand the test of time and symbolize the love you two have for one another. Noel will you take this ring and place it on Lanie's left hand and repeat after me."

Noel slips the ring on Lanie's dainty ring finger and says, "With this ring, I thee wed all my hearts affection, all that I am, all that I ever shall be, and everything that's apart of me, I give to you now, my wife."

Lanie and I both sniffle along with most of the crowd as Noel gets a little choked up at the end as his emotions flood him.

"Lanie, repeat after me..." the pastor has her repeat the same vows as she places a silver band on Noel's left hand. Her fingers shake a bit as she shoves it the rest of the way on his finger.

"Now, I want you two to look deep into each other's

eyes and think back to that moment when you knew this person was the one you wanted to spend the rest of your life with…" At those words spoken by the pastor, I stare at Zach who is watching me intently.

It's hard for me to pinpoint the exact moment I knew he was the one, because I felt a connection with him almost immediately. When I saw all the layers under his macho exterior that's when he really started tugging at my heart. His love is intense and passionate, and I'm ready to receive every bit of it that he's willing to offer me.

"You have stepped into a deeper commitment today, and I charge you to keep true to the vows you've made to one another today. Noel, your bride commits herself into your hands for safekeeping, placing herself into your protection for the remainder of her life. So from this day forward let no word or deed of action cloud her with tears. If there are tears, may they only be of joy."

Noel smiles down at Lanie and wipes his eye as the pastor recites a similar speech to her. "Lanie, you have won this man's heart with your grace, beauty and intelligence. May you comfort him in times of need and remain true. And to the both of you…always remember you're holding your very best friend by the hand right now. Always be quick to forgive one another and cherish the love you have for one another. If you both agree to all of these things, please say I do." Lanie and Noel both answer at the same time before he continues, "By the power vested in me by the great state of Texas, I now pronounce you man and wife. Noel, you may kiss your bride."

Rock My Bed

Cheers erupt all around as Noel leans in and lifts Lanie's veil before wrapping his arms around her waist and kissing her lips.

Noel pulls back and gives her one last peck before she smiles at him and then turns to me for her flowers.

They face the crowd and the pastor says, "May I present to you for the very first time, Mr. and Mrs. Noel Falcon."

Another round of applause and hoots explode at the end of the dock as I watch my best friend walk down the aisle to become one with the love of her life.

Zach approaches me and I hook my arm through his. His grin as we follow Noel and Lanie down the aisle is as big a mine. It's funny how our conceptions about a person can be totally off base. Never in a million years did I think a crude proposition from a rock star would lead me to love. He completely, and unexpectedly, stole my heart, and I was powerless to stop it.

I broke the last rule I put into place for our one-night stand, not to fall in love. It completely flew out the window the moment he opened up to me and showed me a side of him I never expected, but that's okay. Life sometimes works out in ways that's not expected.

The one thing I really thought I wanted was my job, but when forced to pick between my heart and my career, it was no contest. Nothing matters but being with Zach and I know somehow, some way, things will work out as long as we believe in on another and our love. Zach is my forever.

RIFF

I have to hand it to Noel. This reception by the lake is stunning. The white tent under the stars is perfect for their union. The stiffly dressed wait staff scurries about handing out drinks and appetizers while the live band keeps the party jumping.

I'm not one that gets caught up in wedding sappiness usually, but knowing what Noel and Lanie have been through to make it to this moment gets to me. It reminds me that no real love comes easy and I'm going to have to work at this everyday with Aubrey to make this love last forever.

I spin Kitten in my arms as we press close together during a slow dance. "Having fun?"

She grins up and me and trails her fingers at the nape of my neck. "A great time. I'm glad I'm here with you."

I squeeze her tighter against my chest. "There's no one else I'd rather be with."

She raises her eyebrow. "Not even the two women you were with after me."

I sigh. It's time to come clean with that lie. "I was never with anyone else."

There's a puzzled look on her face. "You weren't? So, you lied to me?"

I nod as we continue dancing. "I was trying to get you to see I was no good. I said it to make you angry with me, so you'd move on before I got the chance to hurt you."

She bites her bottom lip. "I never slept with Isaac, either. I only wanted you to think that because I was hurt." She pauses for a moment. "I understand where all that angst is coming from. What happened to your family was a terrible tragedy, but you can't let that rule your life. You deserve to be happy."

"I'm trying to get there. When I found you, I found my heart, Kitten. You're the one putting me back together. You make me feel alive. You're helping me find my soul again, which is something I thought died years ago. It's because of you I want to be a better man. I want to be there for you. I won't ever be able to give you a family, because the accident left me sterile, but *I'll* be there to love you forever if you let me."

She strokes my cheek with her fingers. "I want to be with you, Zach. It's you I love, not what you can or can't give me. I just want you."

"I love you," I tell her before I kiss her lips and we start down the path to our forever. The instant the words leave my mouth something comes over me and I feel a mad rush to not only tell her, but the rest of the world, that I'll do anything to keep her in my life. I pull away from her and hold up a finger. "Wait right here."

The small platform the wedding band plays on is a far cry from the stages I'm used to, but I can't think of a more appropriate place to express to Aubrey what she means to me. I gave Noel so much shit for doing this when Lanie came back to him, but I totally get it now. When you love someone, really love someone, you'll do anything to show them how much they mean to you. I want Aubrey to know my words aren't promises that I have no intention on keeping. I want her for the long haul.

I motion the tall, scarecrow looking lead singer with slicked-back black hair to the side of the stage. He bends down to me. "Hey, man. I hate to steal your show, but I need to sing something."

The man shrugs. "Sure. Do you want us to back you?"

It's been a long time since I fronted a band. The last time was before Noel joined Trip, Tyke and I. Adding the touch of the band may be perfect to bring the song together versus me alone with a guitar. I take a quick glance at Aubrey waiting on me in the middle of the dance floor under the soft lighting hanging in the tent and a song I secretly have on my iPod playlist that reminds me of how I feel about her pops in my head. "Sure. Do you know *I Won't Give Up* by Jason Mraz?"

He nods. "We do. We play that a lot at weddings. Hop on up."

Once I'm up on the stage, the front man hands me the mic before turning to fill in the band. I stare out into the crowd and even though there's a ton of people surrounding me, Aubrey is the only person I see.

Rock My Bed

I pull the mic up to my lips. "This song goes out to a very special lady who needs to know how I feel about her." I give the guitarist a quick nod and he plucks out the signature chords to intro the song acoustically.

When it's time for me to sing, I lock eyes with Aubrey because I want her to know that what I feel for her is real and I don't care who knows I'm totally whipped. The words are perfect as I tell her in song that I won't give up no matter what and I finally know what it's like to be loved and I'm never going to walk away from that.

It's everything I've been missing in my life, and she's given it back to me.

Aubrey wipes tears from her eyes and I step off the platform—the sea of people part before me, clearing my path to her.

I take her hand in mine and tears stream down her face. I fight back the emotion I feel building up inside me, so I can finish the song. The words that I'm still looking up and we have a lot to learn fit us perfectly, but I know together we can get through anything. With her by my side, I'm a better man.

"I'm giving you all my love," I sing and I intertwine our fingers. "I'm still looking up."

The crowd around us erupts in applause and I hear Trips loud ass hooting in the background. I wrap my arms around the one woman who has changed my life forever and I stare into her big, green eyes before I say, "All of it—my love is yours."

She grabs my face and crushes her lips to mine, and I finally allow myself to feel worthy love.

Acknowledgements

I want to thank you, my dear reader, for giving this book a chance. I hope I bring a little joy to you with my stories and I want you to know that I would never do this writing thing without the support of amazing people like you. THANK YOU, from the bottom of my heart.

Emily Snow and Kelli Maine your friendship is priceless. I'm thankful that through thick and thin we're there for one another to see each other through this crazy life we've chosen. Thank you for sharing all your ups and downs with me, and always being in my corner. I love you two to teeny, tiny bits!

Kristen Proby you crack me up, girl! Never lose that crazy sense of humor! It's solid gold!

Jennifer Woods and Laura Sample-McMeeking I can't tell you two how much I appreciate you taking the time to line edit this novel. You two ALWAYS have the best edits and thoughts on plot tweakage! I owe you two big time and it's time both of you get back into writing!

Holly Malgieri you are my biggest cheerleader. I can never thank you enough for all that you do for me. There are some days I know I wouldn't make it through this writing thing without you! Thank you from the bottom of my heart and I am stoked I can call you a friend. Big Hugs! Xoxox

Michelle A. Valentine

Jennifer Wolfel thank you all the insight you gave on this book and reading a million different versions of it! Thank you for sticking with me! HUGS!!

Christine Bezdenejnih Estevez you rock my socks, girlie! Thank you for standing by me and my books! I don't think I can ever truly repay you for all that you do. It means the world to me.

Tanya Keetch, a.k.a The Word Maid, thank you for the awesome line edits and finding all those funky words I like to misuse. You helped me clean this thing up.

My beautiful ladies in the Rock the Heart Discussion Group, you all rock so much it isn't even funny. Thank you for the laughs.

To romance blogging community. Thank you for always supporting me and my books. I can't tell you how much every share, tweet, post and comment means to me. I read them all and every time I feel giddy. Almost to the point where I'm ready to breakout that old Sally Field speech, "You like me. You really like me," because it amazes me every time the amount of love I feel from you guys. THANK YOU for everything you do. Blogging is not an easy job and I can tell you how much I appreciate what you do for indie authors like me. You totally make our world go round.

Last, but never least the two men in my life, my husband and son. Thank you for putting up with me. I love you both more than words can express.

Rock My Bed

About the Author

New York Times and *USA Today* Best Selling author Michelle A. Valentine is a Central Ohio nurse turned author of erotic and New Adult romance of novels. Her love of hard-rock music, tattoos and sexy musicians inspires her sexy novels.

Find her:

Facebook

http://www.facebook.com/pages/Michelle-A-Valentine/477823962249268?ref=hl

Twitter

@M_A_Valentine

Blog:

http://michelleavalentine.blogspot.com/

Rock My Bed

7353